The Cornerpost

Jacqueline T. Moore

ALL RIGHTS RESERVED

Publisher's Note:

This is a work of fiction. All names, characters, places, and events are the work of the author's imagination.

Any resemblance to real persons, places, or events is coincidental.

Solstice Publishing - www.solsticepublishing.com

The Cornerpost

Jacqueline T. Moore

Being crazy rich is one thing. You get to buy whatever you want. Havin' money when you can't tell anyone is altogether different. You just can't go into a shop and lay 'em out on the counter. Someone would notice. After all, a sailor cannot spend what he does not earn.

For all of the women in my family who carry Myra Jane
Langford Keith Galloway's soul strength.

Chapter One
You Want Me To Find You A What?

"Hello, hello, is anyone at home?"

"Why, Missus Annie, do come in." Marguerite Smith swung wide the front screen. "I'll let Myra know you're here."

Annie shook her head. "Many thanks, my dear, but it's you I need to talk to."

"*Moi?*"

"Yes dear. May I make myself at home?" Marguerite waited as Annie lowered herself on the settee. "Please sit with me. I need to ask a question."

Marguerite remained standing. "Care for some coffee and cake? Are you sure you don't want me to get Myra?"

"Goodness sakes, please sit. She cannot answer my question. You can." Annie fiddled with her reticule, digging deep into the contents. She pulled out a folded cutting from the newspaper. "Please look at this?"

Curiosity trumping caution, Marguerite sat next to their guest. The clipping was a square of jumbled print. Annie smoothed it on her lap and pointed.

Marguerite stared at the paper. "*Madam*, this is of no sense."

Annie flipped it over. "There." She handed the article to Marguerite. "Look at that headline. I don't understand it. *NEXT JUNETEENTH CELEBRATIONS BEING PLANNED IN GALVESTON*. The picture shows all colored." Annie shook her head. "Back when we lived in

Galveston, I never heard of this. You're the only colored person I know to talk to. What's Juneteenth?"

Marguerite stared at the photograph. It showed several Negro women dressed up like white society, standing next to a colored brass band. "*Mon Dieu, belles robes,*" whispered Marguerite. She looked at Missus Annie. "Those women have beautiful dresses. I've only seen clothing like that on, er, *les prostituees*. They are not…?"

"Oh, no," Annie assured. "They're colored ladies like you." She tapped the article. "What is this Juneteenth? Is it some kind of secret Negro thing?"

"Not at all." Marguerite stood. "Juneteenth's the yearly celebration we call Freedom Day. It started in 1865 when slavery finally ended in Texas." She shook her head. "The Galveston masters were the last to let go. That's why there is joy to this day."

Annie laid the paper beside her. "Thank you for your information. This is only February, must be last year's picture," she murmured. "And, yes, I'll have a cup. Would you please see if Myra can visit? Is Flossie Mae awake? I'd love to hug 'em both."

"Yes ma'am. I'll get them for you." She looked at the notice. "May I throw this scrap away?"

"Certainly, thank you, my dear."

Marguerite slipped the paper in her apron pocket and climbed the stairs to announce Missus Annie. Soon she was serving refreshments to the ladies. *Colored women in beautiful dresses, h-m-m-m-m.*

Sitting in the kitchen with her own coffee and cake, Marguerite flattened the paper on the breakfast table. She turned on the electric light and read, absently finger combing her smooth auburn hair, braiding and snugging it into her snood. In the article, one woman was quoted as saying they were planning a float with the Goddess of Liberty on it. However, Judge Lenny Fisher said, "Rastus won't be parading down my streets." The article concluded with another lady commenting that God would see them safely through the day.

I wonder if this is done here in LaPorte. I could buy a dress like that if-

"Marguerite, could you come to the parlor?" called Myra. "Missus Annie wants to ask you a question."

"I'm coming." *Thought Missus Annie already did that.* "Do you want more?"

Annie answered for Myra. "Thank you, dear."

"And more cake," chimed in Myra. "The baby's eating mine. Don't forget your own cup."

Marguerite placed the tray on the table and sat. Myra poured Annie's refill and offered her the sugar service. Two lumps and a splash of cream later, Annie turned to Marguerite.

"I know that you're a wife of this household, just like Myra."

Marguerite nodded and refilled her own cup. "Yes ma'am, I am, as best as can be."

Missus Annie smiled "You don't mind me saying, the neighbors are amazed at a two wife, two husband family. Especially since, well, you know…"

"Yes, I know. Jack and I are colored and CB and Myra are white. Our husbands were raised on the *Sallie Lou* as brothers, and Myra and I are like sisters. You and Mister Carlton know that." Marguerite shrugged. "I guess it didn't get announced to the town."

Missus Annie continued, ignoring Marguerite's tone. "I also know that you keep a fine home. CB Ledbetter was a saint to marry our widow Myra with all those children."

Marguerite felt her face redden. "*We* keep a fine house." She nodded to Myra. "*We* are a team." She returned her attention to Missus Annie. "What is this question you have?"

"Well, ever since your---" Annie paused, "ever since your, ah hem, fortune teller sister stayed at our house, I haven't had any help. Your Lulah Marie…"

"*Excusez-moi, Madam.*" Marguerite felt her face flame. "That witch, that *sorciere,* is nothing of mine."

"But your father…"

Myra broke in. "Annie, dear, please ask our Marguerite your question. I know none of us want to remember that horrid gypsy."

"Oh yes, the question." Annie smiled at Marguerite. "I need a colored gal. Can you get me one?"

Marguerite stared at Annie. "*Pardon?* Did you say you wanted me to *get* you a colored gal?" Marguerite stood. "You want me to *get* you a colored gal?" she repeated, an edge to her voice. "You make it sound like you are sending me to the 'colored gal' store." Her face was redder than her hair. "I am sorry but that is a chore you will have to do yourself."

Annie watched, bewildered, as Marguerite slammed out the front door. She stopped on the porch, inhaled loudly, and spoke through the screen. "Myra, tell your guest 'Good bye' for me. I don't want to forget *my* manners."

Myra, after showing Annie out, carried a wiggly Flossie Mae around back. She found Marguerite crying in the gazebo. The baby slid out of her mama's arms, crawled to the close-by rails, and pulled herself onto her feet. Tiny step by tiny step she amused herself, walking ring-around-the-grown-ups. Marguerite watched the child through her tears.

"Myra, Missus Annie hurt my feelings."

"Yes, I saw that."

"Do you know why?" Marguerite kept her eyes down.

"Because she doesn't know any better?"

"Why didn't you say something?" Marguerite looked up, smearing the tears from her cheeks with the backs of her hands just like the children would do. Myra handed her a hanky. They sat in silence, watching the baby. Little Miss sidled a few more steps and plopped down to examine a stray magnolia leaf. Marguerite spoke. "Missus Annie called me a lady one minute, and treated me like a house slave the next." She looked at Myra. "I am your friend. Why didn't you say something?" she repeated.

Myra shrugged. "I don't know. You certainly put her in her place."

"Colored can never put whites 'in their place.' You know that. I just thought, well, I just thought." Marguerite sat for several minutes before she spoke again. "Our husbands think keeping crates of gold coins hidden in the root cellar will bring us happiness." She shook her head. "I want to buy new dresses. I want to look like the lady I'm supposed to be."

Myra nodded. "Humph, I just want to stop pretending to be poor, and have everything the neighbors have." She took her friend's hand. "We. Are. Not. Poor." She bumped their hands down on her apron with every word. "Glory, I hate wash day. Did you know I used Wha Fung's Chinese Laundry when we were moving jewelry on the island? Tee-hee, I wonder if anyone questioned where the money came from for that."

Marguerite looked hard at Myra. "You had money? Jack never said anything about that. He only told me he and CB traded anything of value for the stowaways' travel to the gold fields, and that our home here in LaPorte was one of those payments. He said that your CB bought his half so that he could marry you and house all the children. Thank God LaPorte is north of Galveston and the hurricane didn't touch it." Marguerite quietly crossed herself. "He never said anything else."

"Oh yes." Myra smiled. "CB's sister, Julia Jameson---"

"Who?" Marguerite interrupted. "I thought Miss Flossie Mae was named for CB's sister."

"Julia was her society name, not her real name." Myra chuckled. "Seems being a lady can get you around corners."

"What?"

"Means to get things done on the quiet." Myra sighed. "Oh my, did we have adventures. Maybe it's wrong to say, but I think we made pretty good crooks."

Marguerite pulled Flossie Mae onto her lap.

"Mageet, Mageet," the baby squealed. Marguerite absent-mindedly began to patty cake the child's hands as she stared out over the yard. "Did you ever change out the jewelry?"

"Lord, no. Where in heaven's name would poor little ol' me get jewelry? That would've given it all away." Myra shook her head. "The whole thing worked so well because I was expected on the docks, and Julia was expected to go wherever society ladies went."

Marguerite began bouncing Flossie Mae on her knees.

"Don't worry about the mule,
Just load the wagon.
Don't worry about the mule,
Just load the wagon."

Flossie giggled to the rhythm of the words. "Myra, you loaded the wagon, and Julia was the mule." Marguerite repeated the game, but stopped still half way through the chant. She tilted her head toward her friend. "You know what? We've got a wagon full of gold. All we need is a mule."

Chapter Two
Weneeda Plan

CB and Jack were aware of the fortune, too, since it was their inheritance from William J. Calhoun, the captain of the *Sallie Lou*, and the closest thing to a real daddy either boy ever had. After he died, the Captain left the ship and all its contents to the two; share and share alike. However, he never told them the ship's liquor hold was full of gold coins, not booze. It almost broke the poor mule hauling the crates to their house. However, the men were rarely home from sea, and now that Myra's oldest son, Junior, was part of the crew, the wives and Myra's children living in the house seemed to be doing just fine, including CB's new baby daughter, Flossie Mae. Sure enough, there was gold in the cellar, but neither Myra nor Marguerite ever complained to them. Cookie always said, "Don't stir the pot," and pot stirrin' on ship is his profession. So the young husbands were quite unprepared for what waited when they stepped off the train in LaPorte.

"Daddy CB, Mister Jack, Junior, you're home, you're home." Nora Lee's announcement resulted in the men being covered with celebrating children. Myra and Marguerite stood arm in arm on the back stoop, watching. The ever observant Nora Lee, Myra's first girl and self-appointed big-brother tattler, noticed the wives. "Mama, Missus 'Guite, aren't you gonna kiss 'em?"

"We might." Myra did not break the arm link. "Children, let them have some air." She nodded toward the gazebo. "The grownups need to talk. Carry in the duffels and stay there to play." Their mother's voice was low and serious. She nodded to Junior. "You too, Son."

"And, for heaven's sake, don't wake the baby," added Marguerite.

The women walked to the cast iron settee, sitting side by side in the shade with no husband room. CB and Jack followed, both faces showing complete bewilderment.

"Please sit," instructed Myra, "We need to talk. Don't worry, nobody died."

The men looked at each other and found side chairs.

Finally Marguerite broke the silence. "*Mon Amour*, Mister CB, we are not going to be poor anymore."

"Huh?" Jack stared at his wife. "Of course, we're not poor. What are you talking about?" He looked at CB. "Aren't there cases of gold in the cellar?"

"Aye, aye, sir, there are." CB stared at his wife. "What's all this nonsense about?"

"Wooden boxes full of yellow coins are nothing…"started Myra.

"If you can't do anything with them," finished Marguerite. "We are not going to be poor anymore." She looked away. "*I* am not going to be poor anymore. No one will ever talk to me like some sort of house slave again."

"And I want a laundry man, an auto, and a telephone." Myra stood. "We are ladies who work hard. We deserve…" her voice trailed.

"We deserve better." Marguerite's words were whispered. "*I* deserve better."

Jack held out his arms. "Yes ma'am, *we* do."

Marguerite stood pat. "Myra and I are going to stay up in the sleeping porch all day and all night. We are taking a holiday. Our house working has made us tired."

Jack's eyes went wide. 'You mean no…"

Marguerite nodded. "Yes, no nothing. We work too hard to not have what *we* want. It is your job, gentlemen, to figure out how we can start spending."

"Dagnabit, woman, you both know that a sailor cannot spend what he does not earn." Jack's voice was getting louder. "We cannot draw attention to…"

"Hush your voice." Marguerite stood. "Right now you're drawing attention from the children. You know they don't know." She set her chin. "This bein' poor's got to stop now. You figure out how." She looked at Myra and nodded.

"Flossie Mae drinks from a cup." Myra smiled. "You may bring her to me for nighttime nursing. Other than that, husband dear, you and Jack are in charge of the household." She reached for Marguerite's hand. "Come, our room awaits us." They strolled toward the house. At the back stoop they stopped. "We're due to eat soon. Please put extra coffee on our tray."

The men watched their swishing skirts. Jack shook his head. "Damn, what are we going to do now?"

"I don't know," CB muttered, "but we better do something quick. We've been out to sea a long, long time."

"You're tellin' me." Jack adjusted his cap. "Well, come on mate. We got a ship to sail, and it looks like rough seas ahead."

CB crooked his mouth. "Where's Cookie when we need him? I sure as hell don't know anything about makin' food and keepin' house."

"Or keepin' younguns, for that matter," added Jack.

They slowly made their way along the gazebo path. Nora Lee was waiting outside the back screen door with hands on hips. "We want to know what's for supper. Mama said to talk to you." She looked up at the men. "You two in trouble?"

Jack shrugged, "No, child, I think we're in charge."

"Of what?"

"You." CB took his step-daughter's hand and they all walked into the kitchen.

Junior was sitting at the table with the rest of the children. "What's going on? Why did Mama and Missus Marguerite go up to the sleeping porch? Are they sick?"

"No son, just tired. They left Jack 'n' me boss of the house and y'all." CB looked to the ceiling. "They're staying upstairs until…"

"Until 'those men' figure it out," piped in Nora Lee, "I heard 'em talkin'. They said 'those men'. That means you two, don't it?"

CB shook his head. "I see why your mama calls you Nosey Rosy. Mr. Jack and I are gonna run the house for a while. I'm Captain and Jack's First Mate. You're our crew."

Junior jumped up and saluted. "Aye, aye, sirs, I'll be Second Mate and you can count on us. Come on, men, let's head on out and check the tides in back yard."

Nora Lee stamped her foot. "I'm gonna be a sailor, too, even if I am a girl."

Jack and CB watched the departing parade of shipmen. The backscreen slam brought a cry from the nursery. They waited. There was no scurry of maternal footsteps to be heard.

"Guess I better get my daughter," sighed CB. "You know how to change a diaper?"

"Nope."

"Neither do I." CB headed to the steps. "Let's give it a try."

Jack shook his head. "Your baby, *your* mess." He winked. "I'll see what's in the kitchen for *our* mess. Give a holler for our sailors before you go upstairs. I'll have them ship shape and at their duty stations before you can take care of that wet bottom."

CB did as he was told and headed to his baby girl. Ten minutes later, they were back down to the mess hall, formerly the kitchen. Jack stood in the middle of the floor, tied up in a pink and purple ruffled apron. He looked at himself, swiveled his head around in an exaggerated search, and took a pugilist' pose, feet apart, one fist higher than the other. "Don't you say a word."

CB started howling. "Can't. Laughin' too hard." He gestured to Jack's finery. "Where'd you get that?"

"Closet. Cookie always wears an apron when he cooks." He dropped his stance. "Was all I could find." He swung his arm wide." Notice anything else?"

"No crew?"

"Yes sir, no crew. They never came in. Mutiny, I guess."

"Doubt that. They're used to scatterin' at the thought of work. Here." CB handed squirming Flossie Mae to Jack. "This'un can't do chores, but she can keep us company while we cook."

Jack snuggled his best friend's daughter, kissing her pale blond head. "Well, little one, you gonna sit and watch us silly grownups? You want something to chew on?" He looked in the bread box. "Uneeda Biscuits will do."

Flossie Mae wiggled in his arms. "Caca, caca."

"Yep, Missy, crackers." Jack settled her in the high chair and opened the package.

CB slapped his leg. "Take off that thing. I got an idea. We don't have to cook."

"You plannin' on starvin' the children?" Jack had the apron back on its peg quicker 'n a blink.

"Nope, we're going to serve 'cold milk and cracker soup'." CB laughed. "Just wait 'til our women see how incompetent we are."

Jack set out bowls and spoons in front of each chair. "That won't get us back where we belong, but I did find a pitcher of milk in the icebox."

CB started crumbling handfuls of crackers into each bowl. "We gotta give them a spendin' plan."

Looking at the wax paper covered box on the table, Jack laughed. "They'll give in because they love the children. Hum, Uneeda Biscuits. Yep, we-need-a-spending plan."

Chapter Three
Cold Milk Soup

"Cold milk and crackers? You're feeding our children cold milk and crackers?" Myra stared at her husband.

CB stood at the sleeping porch's door with a tray of milk, crackers, and coffee. "Sorry, Cookie never taught us about kitchens. At least they said grace. Junior changed 'Father, thank you for this food, to Father, bless CB for marrying our mama'. I'm guessin' what we had wasn't really food, and the boy was standin' up for me the best he could." He held out their supper. Marguerite took the offering with a scowl.

Jack stood behind him with Flossie Mae in his arms. She was chewing her fist, tears streaming. "Missus Myra, this baby won't settle for us. She really wants her mama." He held her out, arms' length. The saggy diaper was finding its way south. "Gosh, we can't even keep her britches pinned. She wiggled so much, we couldn't do it right."

Myra stood in the middle of the door opening. "And…"

Jack shrugged. "And us men need to talk about plannin' a plan."

Myra turned to her roommate and crooked an eyebrow. Marguerite returned the look. She lifted the ticking bedside clock. "*Mon amie*, these husbands of ours lasted two and a half hours doing what we do all day, every day. Should we let them in our room?"

"Mama, Mama, Mama." Flossie Mae lunged at her mother, the momentum pulling Jack forward. Myra caught her daughter just in time. The baby instantly nuzzled her mother's neck. "Mama, noose, noose, mulk."

Laughing, Myra sat in the chair by the summer cots. "Yes, my darling, you may nurse." Making herself comfortable, she covered Flossie Mae and herself with a shawl. Marguerite lowered herself on the bed, waiting. They looked at their husbands.

Jack spoke. "We need time. Please give us one turn around to figure this out." He looked at his wife. "Good Lord, was it only two and a half hours? We thought we were in that kitchen forever."

Myra was curious. "The children didn't help? Nora Lee usually runs the show if we ask."

CB shook his head. "Mutiny. Finally got them all in with threats of tattling to you about their behavior. Liked the cracker soup, though."

"Of course, no vegetables." She looked at Marguerite. "Wanna try it?'

"I suppose, but only if our chefs prepare our bowls." She looked at Jack. "*Mon amour*, we will eat this, er, supper. Then, with our stomachs full, it will be decided if we end our holiday this evening."

The very happy couples slept in their own beds that night. The sailors enjoyed the rest of their leave, appreciating their wife's company. The women did not say the words "spending" or "plan," not even once. When it was time to head back to the *Sallie Lou*, CB, Jack, and Junior got their kisses and were on their way to the train.

At the station, CB reached in his pocket for their return tickets, which were wrapped in a sheet of paper. Myra's handwriting said "spending plan." He handed the note to Jack. "They win."

Jack nodded. "Yes, sir, they do."

Junior perked up, interested. "Who's 'they'?"

"Son," CB cautioned, "When you get married, you must remember that the woman always wins."

"Oh, gosh, I figured that out when Mama and Missus Marguerite came out of the sleeping porch."

CB grinned. "You're learnin' fast, boy."

WHOOT. WHOOT.

"Train's a'callin', step lively."

"Aye aye, Captain."

Junior raced ahead to the train and was feigning sleep when CB made his way between the seats, sitting beside the boy, while Jack settled into the colored coach. The trip was spent in silence, watching the passing scenery.

"GAL-VEE-STON, GAL-VEE-STON, TEXAS," hollered the conductor. "End of the line. Watch your step."

Chapter Four
Baby Baptism Blues

Ada Dickenson had a bee in her bonnet. Nope, not a bee, a whole hornet's nest was a buzzing around her head. It started before church.

Linda Sue Nicholson, the pastor's wife, was waiting in the narthex for her. That was unusual. Linda Sue usually stood with her husband, greeting their parishioners. "How is your dear niece and her sweet new Flossie Mae doing?"

The Galveston Methodist Church survived the Hurricane of 1900, but flooding ruined the contents. Eighteen months later the wonder of rebuild and repair was finished, and the rhythm of the Women's Guild was once more the heartbeat of the church. Unknown to Ada, the ladies had been gossiping about her beloved Myra and her family up the road in LaPorte.

"Fine. If there was any problem, I'm sure Myra would send for me." Ada pulled her crystal beaded hat pin. "Why do you ask?" She rewove the weapon through silk-covered straw of her Sunday best and down through her white curls.

"Has she found a home church? We do miss seeing those children." Linda Sue smiled. "They're quite a handful, but they are missed."

Ada tilted her head as she gave the pin a final jab, sending it through the other side of her hat. Straightening up, she looked at Linda Sue, one eyebrow crooked.

"Who've you been talking to? I truly don't believe the Guild would be asking *that* question." Ada snugged her gloves. "However, thank *you* for your concern." She decisively walked to her pew and sat with a less than ladylike 'thump.'

"Hens?" Harry knew his wife. He reached for the hymnal.

"Number 213, 'Lift Up Your Heads,'" was all she said.

Yes, Linda Sue sure did set those hornets to work. They circled Ada all the walk home, and kept swarming in the kitchen. "How can they find anything to talk about our Myra? She's better off than most since she got married." Ada was getting out the Sunday dinner china, grumping and mumbling. "Harry, darlin', would you see if the rice has set up?"

"Only if you tell me what happened in church. You're really out of sorts."

"Linda Sue."

Harry peeked under the rice pot's lid. The starch was still floating. "I'm a'guessin' another ten minutes. Want me to stir?"

"Don't touch it 'til the holes bubble."

"Yes, ma'am." Harry settled into his spot at the table. "What about Linda Sue? She's not one to rile you like this." He picked up his water glass. "Can I fill yours, too?"

"Thank you. Half full." Ada pulled out the oven rack and slowly lifted the pork roast to the stove top. "My goodness sakes in a bucket, that smells good."

Harry put two topped off glasses on the table and sat back down. "Sure does." He licked his lips. "Would you cut me a taste?"

"No. You know it has to rest to keep the juices in."

"How about a turnip? I'm 'bout starved."

"You are not." Ada forked the juice covered vegetable to a saucer and set it atop Harry's dinner plate. "Here, don't get the meat drippin's on your suit."

"Thank you, ma'am. It looks mighty good." Harry cut into his appetizer. "So, what did Linda Sue do that fired you up?"

"She asked of Myra." Ada felt that covered it all.

"Huh?" Harry chewed on his turnip. "You're all het up over that? Woman, that just don't make sense." He looked hard at her. Her curls were coming loose. "Sit down here and tell me what's really going on."

"Checkin' the rice."

"Sit down right now." Her husband used his 'I've had about enough of this' tone. Ada sat.

She broke into tears. "Flossie Mae's going to hell."

That bit of news sent his most recent bite across the table. Once the coughing fit subsided, he handed over his breast pocket handkerchief. They both smelled the scorching rice. Harry pointed at his wife. "Do not get up. I'll save it."

The top two inches of the potful was palatable. The rest would go to the rats in the rot dump. Harry spooned the rescued rice into a serving bowl, lifted the roast to the sideboard, and cut four slices. He put the browned carrots, turnips, and meat all on the same platter. "You want pan gravy?"

"I'll make it." Sniffling, Ada stood.

"Sit. You are not leaving this table until you tell me just what in the devil you mean about Flossie Mae. Did Linda Sue say she was going to hell?" Flour, salt, and pepper went stirring into the pan. Harry used water to get the right consistency, and, slick as a whistle, Sunday dinner was ready.

Harry sat, Ada prayed, and the plates were filled. Ada stared at her pork.

"Talk, woman." Harry poured his gravy and stirred his rice.

"What are we going to do? Flossie Mae's going to hell."

"She is not. You're not thinkin' straight." Harry cut his carrots and added them to his rice gravy mix. He scooped the whole mess onto his slice of meat and dug in with his knife. He noticed his darling, deranged wife had not taken a bite. He set down his utensils.

"Talk, woman."

"Oh, Harry, we have got to get that baby baptized. I don't think Myra's even though about it." Tears started again. "Her least'n Franky almost died. You just don't know about babies these days."

Harry, leaning across the table, took his wife's hand. "Sooooo, Linda Sue did not say the child was going to hell?"

Sniff. "No."

"Did anyone in that church tell you the child was going to hell?"

Sniff. "No."

"So-o-o-o, you have been buzzin' and flyin' all around this place over something nobody said?" Harry gave her hands a hard squeeze and turned them loose. "I'm eating my dinner, and so are you. We will take care of this after dessert. Pass me the turnips."

Ada served sponge cake with dewberry sauce and hot cups of java in the parlor. After a bite and a sip, she spoke. "You know we made sure all the other children were churched. Myra, bless her heart, at least gave them Saturday baths and got them all to service on Sunday. We didn't get the new one baptized. It will be our fault if, God forbid, she..." Ada closed her eyes. "It will be our fault Flossie Mae can't become an angel."

"Don't start crying again." Harry put another forkful of the fruit juice-soaked treat in his mouth. "You need to get on that train tomorrow and go up to LaPorte.

You don't know. They might have taken care of this and not told us." He lifted his china cup, set it back down, and stood. "Woman, you know I drink out of a mug. You want one?"

"No. Today's Sunday."

He brought both breakfast mugs, steaming. "Here." Harry sat back down and broke off another piece of cake. This time the dewberry sauce was forgotten.

Ada glowered at him. She pointed at the mug. "You don't listen to a word I say, do you?"

"Huh?"

"Never mind." She lifted her china cup and drank it empty. "Do you actually think she would have gotten that child baptized without borrowing back your baby gown? Every one of her young'uns, even the twins, wore it. Remember how little Frankie wore the under slip 'cause he was so tiny, and Benjy wore the over dress?" Ada smiled at the memory. "I made those boys matching caps out of handkerchiefs. No one said a word." She sighed. "No sir, I'd have known if they did it in LaPorte." She held out her unwanted mug. "Husband, do you want this?"

"You betcha."

Chapter Five
Lonely LaPorte

The next morning Ada bought the ticket. She sent a telegram saying she was coming for a short visit that afternoon and needed one of the children to meet her. Myra sent Theo.

"Mama said almost-ten was old enough to walk to the station alone. She said it would help my extra energy." Theo was the youngest boy in the house. He swaggered with the importance of carrying Aunt Ada's valise. "She doesn't know why you're here, told me not to ask." He grinned at her. "So I'm not."

"So I won't tell."

Aunt Ada's arrival on Lobit Street was met with the usual kisses, hugs, and observations about growing like weeds. Theo ran the bag up to the sleeping porch, and was off to play. Hello squeezes waited for the napping Flossie Mae. Myra finally shooed the children outside with warnings about slamming the screen, and invited her aunt into the kitchen. Marguerite was off to market and the women relaxed with the obligatory lemon zest pound cake. Myra had been baking all week in anticipation of CB, Junior, and Jack's eminent return. Three bites in, Ada set down her fork. She gazed at her niece.

"We've got to get that baby baptized right now. She could go to hell." Ada picked up her mug. "You haven't saved the soul of your child." She sipped, stood, and brought the galvanized coffeepot to the table. "You want some hot? Mine's coolin'." She topped her brew. "I'd know if you had it done. You'd have sent for the gown."

Myra loved her aunt more than life itself, but that last statement set her back. She took a deep breath, counted to five, taking in what she'd heard, and drank an inch of joe straight down. She set the cup on its saucer with a clunk.

"Auntie, I…"

"Yes or no, is that girl christened?"

Myra stared at her cake plate. "No, ma'am."

"That's what I thought." Ada tested her coffee with a small sip from her teaspoon. "Too hot. Do you have a congregation way up here?"

"No, ma'am."

"Thought not." Ada sat very straight. "Child, you can't let your family become unchurched just because of a hurricane and a different house." She pulled and reset her comb, a signal the family knew all too well. "Where are Missus Annie and Carlton attending? She was so active in our church before she wed."

"I don't think they are. Auntie, there are only a few churches here. I think there's a Catholic and maybe a Baptist, and that's all. You know we can't go to those."

Ada nodded. "I see your point." She sipped another spoonful. "Ah, just right." She smiled. "Would you like to come to the island and have our Reverend Nicholson do it? Everyone would love to see you all again."

"I doubt that, but it sounds wonderful." Myra cut another slice and left it on the serving plate. "Marguerite might want some when she gets back."

"How is it going with the neighbors?" Aunt Ada knew that the Ledbetters were walking a fine line, sharing their home with a colored couple. "Y'all have any problems?"

"Aunt Ada, LaPorte is so hateful. Marguerite and I mostly stay to ourselves." Myra made a wide gesture. "This whole section was built about four years ago for rich people. They call it 'New Town'. When someone hears you live on Lobit Street, they immediately know you weren't born and raised here." She wrinkled her nose. "The 'Old Town' people won't talk to us and the New Town people treat us like dirt because our husbands are sailors. They're more polite to Marguerite than they are to me 'cause they think she's my help." Myra sighed. "Missus Annie and Carlton are the only ones around who know and accept us as a mixed household. And they live in Old Town."

"That makes sense, darlin'. Annie told me that Carlton bought his house many, many years ago. She said that's why she's invited to things, even though they just got married. People know him, and welcome her." Ada squinched her mouth. "And to think we all thought she'd die an old maid. Wonder if her sisters get invitations?"

"Doubt it. They never come downstairs when we're invited. I always figured it was about sitting with Marguerite and Jack."

"You mean to tell me that *all* of you are welcomed to their table?"

"Yes ma'am, even the children."

Ada smiled. "Well, I'll be." She looked over her shoulder toward the staircase past the dining room. "Did I hear a peep?"

"Just wait. She knows how to holler 'Mama' and stand in her crib. When that all happens, I go get her."

"Oh my stars, if she's that big, she'll never be able to wear the gown." Ada stood. "I have it in my satchel." Looking all around, she took a step to the dining room door. "Where did that boy put it? I had it with me."

"Where you always stay, in the porch." Myra raised an eyebrow. "Are you gettin' forgetful in your old age?"

Ada shook her head. "No, but your Uncle Harry is. Darlin', I tell him one thing and he does whatever he wants," she harrumphed. "Sometimes I wonder about him."

"Well, at his age…"

Flossie Mae interrupted her mother's thought. "Mama. Mama, Mama."

The women stood. "I'll get her cleaned and presentable. Auntie, why don't you sort through your things and bring down the gown." Myra shook her head. "Nora Lee was the last child to wear it, and she 'bout popped the seams. This baby's much bigger."

"Well, darlin', you can't rightly stop feeding her."

Chapter Six
Father Daughter Heathens

Ada slowly climbed behind her niece to the sleeping porch, grumping about her 'old bones'. She rummaged through her case. Below her personals was the tissue wrapped garment. Gently she carried it down to the parlor.

She was so intent on her treasure that she did not notice the front door opening. Only when light from the side window was blocked did she look up. A tall, dark-haired young man in sailor's garb was standing smack dab in front of her, grinning to beat the band. Ada blinked.

"Junior?"

"Shhh, Auntie. We want to surprise Mama and Missus Marguerite." Then that tall, grown man of a boy collapsed to his knees and buried his head in his great aunt's lap. After a long time, Junior looked up, blinking tears. "Oh, Auntie, do you forgive me? I am so sorry I broke your and Uncle Harry's trust."

"And my broom," Ada added.

"And your broom." Junior stood. "I didn't know you were here or I would've brought you one from Panama."

Myra's first-born, Junior, after a violent fit of anger against his new step-father, was sent to live with Ada and Harry. There he'd gotten in trouble for sneaking out the back storeroom window to drink beer and kiss girls. One evening his auntie slammed down the pane and beat the trapped bottom with her broom until it broke. The family arranged to have Junior arrested, jailed, and 'judged' by Captain Calhoun wearing robes. He was 'sentenced' to one turn around on ship with the man he hated. Those three months changed the boy into a man.

"I forgave you the day you went to jail." Ada smiled. "Now what have you forgotten?" She tapped her cheek. His kiss was prompt.

"Where's everybody?" CB and Jack strolled in from the kitchen. "Oh, Auntie, I didn't know you'd be here."

"Ma'am." Jack tipped his cap, looking around. "Where is that beautiful wife of mine?"

"Myra said she went to market. 'Spect she'll be back soon." Ada returned her attention to the boy. "Young man, what did you do with my Junior? Last time I saw him, he was scrawny armed and ratty haired. You are a strong, handsome man."

The strong, handsome man giggled. "Silly Auntie." Junior leaned down and planted a smooch on the other cheek. He cocked his head toward the steps. "Flossie Mae?" Ada nodded. Taking two steps at a time, quick as a flash Junior was back with his screaming sister, their mama chasing them both. CB stood at the bottom, arms wide. Myra got her kiss and CB got his daughter. Only then did Flossie Mae stop crying. She snuggled her daddy's neck, and settled into the crook of his elbow.

"Been gone three months. Guess she didn't know me," observed Junior.

"Guess not. Get over here and hug your Mama."

The back screen slammed, and a thunder of children rumbled into the house. "Junior." "Daddy CB." "Mr. Jack." They swarmed the men with hugs and kisses. Nora Lee grabbed Jack's hand and dragged him toward the kitchen. Marguerite was pulling her wheeled market basket up the stoop steps. Nora Lee flung open the screen. "Lookie. Lookie."

"*Mon amour.*" Marguerite passed the basket's handle to the child and fell into her husband's arms, red hair escaping her straw bonnet. Nora Lee watched intently as the couple kissed. When the embrace did not end, the child shrugged and got the groceries into the house. The children had all the parcels put away and were out to play by the time the couple entered. Jack left his valise at the bottom of the steps.

"Halooo, you two, come into the parlor. Aunt Ada is here." Myra tilted her head toward the settee. Ada was showing the christening gown to a frowning CB.

"We can't get her baptized." CB's voice was deadly quiet.

"Whatever are you talking about?" Ada's tone betrayed a mixture of confusion and incredulity. "Of course we can get her baptized."

CB slowly shook his head. "No we can not."

"Why?"

"Because I'm a heathen."

CB's statement was met with silent stares. Flossie Mae squirmed, trying to reach her daddy's chin.

"Ma Ma?"

"No precious, Papa." CB kissed her fair hair. "I'm your Godless papa."

Marguerite held out her arms. "Come to me, *mon petit enfant*. Your papa is talking *foufou*." She carried Flossie Mae into the kitchen. "*Mon amour, Jacque*, let's look for some cake, and a cup of milk and a spoon. We will make sop with my crumbs and share my dessert with her."

CB, shaking his head in misery, sat beside Aunt Ada, fingering the lace around the edge of the christening gown. She shifted to face CB. "Tell me, son, why do you think you're a heathen? I did not ride all the way here on the train, getting my rheumatism up with all that joggling, to hear what I just heard." She picked up the gown's embroidered under-slip and fluffed it across her lap. "I don't believe you're a heathen. My Myra wouldn't entrust her family to a Godless man."

CB looked at his wife and then at Junior. He took Aunt Ada's hand. "My wonderful family, I have a confession to make." He hugged her hand to his cheek and let it go. "The very first time I was ever in a church was the day I found you all sheltered with the Catholics after the hurricane. My daddy wouldn't let us go to any services or meetings when we were growing up. He sent me to sea when I was nine." He shrugged. "There are no cathedrals on the ocean."

Myra knelt in front of her husband and kissed his knuckles. "You know all the hymns and prayers. Where did that come from?"

He tilted his head toward to kitchen. "Jack taught me to read and to sing, and to praise. That doesn't matter. I'm unconsecrated."

Myra looked straight into his eyes. "What does that have to do with this?"

"I thought you could only baptize a baby from a dedicated family. I'm not."

"Good grief." Myra stood. "Jack," she called over her shoulder. "Jack, could you come here?"

"Yes ma'am, I've been listenin'." He walked into the parlor.

"Did you tell him this garbage?" Myra stepped back from her husband.

"No, ma'am." Jack looked at CB. "Where did you get a notion like that?"

"My daddy said we wouldn't ever go to heaven because God wouldn't take us, so why bother goin' to church." CB looked at Junior. "Son, I'm so sorry to let you down."

Junior smiled. "Daddy CB, you'll never let me down."

"You did not let anybody down." Myra was losing her patience. "You were sired by a filthy polecat, but you and Jack were raised right on the *Sallie Lou* by Captain Calhoun and Cookie. I had no idea you put so much stock in the words of that lowlife, boy-sellin' skunk."

"But..."

"But, nothing, did that man ever do anything for your soul?"

"No."

"Then for heaven's sake, husband, why do you believe his word?"

"I don't know."

Ada looked at Jack. "Are you and Marguerite baptized?"

"Yes, ma'am, she always was and her priest did me before we were married at St. Mary's on the island."

"So the Catholic church took you as a grown man?"

"Yes ma'am, it did." Jack looked at his best friend. "Hm-m, wonder if the Methodists will take on a white daddy? After all, the Catholics took on a colored bridegroom."

Ada smiled. "That's exactly what I was thinkin'. Thank you, Jack, for your wisdom."

"Yes ma'am." He nodded. "Excuse me, everyone, I've got a kit to unpack." Jack's long legs had him out of the room and up the steps in two shakes of a puppy dog's tail.

Well," Ada declared, "that fixes that. We'll get you both blessed." She folded the under-slip, wrapped it in its tissue, and tucked back in the box. "I'll telegraph Reverend Nicholson tomorrow and get the whole thing set up."

"Hold your horses, Auntie." CB stood and faced her. "You forgot something."

"I have?"

"Yes, you have." There was a very small twinkle growing in CB's blue eyes. "You forgot to ask me if I wanted it."

Myra spoke softer than a whisper. "Husband, do you want to be baptized?"

"Oh yes, my darling, yes."

Ada crooked her head, cupping her ear. "What did you say?"

"I want to be baptized!" His response echoed through the house.

"That's what I thought you said."

Chapter Seven
No Checkers In That Church

Reverend Nicholson's return telegram expressed joy and willingness to do the job. He had only one question. "Does CB want to get sprinkled, poured, or dunked?"

"I'm a grown man who loves the sea," he answered. "Make it dunked." The family was seated around the evening supper table, enjoying the leftovers from their dinner. With the addition of four more mouths to fill, Myra and Marguerite turned the kitchen into the heart of the house. Every noon meal had three meats, hot vegetables, plus the ever-present mounds of breakfast rice, biscuits, and cream gravy. The meal ended with whatever sweet was created. Junior still loved biscuit and honey dessert, and his mother kept the pot on the table.

"I wish I'd been dunked," commented Jack. "That priest just poured some holy water on my hair and painted oil on my forehead with his thumb." He smiled at Marguerite. "Can't complain about the results, got us married, didn't it?"

"*Oui.*" Marguerite turned in her chair. "Excuse me, Missus Ada, will we be allowed to witness this *bapteme*?"

"Of course, why do you ask?" Ada smiled. "Methodists even have open communion."

"But will Jack and I be allowed? It's a white church."

Ada set down her fork. "Oh my, never thought about that. The only colored I've ever seen there is the cleaning man, and he comes in the evenings." She lifted her cup. "Oh, my."

"And what about Julia's brother?" CB added. "He's gone full blown Hebrew. Does your Reverend Nicholson let Jews in his church?"

Myra patted her husband's arm. "Now, now, darling, I'm convinced Aunt Ada will figure this out, won't you Auntie?" Myra's pointed tone said it all.

"I, um, I'll have to do some thinking about this." Ada sat down her unsipped cup. "I just don't know what to say."

"Well, I do." CB stood. "If my brother Jack and my brother-in-law Isaac are not welcome in this church, than neither am I." He nodded at the table. "Excuse me. Somehow I'm not so hungry anymore."

The children stared at his departing back. Junior spoke. "Mama, if Daddy CB won't get baptized, I don't want Flossie Mae gittin' it, either." He left the table without his 'Excuse me' and followed his step-daddy out the door.

The rest of the children stood.

"Sit before I get me a switch." Myra glared at her brood. "You will finish your suppers now. You will not stand until I say so. I am sure that Aunt Ada will let us know as soon as she knows. This has been her project from the beginning." She pursed her mouth and looked at her aunt. "You will fix this as soon as possible. I will not have my husband's soul left to the devil." Myra looked at Jack. "When does he have to get back to his captaining? Is there time?"

"This is a long turn around. The *Sallie* is getting her rump rouged."

"What?"

"Huh?"

"Pardon me?"

Myra hushed her children, and her blushing auntie. "What Jack means is that the *Sallie Lou* is in dry dock for her annual going over. Isn't that so?"

"Yes ma'am, our girl hasn't had the best of care. CB and I are changing all that."

"*Our* girl?" Ada looked surprised. "I thought CB was captain now."

"Auntie, I *told* you that CB and Jack inherited the *Sallie Lou.* It's share and share alike."

"You did?" Ada's voice had a question in it.

"Yes, I did. CB is captain and Jack is first mate." Myra gave Marguerite a look of apology and frustration. "Just like this house, that ship is checkerboard."

"Oh. I think I knew that." Ada smiled. "Just forgot."

Jack nodded. "We live together and sail together."

"And Auntie, it is up to you to get us together in that church."

"Mama?"

"Yes, Nora Lee."

"May we be excused?"

"Scoot."

Jack went outside with the children. CB and Junior were sitting in the gazebo.

"Hoy," Jack called.

"Hoy," the unison reply rose from the shade. "Seas settled?"

"Myra told Missus Ada to fix this. I'm a'guessin' there will be a few more waves before all is well." Jack sat next to Junior. "You forgot to excuse yourself. Your mama was a tad puckered." He smiled. "Don'cha think you'd better make it right?"

"Mister Jack, I walk with my Daddy CB."

"Son, I thank you for that." CB nodded toward the back stoop. "How 'bout gittin' us men some pie. I saw the safe had two." CB raised an eyebrow. "You might see if your Mama needs an extra chore done to make up for the both of us leavin' the table."

Junior returned with two pieces of fig pie. Jack looked at the plates. "Again?"

"Myra says the big shots runnin' LaPorte think fig trees are God's gift to the town. That's why every backyard has 'em. She says we might as well use God's gift."

Jack buried his fork in the back crust. "Did those boss men ever think about what all those seeds do to a man's morning constitutional?" He took a bite and grinned. "They hit me just like raspberries."

"I know what you're sayin'." CB gestured with his fork. "Why you eating your pie backwards? Only makes sense to start at the point." CB dug into his pie the 'right' way.

"My mama always said, 'Boy, bite your crust first. That way, if the fruit's bad, you at least had one taste of the good'." Jack put some of the filling in his mouth, turned, and spit it on the grass. "Ugh, that stuff is not fit for man or beast." He went back to the crust. "I know this part is Marguerite's doin'. I can taste the sweet love she puts in it. I'll tell her how good it is."

CB's plate was almost clean. "How you gonna explain that mess of fruit left?"

Jack handed over his dessert. "Won't have to."

Chapter Eight
Oh, Preacher Man

Aunt Ada was on the first train to the island. "What in tarnation have I gotten myself into?" She kept her muttering under her breath. "Humph, Jews and colored aren't allowed in the church. Reverend won't hear of it. Linda Sue'll have a fit. Blast her, startin' this mess." She kept the grumping going all the way home. Some of the passengers were starting to look funny at her. The hack driver from the station asked if she felt well. It was only then that Ada hushed.

She repeated the whole story to Harry. They were sitting toward the back of the mercantile, using the checkerboard as a table. Harry nodded and sipped, nodded and sipped, not saying a word.

"Did you hear what I just said? That boy won't get baptized without half the world represented." Ada was unusually loud. Two customers looked their way.

"Hush, woman. I hear you, and so does the rest of the store. Look who's over there in dry goods." He cut his eyes to the left. "Lower your voice. You don't want to get in a pickle with those two gossips."

The shoppers were wives of Masons in Harry's Lodge. While the men kept 'on the square', the women had no vow. Gossip could run wild if the fuel was hot enough. Harry's warning was too late. The women may not have heard all the words, but they sure did catch the tone. "Mister Harry, Ada, it is wonderful to see you. Darling, how are things in LaPorte? Are the children well?" They swooped in like buzzards. Kathryn crowded up to the game barrel. Ada scooted her chair back.

Harry stood. "Afternoon, Missus Kathryn, Missus Penny. Can I help you find something on your list?" He skillfully guided the two toward the bolts of fabrics. "Ada, would you please go in the back room and straighten up the spice tins? That new clerk doesn't know cinnamon from sassafras. "

Ada's grateful nod said 'thank you' for the escape plan, and she was gone. *No carrion pickin' this go-round.*

He spoke to his customers. "Ladies, please remind my Brothers that meeting is tomorrow evening." He gestured toward the candy case. "Let me put a root beer sweet in your shopping totes." He winked. "Just don't tell your husbands you got beer at Harry's place, no cold cash needed."

Soon the giggling ladies were out the door, sucking on their candy sticks like cigarette fiends.

"All clear," Harry called. "I buttered them up with candy."

The next morning, at the early hour of nine o'clock, Ada knocked on Reverend Nicholson's office door. The pastor was behind his desk in his shirt sleeves, reading the paper. She entered without a 'come-in'.

"Good morning Missus Ada, let me make myself presentable." He stood, trying to get his generous girth into his suit jacket.

"Pshaw, Reverend, stay still. I've seen you in your shirt before." Ada sat without invitation. "You're just fine."

He settled back in his chair. "You seem to have something on your mind. What may I do for you?"

"I'll come right to the point. Can you baptize my children with a Jew and a Negro as witness?"

"What in the world are you talking about?"

"Can you christen CB and his daughter with a Jew and two Negroes in attendance?"

Reverend Nicholson shook his head. "Of course not, you should know that. They stay to theirs, and we got ours. There has never been any mixing under this roof." He slowly folded his newspaper. "Never will be."

"Sir, you are wrong." Ada was starting to steam. "You had a Jewish man who attended services every Sunday for years. Now if that ain't mixin', I don't know what is."

"Who?"

"Ike Jameson. Born, bred, and beanie-wearing, Ike Jameson, now known by his real name, Isaac Jacoby." She pointed at him. "You married him and Julia. Didn't you ask for his baptism certificate?"

"No, took him at his word."

"Well, Julia was never baptized either, so I guess it was even."

The reverend took off his glasses and polished them on his shirt sleeve.

"Stop that," Ada scolded. "I know Linda Sue starches your shirts. The sizing will scratch 'em." She pulled a handkerchief from her bosom. "Use this."

After huffing moist breath on the lenses and cleaning them, he handed back her cloth. He adjusted his spectacles on his nose and sighed. "You are so worked up. My dear friend, tell me why you're really here. You knew the answers to your questions before you opened my door." He slowly shook his head. "And, no, I didn't know about Ike and Julia."

Ada started to cry. "Oh my poor family, my poor family is going to hell. CB and the baby need to be blessed now."

"I know."

"No you don't. You don't know." Her sobs were getting louder.

"Hush. You'll wake up the dead." He looked at the door. "You don't want this to be heard down the hall. You know how close we are to the hen house."

Ada took several deep breaths. "CB won't consent to either ceremony unless Jack Smith and his wife, Marguerite, attend."

"Who's that?"

"The colored boy he grew up with on the *Sallie Lou*. The couples live in the same house." Ada turned her hands up. "They've caused quite a stir in LaPorte."

"I bet they have."

"Marguerite acts as their house girl to help with the passin', but all the close neighbors know that a white man and a colored man come home from the sea every three months." Ada dabbed her eyes. "These modern times…" she drifted off. "Anyway, CB won't do it if Jack and Isaac can't be there." She looked the pastor in the eye. "How are we going to fix this?"

"Hmmm, I'm not sure." Reverend Nicholson scratched his head. "Let me talk this over with Linda Sue."

"Don't you dare."

"Why ever not?"

Ada stood. "She caused this whole mess. I will not have her involved." She picked up her reticule and turned to the door. "Figure this out. That's all."

The reverend watched his parishioner leave. He knew his Linda Sue and wondered what Ada was talking about. "Whatever's happening in the hen house is spilling into my study," he thought. "Guess I better think of something quick."

Chapter Nine
CB has a Plan

A telegram waited when Ada got back from the church. CB was on the train south and would be in at 4:20 PM. Could he eat supper with them? He would bunk on the *Sallie Lou* up in dry dock. The Dickensons had no idea what was going on, but Ada set an extra plate.

"You think something happened to the ship?" Ada was filling three water glasses. Oh how she loved plumbing. The hurricane took their store and house. Thrifty-minded Harry used the old plans for the new mercantile but had the second floor built into living quarters instead of a Masonic Temple. This new building had a real bathroom up in the apartment and a toilet down in the store area next to a working sink.

"Don't know." He drank his water straight down and held it out for a refill. Susan, the regular clerk who did know cinnamon from sassafras, was minding down stairs while the proprietors awaited their early dinner guest.

Ting. The front door bell rang each time it was opened.

"Ahoy, up there."

"Hello, dear," Ada bustled to the top of the stairs and waited. "Come on up. Supper's waiting."

"Aye, aye, ma'am, I'm really hungry." CB planted a big kiss on her cheek. "Where can I wash my hands?"

She showed him the bathroom. After a proper clean-up, CB found the dining room.

Harry extended his hand across the table. "You seem happier than the last time Ada saw you."

CB grinned. "I want to apologize for that. I was pretty het up."

"Yes you were." She passed him the cold meat. "You better, now?"

"Oh, yes ma'am. I am sorry for my rude behavior."

"What behavior?" Ada winked. "You are forgiven for everything I have forgotten. Would you please ask the blessing?"

"Yes ma'am." He recited his favorite seaman's prayer. "Amen."

"That was nice. Would you like some bread? Our suppers on work days are usually sandwiches."

"Thank you, ma'am, sounds wonderful to me."

Harry plopped a generous spoonful of chow-chow on his plate. "Son, try some of this on your sandwich. Put it top of your meat, not the bread. Gets soggy if you don't." He demonstrated. CB followed suit and took a bite.

"Kinda tastes like souse, what with the vinegar." He licked his lips. "Picklier. I like it." He added more to his plate and loaded his fork. "Good plain, too." He had another bite of the meat and bread, chewing slowly. "Bet this is good on rice."

Harry thought about it. "Probably." He turned to his wife. "Any in the pot?"

"No. We ate it all for dinner." She smiled at her nephew. "Tell us, son, why are you here? Is there trouble with your ship?"

"No, ma'am, all's right with our girl. She's not why I came down so soon." CB looked at the meat platter. "May I?"

"Of course, and here's more bread." She handed him the chow-chow without his asking. "As I was saying, why are you here?"

"Aunt Ada, Uncle Harry, is the rule against Jack and Isaac about the church building or about the church? I figured out this baptism thing. We can do it with Jack and Ike, er, Isaac there."

"How?" Ada was curious. "Reverend Nicholson was stumped."

CB cleared his throat and sang.

"Yes, we'll gather at the river…"

Ada set down her napkin. "Oh, I see, do it outside." She relaxed in her chair. "Harry, do you think Reverend Nicholson would object?"

"Better not, Jesus did it." Harry reached for the honey pot. "Pass the bread. Dessert anyone?"

"Husband, wait just a minute, this meal's not finished." Ada stood. She returned with a bowl of berry compote. Mixed in was a fruit Harry had never seen before. "Let me get the sauce dishes."

"Woman, what are those round green things? Never seen them before." Harry poked at one with his fork.

"Gooseberries. Susan brought me some from her yard. Said they're really hard to grow."

Harry honked. "I'm not a goose."

"Hush." Ada filled each bowl, and pointed the serving spoon at CB. "Go on with your idea."

CB popped a gooseberry in his mouth. "Yum, they're good." He eyed the bread and honey. "Now?"

"Serve your uncle first."

"Yes'um. Here you are."

"Thank you, son." Harry nodded toward Ada. "Your auntie asked you a question. Just what is your plan?"

"If the reverend is agreein', we can do it down at the harbor when the *Sallie* is ready to sail. He can sprinkle the baby and dunk the daddy. You know, you can't stop anyone from going to the harbor." CB dripped the honey on his own cut of bread. "Then the crew can watch, too."

Harry's eyes lit up. "And the Brothers would come. Ike, er Isaac, could wear his beanie standin' next to Rabbi

Joe. After all," he chuckled, "those two birds of a feather *should* flock together."

"Hummm," Ada wrinkled her brow, "Did you and Myra think about godparents for our angel? They have to be there, too."

"Sure did. Jack and Marguerite."

"Are you two out of your minds? Colored can't raise a white orphan." She cut her eyes at Harry. "We are the godparents of all the other children. We will be Flossie Mae's, too."

"No." CB set the honey pot on its stand. "I want our daughter to be in the hands of my brother. She's my child, and I pick Jack. Besides, most plantation children were raised by colored. This is no different."

"Please. Excuse. Me." She nodded to her husband, ignoring CB. "I'm not feeling sociable. I'll be in our room."

CB's fair skin reddened as he watched her leave. "Uncle Harry, I am sorry Aunt Ada's upset, but this is something Myra and I agree on." He took a deep breath. "We love you both so much, but...well...," CB's voice drifted to a whisper. "We worry about your ages."

Harry slid back his chair. "I'll handle this. I'll remind her of her rheumatism, and ask her how she plans to handle a house full of children when she can barely get up from the settee." He smiled. "She'll come around." He stretched his back. "Wait here."

By the time Ada and Harry returned to the table, the dishes were scraped and stacked on the sink drain board. The washing water was heating in the kettle and CB was shaving the Ivory soap into the dishpan.

"Here, son," Harry indicated the empty chair. "Let that go for now. We need to talk with you."

"Yes sir." CB sat and turned to his aunt. "I'm sorry if this decision upset you."

"It did, but now I understand." Ada smiled at her husband. "A very wise man helped me remember my creaky bones and tired muscles."

"And a very wise woman helped me remember that sometimes I don't remember." Harry took her hand. "Son, we have a very important question for you."

CB waited.

"Your dear old aunt and uncle want to know if we may pass the care of all the children to Jack and Marguerite." The held hands squeezed. "Would you ask your household if they would cotton to this arrangement?" Harry released his grip. "We love them too much to not let them go."

Ada grinned. "After all, neither of us could chase 'em with a switch if we tried."

Chapter Ten
Let Us Gather at the River

As soon as she waved CB goodbye at the station, Ada bee-lined to the church. Reverend Nicholson smiled at the news of the harbor side ritual. He opened his appointment book. "When do you want it done?"

Ada leaned across his desk, peering at his calendar, trying to read up-side-down. "CB said right before the *Sallie Lou* sails. He wants the crew to witness." She pointed at the page. "See if the Guild has anything scheduled. They should be invited." *Even if they won't come.* "Please make sure Linda Sue is with you. She has always shown great concern for my girl." *That'll shut her up.* Ada walked around to the right-side-up of the book, and tapped next week. "Harry said he ushers Sunday. I don't see him here."

She watched the reverend run his finger down the list of names. He flipped the pages. "No, he's not working this month at all." He looked at Ada. "You tell him he can take a vacation." Reverend Nicholson shook his head. "Has he been forgetting things?"

"Yes, but I try to keep him straight."

"You're a good wife." The pastor shut his book and stood. "My dear, let me know when the boat is ready. Everything'll work out." As he watched her leave his study, he murmured, "Thank God for small favors. This will keep the hens *and* the Bishop away."

Ten days later, the *Sallie* was pitched, polished, and ready to be loaded. She almost smelled new, almost. Her crew was called in and told about the baptism. Cookie made sure they were in their best uniforms as the men stood on deck, waiting for their captain and his baby girl.

Harry, Ada, Isaac, and the Masons watched for the Ledbetters. They stood with the Nicholsons by the new counting house near the mouth of the pier. They could hear the family long before they saw them. Nora Lee and Junior were singing at the top of their lungs. Flossie Mae was screaming, and Myra was hushing. Marguerite was trying to keep the rest in some semblance of an organized parade. Jack and CB walked behind.

"Y'all look like someone's trying to stuff pillows in the wind," commented Jack.

"Get up here and help," hollered Marguerite over her shoulder. "You're the godfather, for goodness sake."

"Yes ma'am."

Jack joined his wife and began the hymn from the beginning. The children immediately took his lead and lowered their voices to a proper level. Miraculously, the maiden of honor stopped squalling, soothed by the hymn.

"Shall we gather at the river,
Where bright angel feet have trod,
With its crystal tide forever
Flowing by the throne of God?"
"Yes, we'll gather at the river,
The beautiful, the beautiful river;
Gather with the saints at the river
That flows by the throne of God."

Once assembled in the counting house, the three sailors stowed their duffels. Reverend Nicholson smiled, spread his arms, and spoke. "Thank you all for coming. Today is a very special day." He looked at Myra. "My dear, it is especially nice to see you." Myra nodded. The Reverend smiled. "I have never met your husband."

CB stepped forward. "I am CB Ledbetter. Thank you for baptizing me and my daughter."

"You are welcome. However we have a small concern."

Ada stiffened, her eyes flashing. "Reverend Nicholson, you assured me that there would be no problem. I took you at your word."

"My dear, my word has always been good. It's the circumstances that are the problem." He pointed out toward the harbor. "Take a gander at how tall this pier is." Reverend Nicholson looked at CB. "I cannot dunk you without drowning us both. We are too high, and with all the work being done on the new seawall, the water by your ship is just plain filthy. Even if I could, I wouldn't dunk you here."

CB looked to Myra and then nodded. "You're absolutely right, and I know what's in bilge, just never thought about it. Could you sprinkle me when you do Flossie Mae?" He took his baby girl from her mother and headed to the door. "Come on, family, let's gather at the river." He led them all to the far end of the wharf where their ship was moored. The reverend spread the altar cloth over a barrel, set out his mason jar of holy water, and began. The baby did just fine, but her daddy cried through the whole ritual. When Reverend Nicholson called for the congregational pledge, *Sallie Lou's* entire crew responded with a hearty "We do."

Jack Smith was the loudest.

After closing prayers and blessings, the families returned to the counting house. There Cookie set out a delicious looking yellow sheet cake, along with plates, napkins, and forks for the celebration. He'd lay the repast on the largest surface, not knowing the significance. Isaac stood proudly at his desk and served his newly baptized brother-in-law the first cut. Holding out his arms for Flossie

Mae, the proud uncle took a finger full of the butter caramel icing, and fed his beloved niece a bit on her lips.

"Oh, my beautiful child, your Aunt Julia would've loved to have been here." A silent tear escaped his left eye at the memory of her death in the flood. "You are a testimony to her." He cleared his throat. "I, uh, I am so happy that her God-given name and family lives on." He touched his yarmulke. "Thank you all for inviting me."

"Mighty welcome, sir." Jack took up the cake knife. "You've got your hands full. Can I help you?"

"That would be wonderful." Isaac snuggled the baby. "She really brings back the memories of our..." He blinked his tearing eyes.

"Do you need me to take her?" CB's voice was soft.

"No, I want to hold her." Isaac lifted the baby to his face. "I love you, little darlin'. I think you look a tad bit like your Aunt Julia, rest her soul."

Flossie Mae stared at her uncle. "Hat?" She reached for his head.

Isaac looked around, laughed, and plopped his yarmulke atop her christening cap. "Yes precious, my hat." Flossie Mae pulled the beanie off and started chewing on it. "How does it taste, little one? You know it's kosher."

Manners set aside, Mrs. Nicholson sidled up to Isaac. "Where's your son? Last time we saw Ikey was at Julia's funeral, rest her soul. Hasn't been to church since."

"I can't keep him right now. I'm living in a boarding house, so he's with Joe's family."

"*Rabbi* Joe? But what about his Christian..."

Reverend Nicholson heard her tone. "Linda Sue, we need your opinion over here. Ada just asked me about ..."

A boson's whistle was sounding from the *Sallie Lou.* CB and Jack nodded to each other. The call was 'side galley', the standard officers' beckoning. CB embraced his brother-in-law and his daughter. "It's time to go, baby girl, time to go." The children crowded the three departing sailors, hugging legs, middles, or anything else they could grab. The calling repeated.

"Marguerite, will you escort me to the plank?" Jack slung his kit over his shoulder and hooked arms with his wife. She tiptoed and whispered in his ear. Jack shook his head. Myra and CB followed in like fashion. Junior looked around the counting house, shrugged and walked behind. He kept a proper distance from the kissing couples when they all said "goodbye." As the women turned to leave, Myra blew her son a silent smooch. "Fare well, young sailor, fare well."

Junior saluted, turned, and scampered up the ramp.

Myra smiled as she joined Marguerite. "What did you say to him?"

"Spending plan."

Laughing, she gathered the baby and looked around for her scattered brood. "Our house will be a bit quieter."

"*Oui*, thank heavens. We could use a little peace."

"Amen to that." Rubbing right above his brows, Harry stepped up to the group.

Ada followed. "Is your head hurting again?"

"Shush, woman, just need to get away from all this commotion." Harry gestured with his chin toward the running sounds of children out on the boards. "Time for the train?"

Myra nodded. "Auntie."

"Yes, darling?"

"Thank you for making this happen."

"You are welcome." Ada gathered both nieces to her and gave them a bosom-squashing hug. "We love you all so much." Releasing her embrace, she slid her arm through her husband's. "Come on, Sir Grump-a-Lot, let's go home."

Chapter Eleven
Ikey

Ikey hated his father.

Things had been just great before the hurricane. Every Sunday they'd gone to the Methodist Church, where his mother spent the rest of her week days with the ladies of the Guild. His father was lead counting man in an office on the docks and always worked arithmetic with him in the evenings. Then his mother, Julia, got killed, their house got flooded, his father turned all Jewish, and even wore a stupid little hat. Worst of all, Ike Sr. changed his name to Isaac Jacoby, and dumped Ikey with a rabbi's family that did all that Jewish trap.

Now it's a year later.

Yep, Ikey Jameson hated his father, who was too busy with his work to come visit. He hated the family he was put out to. However, he didn't hate the rabbi's daughter, Sarah, who was almost three years older than him and liked beer and kissing. Nobody in the house knew what was going on out by the bushes. However, Sarah worried Ikey. She was always trying to get a rise out of him. This was one big problem, because she had titties. "You know," she'd whisper, "You can feel on me if you want. The folks won't know."

Ikey had no buddies to talk to about all this. His friend, Junior Gallaway, the only one around from his old life, got sent to jail for drunkenness after one of their kissing nights with Sarah. Ikey never knew what happened to him when he was taken to the courthouse. Some people in the neighborhood said Junior got shipped out on a work gang. Some said he got hung in Austin. *They don't hang twelve year olds, do they?*

That night she started again. The two were sitting out back by the oleander hedge. Ikey had spent a nickel for a half bucket of beer, and they were sneaking kisses and drinks. "You want me to feel on you?" Sarah put her hand on Ikey's knee, and started finger walking north.

"I just want to drink." Ikey put her hand back where it belonged. "You need to keep to your drinking. Don't need to feel nothin' but dizzy." Dipping into the bucket, he handed her a foaming china teacup full of beer.

She drank it straight down and dipped some more. "Same at 'cha." Her smile was crooked. "You sure ya don't wanna play?" She leaned over and stuck her tongue in his ear.

"No, just drink."

Sarah slurped her beer. "Ya know," she said, handing him the cup, "fosters don't count in that stuff about first cousins."

Ikey slurped his own. "We gotta stop this. You go lickin' my ear, feelin' my leg, and the next thing ya know, we could be in trouble." He held up the empty cup, nodding for more. "I was told to never get started 'cause a boy can't stop, and then there's a baby. I don't want no baby." He drained his drink. "Dang, I'm almost fourteen. You know any daddy who's fourteen?"

"Nope, just some girls with babies." Sarah stood up. "I'm goin' in. Ya comin'?" She swayed and grabbed at the hedge, but that didn't break her fall. Ikey offered his own unsteady hand and pulled her out of the bushes.

"Ya got twigs in your hair. Let me get 'em." Ikey pulled oleander from her braids and handed her the leaves.

Sarah started giggling. "Thank you, kind sir." She wiggled her eyebrows. "I should give you a special kiss."

Ikey shook his head. "Naw, not now." He headed toward the house. "Leave the bucket and cup. I'll get it tomorrow."

Sarah sniffed the leaves. "Wonder if they would make the beer taste different?"

Neither child knew about oleander. They would learn.

Chapter Twelve
Snuff's Enough

All the boys did it, even some of the girls. Ikey had his own in his pocket. Tube Rose Sweet Scotch Snuff was his favorite, but it cost too much. W.E. Garrett was much cheaper. Besides, dip made your teeth brown, and the adults would know, but nobody could see up your nose.

"Dang it, fellas, how do you keep from sneezing?" The boys were off to the far corner of the school yard. They gathered there every day after dinner break, before the bell rang them in. They were passing the can, and several boys had exploded their pinch before they could breathe it all the way in.

Ikey grinned. "Practice." He flared his nostrils, showing that there was no residue to be seen. "I've been usin' since…"

"Yeah, we know, since Jesus grew hair." The boys laughed. "We're gonna need more 'en a snort this afternoon," said Jay Jay. "I heard there's a surprise test on yesterday's homework." He grimaced. "Any of you guys actually do it?"

"Nope," was the almost unison reply. Ikey stood silent. All the rest took another snort. Just then the second bell rang and they straggled toward the school door.

Sidling beside Ikey as the boys stood lined up outside the classroom, Jay Jay hissed, "You gonna make us look bad?"

"Whacha talkin' about?"

Jay Jay knuckle-punched him in the arm. "I'm a'thinkin' you studied. Ya better hadn't, that's all I gotta say."

"Hey." Ikey rubbed the sore spot. "Rabbi Joe makes us. He questions us on everything we study."

Jay Jay looked at him. "Who's *us*? I thought you were in some sort of orphanage, or something."

"I stay with my father's friends. The Cohen's have a girl a couple of years older than me. She has school at home. Even then, she has lots to study." Ikey cricked his eyebrow. "Sometimes her 'n' me do *home*work, if you get my drift."

"Um, I gue..." Jay Jay's next words were drowned by the final bell. They slid into their assigned seats just as the teacher turned from the chalk board.

"Ladies, gentlemen, please take out your pens. There are a few questions about what happened at the battle of San Jacinto waiting for your wonderful answers."

Ikey went home with an A minus paper and another bruise on his arm. *I gotta show them I'm not a pansy.* The next day he bought some Mail Pouch.

Chapter Thirteen
Sweet Oleander

Three days later Ikey spent a nickel for another half bucket. The pair met at their usual place. Earlier, Sarah'd brought out the old chipped teacup, the one she knew her *muter* never used, and left it under the bushes. Ikey carefully carried the pail from its hiding place against the garden shed, and they settled in, close to the leaves, for an evening of drinking and kissing. The days since their last chance to be alone were very busy with Ikey's schooling, Sarah's *shul*, and her housekeeping chores.

Ikey dipped out the first cupful and handed it to Sarah.

She took a sip. "I want to try something."

Taking another dip, Ikey winked and drank straight down. "You always want to try something." He handed her the cup.

She giggled. "No, you silly goose, not *that*, I want to try something with the beer." She reached above her head and pulled off a branch. "I want to see if the beer tastes better if I put some leaves in it."

Ikey made a face. "Why would you want to ruin the beer? It tastes good as is."

Sarah dipped her own cupful and dropped two leaves in it. They swirled slowly in that sea of foam. Sarah took the end of the stick and sank her miniature ships, stirred the whole thing for about a minute, then fished the greenery.

"Here goes nothing." Sarah took a tiny sip. "Hmmm." She took a deeper drink and finished the cup.

"Tastes like beer, only sweeter. Thought it would taste like the flower smells." She leaned back. "You wanna try?"

"Naw, I'll drink mine regular. I like the taste plain." Ikey dipped his own and threw it back like whiskey. He looked over at Sarah. "Ya wanna kiss?"

"Uh huh." She crawled to Ikey and threw herself across his lap. "You make me dizzy, lover boy." She pulled his head down and kissed him hard. "Here." She grabbed his hand and put on her left breast. "Feel my heart beat."

Ikey jumped up, his face flaming. "Are you crazy? I told you we can't do that." He grabbed the bucket and started toward the shed, making a show of trying to dump the beer.

"I'm sorry," Sarah called, patting the dirt beside her. "Come on back to the bushes. I'm thirsty."

"No funny stuff." Ikey sat down and dipped the cup.

"Thanks." She drank it quickly. "I'm really dry. Can I have more?"

"Just a little, I want some, too."

"Gonna put more leaves in," she said. "Might make it sweeter." Sarah rubbed three leaves between her palms and dropped the mess into the half-full cup. This time she stirred with her finger.

"Hey. Don't do that." Ikey made a disgusted face. "I don't want mud in my beer."

Sarah set down her stewing cup and swiped her hands along his sleeve. "See, I'm just dusty, not dirty." She returned to stirring. Then she drank.

Ikey took the cup and threw away the leaves. Pulling his shirt tail loose, he studied the porcelain and wiped it clean. There was just enough in the bucket to fill 'er up. He leaned back on one elbow and stared at Sarah. She had red cheeks and eyes were closed. He slowly drank the dregs. "What 'cha thinkin'"?

She looked through lidded eyes. "I thin' I'm drunk, 'n' I thin' I like it." Her head fell to her chest and her mouth went slack, drool dripping.

"Good God, girl, wake up." Ikey shook her arm. "Ya can't sleep here. The folk'll come lookin'."

She opened one eye, grinned, and blew him a lopsided kiss. "Lemme alone, I'm busy bein' dizzy." The other eye popped open. "Hee, hee, busy bein' dizzy. 'At was funny." Down went the lids. "Busy bein' dizzy, dizzy bein' busy. Busy..." She snored.

Ikey stood on his own unsteady feet. He hid the cup and the pail in the oleander. "Jesus Christ, she's really drunk. What'm I gonna do now?"

"Quit prayin'," she mumbled. "Ya know I'm Jewish. It don't work on me."

He squatted behind her and stuck his arms through her pits. "Can you get up? You're too tall for me to hoist."

She leaned her head back on his chest, looked up, and burped. "Ya wanna kiss, lover boy? My heart's beating hard for you."

"No, dammit, get up." Ikey jerked his arms back and shoved out with his chest. Sarah's head flew and the momentum tumbled them face forward. Ikey scrambled off her back. "Get up, dammit it, get up and walk." He stepped in front of her and offered his hand. "We're gonna get killed if the folks see us come in together."

"Uh huh."

"So stand up."

"Uh huh."

Ikey pulled hard. Sarah found her feet, and the momentum sent her shuffling toward the back porch. She landed on a stoop step. Ikey watched from the hedge as, after a bit, she stood, touched the *mezuzah* and made her way into the kitchen.

Once the screen was closed, Ikey circled the house, quietly slipping through a barely-opened front door, ignoring the charm posted there. He burrowed under his sheet and covered his face with the pillow. Once again the grief hit him. *Oh Mother, oh Mother.* Late in the night, Ikey Jameson fell asleep.

Chapter Fourteen
Bitter Brew

"*Oy,* how did I get here?" Early dawn light drifted through the kitchen curtains, not yet shining under the table where Sarah lay. "*Oy vey, ikh bin in konflikt.* I gotta get upstairs before there's trouble."

Silent tip-toeing got the girl into her room seconds before her mother shuffled past, on her way to start the morning's chores. Slipping out of her yesterday clothes, Sarah put on her nightgown and wrapper. She wandered back down into the kitchen.

"*Muter.*"

"*Yo meyn tokhter.*" Esther eyed her child. "Why are you up so early?"

"Is there any yesterday bread? I'm overly hungry." Sarah smiled at her mother. "Would it be all right if I eat something before breakfast?" She sniffed. "And a cup of coffee to wash it down?"

"Of course, my darling." Sarah made the slightest recoil as she felt her mother brush back the wisps that were escaping her braids. "Child, when was the last time you reworked your hair? Somehow you have twigs caught up in your plaits." She picked out the few sticks. "Just where have you been, playing in the bushes?" Wagging her finger, Esther said, "A lady wears her *babushka* when she goes out. It keeps things neater."

"But *Muter,*" Sarah whined, "Some of the *shiksas* tease me. They call me names."

"You should be proud." Esther began rummaging in the cupboard. "Where is my teacup from Brooklyn? The one with the chip." Sliding several cups aside, she continued to search, even looking behind the Seder dishes used for *Pesath*.

Sarah kept a passive face. "Why do you want that old thing? You said the chip scratched your lips."

Placing two everyday china mugs on the sideboard, Esther poured. She brought coffee, the heel from the yesterday bread, and a jam pot to the table. "You are right about the chip. It does scratch my lips. I never use it, but I love it just the same."

Sarah *schmeered* the jam. "Why?" She took a big bite.

"It is the only thing that survived when the family fled to America," Esther said with a winsome smile. "The cup is from my Brooklyn *bubbe*. It was her first milk cup."

"And…"

"And you are from Brooklyn, too."

"So?" Sarah blew her coffee, as she was just learning how to drink it without scalding the roof of her mouth.

"So, like my grandmother's chip and its scratch, your *babushka* tells your story." Esther took her first sip full-heat. "Don't ever be ashamed of who you are." She reached across the table and stroked her daughter's face. "Oh my *tokhter*, you are growing up so quickly." She lifted Sarah's hands and kissed her knuckles. "Finish your bread and go work your hair. You do not want your *abba* seeing you all bushy." She smiled. "No father wants to look across the study table at a messy daughter."

Sarah stuffed the rest of the heel in her mouth and carried her drink up to the room. An hour later she was combed, braided, and dressed for the day, leaving the mug hidden in her stocking drawer. Ikey was sitting at the breakfast table, working on pancakes and a glass of milk. He looked up from his plate and opened his eyes wide.

Sarah tilted her head toward her mother and didn't say anything, then nodded toward the back door.

After a few minutes, the two met by the shed. "*Muter* wanted her chipped cup this morning."

"That's something new."

"I know. She's all talk about Brooklyn and old things." Sarah rolled her eyes. "I gotta sneak it back in with the others. You'd think Queen Esther used to drink from it instead of mother's *bubbe*."

The back screen squeaked open. "Ikey," Rabbi Joe called from the stoop, "time to get a-walking. School won't wait for you to get there." He swung the strapped school books back and forth. "Come get these and don't forget your dinner bucket."

"Yes, sir, I'm comin'."

Joe handed over the books and food. "You too, young lady, come in for our Hebrew lesson."

"Aww…"

"No *kvetching*."

"Yes, *Abba*, one minute."

"Don't make it a minute and a half." Joe smiled, and he disappeared back into the kitchen. Sarah slipped the cup in her apron pocket. Halfway through the morning, she hid it behind the regular mugs. Later on, she "found" it in the cupboard when she set the dinner table. Without a word, Esther placed it on the mantle, the side with the chip on display.

Two days later, Ikey raised his breakfast milk glass like a toast. Sarah knew that meant there would be beer in the shed, waiting. She lifted her own glass, and nodded. She had a plan.

Come evening they met in their usual place. Sarah was wearing her *babushka*.

"Why've you got your hair tied up?" Ikey'd only seen her that way when she was helping with the house cleaning. "You look like you're supposed to be washin' windows."

"*Muter* fussed at me when she saw the twigs in my hair from last time we were here." She wrinkled her nose. "Take it off as soon as I get away from her." Sarah patted the lumps in her apron pocket. She pulled out the mug. "Here, we gotta use this. She turned the teacup into a kind of shrine or something. Every time she sees me in the parlor, she points at the mantle and says 'chip'." She looked around. "Where's the beer?"

"I'll get it in a minute. First I wanna do some kissin'." He scooted closer. "We gotta do our kissin' before the beer gives you any wild ideas." He leaned in and puckered. She put her finger on his lips to "hush" him. He kissed it.

She grinned. "That's all for now. Get the beer, I've got a surprise." She crooked her head. "You're gonna like it."

When Ikey returned, he found Sarah holding a corked bottle. It was full of a dark green liquid with some leaves in the bottom. She sloshed the contents side to side. Without a word, she pulled the stopper and dumped it into the beer.

"What the hell is that?" Ikey stared.

"Shhh, I said you're gonna like it." Sarah took the mug and stirred the beer around. She pulled out a cupful and drank several swallows. Smiling, she handed over the rest. "Here. It's yummy."

Ikey's tentative sip registered nothing but beer. He finished it off and held out the mug. "More?"

"Sure." She dipped, and he drank. He dipped, and she drank.

Ikey settled back. "Damn, girl, wha's that green stuff? The dizzies are here already." He tilted against her.

"I know, feels good." Sarah handed him a full mug. "Wan' s'more? Bottoms up, then you c'n feel on me." She giggled as he finished, dipped out her portion, and drank. She opened her blouse five buttons. "Come on, lover boy, yer honey mama's waitin'."

She took his limp hand and put it against her skin. He did not move. She shimmied her shoulders, jiggling her breasts. No reaction. Sarah left his hand there, reached around Ikey, and filled the mug. That movement dislodged his hand, and he folded sideways onto the dirt, the dust covering his colorless lips.

Once more she drank straight down. "Woah, good dizzies. Gonna nap, too." She cuddled beside him, throwing an arm around his middle. "I feel your heart beat. It's fas' like…"

Joe and Esther found them early the next morning. The children were barely breathing.

Chapter Fifteen
Death Bed

Dr. Shien didn't know why, but he did know what happened to the children, saying they had been poisoned by the oleander syrup in the bottle found beside the bucket out where they lay. The only way to save them was to make them pee. And pee. And pee. Their systems had to be flushed clean. NOW.

"How do you make him drink when he won't wake up?" Isaac was called in from his boarding house to attend his son. On the way, he stopped by the docks to let his men know there was an emergency and that Mr. Thomas would fill in for him. "Oh God, I can't lose my child, too." He was crying so hard that Esther had to take him away from the bedroom where the sheeted children lay side by side. She walked him down into the kitchen table, and sat with her old friend.

Joe and the doctor were doing frightening things up upstairs. Tubes had to be inched down each child's throat so that water could be dripped into their stomachs. Oleander poisoning causes a heart to stop. Vomiting with the hose down their throats would kill them.

"Isaac." Joe was calling from above. "Esther. We need you both right now."

Isaac startled. "They're dead. Oh my God, they're dead."

Joe called out again. "Bring water."

"Oh God, oh God, they want to wash the bodies." Isaac was blubbering.

Esther was at her wit's end. "Shut up, you idiot. Did he say 'Isaac, come here and close your son's eyes?' No, you imbecile, he called for water. He must be ready to give them life." She rummaged through the pantry and handed him two tin pitchers, pointing at the pump by the sink. "Do it," she commanded, and ran up to see what had happened.

Careful not to splash, Isaac followed with the water. Esther brushed past him, heading down. "Funnels, they need funnels." She moved so fast that the water and two funnels arrived at the same time.

Dr. Shien asked Esther to step out into the hall. "We will know soon if this works." The doctor lowered his voice. "They will wet themselves. I know you don't want your mattress ruined."

Esther nodded.

"Do you have an old oilcloth we can put under them and towels to use as diapers? The kidneys must function to save their lives." He took her hands. "We had to undress them, and I saw their bodies. They are no longer children."

Esther squeezed his hands. "I know."

"Please consider the consequences of an unrelated, uncircumcised Gentile and your *tohkter* living under the same roof." He shook his head. "I do not want to come back here to attend a birth."

"I know." Esther released the doctor's hands. "I know."

"If they survive, you know what you must do."

"Yes."

"Let's get back to work." Dr. Shien returned to the sick room.

Esther found an old table cloth in the kitchen pantry and towels in the linen closet. She collected them all, along with two of her husband's nightshirts from his chifferobe. Setting the tubes aside, Joe and Isaac lifted the covered bodies and slid the protection under them. The men were instructed to step outside.

Dr. Shien helped lift as Esther diapered. "You see?"

"Yes sir, I see. I just didn't realize." She pinned each towel in place and wrestled the nightshirts over their bodies.

"You have the task of checking for wetness." He shook his head. "If the water doesn't move in the next twenty four hours, they probably won't survive. When they're wet, write down the color. If you see pink or red, find me right away. Light orange is acceptable. That shows the poison is moving through."

"*Nebekh das, nebekh das,*" sighed Esther.

"Yes, you are the mother of those poor things. However, you are the strength. Joe will need you later, but Isaac needs you now. I know about his dead wife." He pulled the sheet over his patients. "My advice is to keep him busy, away from his old memories. Word is out that he is not over this. Some say that he may have lost his…well, let's just do the best we can to bring him back to a good state of mind."

Esther nodded. "We were children together long ago. I knew his *bubbe.* I will try to remember some old recipes for him while he is here."

"Yes, good food always helps." Dr. Shien opened the bedroom door. "Come in, gentlemen. Our young ones need you."

Dr. Shien soon had the men sitting on either side of the bed, ready to slowly, slowly pour water through the funnels, down the tubes, and into their stomachs. The pitchers were too large for the slowness of the job, and Esther was sent to fetch smaller containers. She brought back a mug for Isaac and the chipped teacup for Joe. "My *tohkter* will learn the meaning of the chip," she told her husband. "One day it will be hers."

"Today it may save her." The doctor took the cup and filled it almost full. 'Watch." He tipped it into the funnel Joe was holding. "Pour slowly. Too much will harm her." He demonstrated, then looked at Isaac. "Now you."

A half hour later, Dr. Shien was satisfied with his helpers. "You three hold their care in your hands. I will come back tomorrow morning."

Joe nodded. "*Adank*."

Esther showed the good doctor down the stairs. "Yes, thank you."

Dr. Shien took his hat from the hall tree. "Missus Esther, we all are counting on you."

She opened the front door. "I know, *oy*, I know."

The doctor turned to her at the bottom of the porch steps. "Oh, by the way, when you cook, save me a *nosh*."

Esther smiled. "I will."

Chapter Sixteen
To The Store

Esther needed to cook. "I know my Joe'll be hungry. I'll make him fried noodles." There were sheets of dough draped over the back of an extra kitchen chair, ready for cutting. She had the root vegetables, but no fresh chicken for the fat. That meant a quick trip to the market. Taking money from the cookie jar, Esther put on her hat and ran up to the men. She did a quick diaper check. Nothing.

"Going for a chicken," she panted. "No time to wring and dress one of our own."

"But the cost?" asked Isaac. "Let me." Balancing the funnel contraption with one hand, he reached for his money clip.

Esther jingled her apron pocket. "No need." She quick-kissed her husband and was down the steps and out the door.

Long strides got her to Dickenson's where she ran smack-dab into a departing customer. The lady's groceries went everywhere.

"*Antshuldigt mir,*" Esther apologized. "Let me help you." She scrambled around picking up wrapped meat and rolling oranges. The lady stared.

"What did you say?" She held open her cloth tote. "I've never heard that kind of talk before."

"Oh," Esther smiled. "That's Yiddish. I'm Reform Jewish."

"Hmmm," murmured the lady. "My husband knows a Jewish man from his Lodge. Calls him Rabbi Joe."

Esther dropped the last of the stray fruit into the sack. "That's my husband. My name is Esther Cohen. Perhaps we've met at family events."

"Perhaps. My name is Margery Butler, husband's named Scott." Margery adjusted the straps of her load. "Almost dinner time. Gotta get home and start cookin'." She shook her head. "Twelve o'clock gets here quicker every day, and those young'uns come in right hungry." She tilted her head. "You have children?"

"Yes, but they're very sick." Esther's chin started to tremble. "Pleased to meet you, Margery. I must hurry to them." She nodded and headed to the meat counter.

"I'll say a prayer," called Margery from the front door.

"Sister Esther, what's this you say about sick children?" Harry was busy cutting pork chops on his butcher stand. "What's going on?"

"Oh, Harry, I need a chicken for *schmaltz*. Sarah and Ikey both got into oleander and are poisoned. They might die." The chin tremble exploded into sobs.

Harry was not quite fast enough to catch her as she collapsed. "Ada," he hollered, "Get in here. Now." He stood over her, not knowing what to do. "Esther needs help. She fell down."

Ada's words preceded her. "For God's sake, Harry, what's the matter with you? Get her up, or her dress'll get ruined." She rushed past the chopping block and stood on the other side of Esther. "Don't touch her."

"Huh?" Harry looked from woman to woman. "First you say get her up, then you say don't touch her. Just what in hell am I supposed to do?"

"Dammit, Harry, look at your hands. Go wash them. You were cutting chops."

"So?"

"So she's Jewish, for God's sake." Ada squatted down to Esther. "You're not allowed to touch pork, are you, my dear?"

Esther shook her head 'no'.

Ada looked up at her husband. "I thought you knew that. Now help me up so that I can help her up."

Harry just stood there. "But you said not to."

"Jesus, man, I'm not Jewish. Get *me* up, not her."

"Good Lord, woman, you're giving me a headache."

By the time Harry returned with clean hands, the women were looking through the glass at the chickens lined up in their butcher paper beds. Esther's tears were slowed.

Ada walked behind the counter. "You must take the fattest one." Concentrating on tying the cotton string, Ada's own tears were blurring her sight, slowing the packaging. She'd wrapped their best hen and refused payment.

Esther rushed home, left the meat on the drain board, and ran up the stairs.

"Hello, my dear." Rabbi Joe's voice was soft. He nodded to Isaac, who was slumped, snoring in his chair, the hose still upright in his hand. "Did you get a good one?"

"Yes." Her reply was just as quiet. "Harry and Ada send their love and gave us their fattest hen, no charge." She gestured toward the children. "Have they...?"

"Didn't check. Afraid to, I think."

With gentle movements, Esther pulled back the sheet covering the two, still forms. She raised the nightshirt on her daughter. The towel was dry. Doing the same to Ikey, she found a small, light orange stain.

"He peed, he peed." Esther's jubilance startled Isaac.

"Whaaat?" He dropped the funnel. "Did you say...?"

"My dear friend, your son is wet." Joe pointed. "It's starting to work."

Esther quietly covered her daughter. No celebration there. Joe's mouth turned down in acknowledgement. She backed out of the room. "I will cook now."

In the kitchen she banged the pots to cover the sounds of her sorrowing.

Chapter Seventeen
Chicken Soup

Esther knew noodles would take more time than the men could wait. It was daybreak when the children were discovered. There had been no breakfast, not even coffee, so she decided to change around the day's foods. Perhaps that would change her daughter's luck. Esther set the chicken to simmer with the vegetables, salt, and garlic. The pot was put to boil and the stove heat warmed the oven. Twenty minutes later, she made a slight breakfast tray of coffee and warmed left-over biscuits with butter and jam.

"I know it's dinner time." Esther touched her husband's cheek. "You can't rush a good chicken." She indicated the three waiting mugs. "Gentlemen, lay down your devices, and, if need be, stretch your legs." She smiled. "The brew's plenty hot in the pot. It'll wait."

"I'll show Isaac the necessary." Joe led his friend out the door. "Come, *gut fraynd*, right down the hall."

As soon as the men were gone, Esther checked her daughter again. Nothing. She quietly prayed the *Mi Shebeirach,* begging for healing while unpinning the barely damp towel around Ikey in preparation for his diaper change. The men would have to lift him, so she waited. She stroked the boy's cheek and forehead, murmuring the prayer. She absently tickled her fingers behind his ear. Ikey's eyes popped open and he started choking, the tube making him heave and gag. Esther pulled and it flew across the bed.

"I gak ga, I gak ga go," Ikey croaked. The spot on his diaper grew. Screaming for her husband, she threw a fresh towel over the soaking mess that covered the boy. Ikey started to thrash in the bed, hitting Sarah.

"Joe, Isaac, help me. He's awake, he's awake." Esther flung her body across the child to pin his arms. Her weight calmed him.

In the smallest of whisper, he sobbed, "Mother? Where's my mother?"

Silence.

Isaac watched as Joe gently lifted his wife and led her to a side chair. "Father is here, my son," Isaac said." Oh, my child, I am here."

"Mother?" Ikey's words were soul wrenching.

"Gone." Isaac laid his head on his son's chest. "But she gave you life, and I hear your heart beating. Your mother is in your heart now and forever."

"Father?"

"Yes, son?"

"Don't make me go away anymore."

"I promise." Isaac lifted his head and kissed his son's cheek.

Closing his eyes, Ikey appeared to doze. Esther poured and handing Isaac his mug. "Father, I smell coffee. Is it time to wake up?"

"Yes, my son, it is."

Ikey was moved to his own bedroom. His father never left his side, watching him sleep.

Joe and Esther took turns with Sarah's tube. She still had not passed any water, nor shown signs of awakening. At two in the afternoon Esther went down to the kitchen to check the stew pot. The hen's meat was completely off the bone, juices simmering below that wonderful rich fat. She lifted the pot to the center of the stove and closed the burner. Wrapping her shawl around her, she stepped out into their back yard with her egg basket and a handful of the day old biscuits not eaten in the sick room. Standing by the fence, she threw her bantams some crumbs in the pen yard.

"Here my chick chicks, have some old dinner and breakfast." She smiled at their frenzy. "One, two, three…" Esther counted them as she did each day. She did not like having to reach under a broody, kidnapping her eggs. "Four, five, six…hmmm, ladies, where's your husband?" The rooster was not out with the others. Then she heard his 'cock-a-doodle'. The king of their realm was perched atop the peak of the hen house, crowing his displeasure for her gathering the eggs.

His call brought the memory of her beautiful little girl, helping with this chore. Sarah would crow back at the rooster, 'cock-a-doodling' louder than the bird. Sometimes she would yell the 'doodle-do' with such force that the hens would run to their house in fear.

She sighed. "My girl, my *tohkter,* where is your crowing now?"

Esther sucked in breath and crowed. It echoed off the nesting boxes. She crowed again as she left the hen house, this time louder. King Rooster flew from his castle roof, landing in the middle of his biscuit-eating wives. Esther crowed all the way through the kitchen, up the stairs and into her daughter's bedroom. Joe stared at his wild-eyed wife, standing at the foot of the bed, cock-a-doodling over and over again, the egg basket long forgotten on her arm.

Sarah gagged and flailed, pulling out her own tube. "Gok a goga goo. Gok a goga goo, *Muter.*" She smiled, vomited, and flooded the towel, the oilcloth, and the sheet over her. It was the best mess Esther and Joe ever cleaned up in their whole lives.

Esther drained the broth and fat into a bowl and set in the cool root cellar. Pulling the meat off skin and bones, she put that in the icebox for later. Unfortunately the noodle dough had been drying a bit too long to make good cuts, so she did the best she could with the wettest parts.

When the *schmaltz* was floating, perfect for lifting, Esther spooned that delicious fat into her skillet for the frying. She poured all the wonderful broth back into the pot. Soon it was ready. Her husband liked his noodles boiled soft and fried softer.

The cooking was almost done when Joe called joyfully from above. "Bring the soup. We have two hungry children to feed."

"Yes sir, will do. I'll carry up our plates and we can have a bedroom banquet." Esther shredded meat on each pile of noodles, and set the tray with silverware, napkins, and bowls. The smell of the soup whetted everyone's appetites.

Isaac slowly fed his son. Ikey asked for some of his father's noodles, but was told he'd have to wait until the doctor came in the morning.

Plates empty, Esther went to the kitchen for more. She served the extras first to her husband, and after a quiet exchange of words, brought the bowl to the boy's room. Joe followed and watched as Esther sat by Isaac. "My old friend, we have to ask you to take your Ikey home." She gestured. "Your wonderful son is a young man. My wonderful *tohkter* is a young woman. It is not right that they live in the same household anymore."

"You will stay here with your son until..."

"Until he is well." Esther finished her husband's thoughts. "That will give me time to teach you how to cook some things." She smiled. "I cannot let you starve. After all, your b*ubbe* taught my *muter*. I will close the circle."

"I understand. I need to find a house for us." Isaac looked first at Ikey and then at Esther, smiling. "And I need to learn how to make chicken soup."

Chapter Eighteen
Brotherly Love

At Lodge that night, when time came around for new business, Rabbi Joe spoke. "I need to find a decent rental house, and I need it now." Word had traveled fast about the near tragedy, and the Masonic Brothers were waiting.

Harry Dickenson stood. "We are all grateful that the children survived. I know that my beautiful grandniece's uncle is setting up housekeeping." Harry looked around the Lodge room. "My Ada squeezed the Methodist ladies, and we have enough pots, pans, dishes and all that's needed for a kitchen. She has a crate of sheets and towels sitting in our back storeroom." He chuckled. "I'm a guessin' we all just didn't think about where he was gonna put it."

Sitting where he always sat, in the middle of the North, Constable Robearde Turner nodded to Harry. He stood, faced the East, and saluted. "Worshipful Master, Wardens, Brothers, I have a two bedroom furnished house for Isaac."

Joe nodded. "Thank you, Brother. What are the terms?"

"Six months, gratis. After that, I'll talk to him." Robearde spread his arms wide. "Gentlemen, this is a family without a mother. Isaac is not a Brother, but he is one of us, just the same. The boy, Ikey, is very close to straying. We must light his path."

After the meeting was closed, all the members gathered in the kitchen for coffee and three kinds of cake, thanks to the wives. There was an up-side-down hat sitting in the middle of the table.

"We're talking about a man who has eaten double-nickel diner meals since he was widowed." Joe gestured toward the hat. "He will need to fill his pantry, thanks to my Esther who has started teaching him cooking." Joe pulled out his wallet and dropped two dollar bills in the hat. "Soon he will have to go back to work."

By the time the cake plates were empty, the hat was full. A curious counting followed. The men had donated the goodly sum of one hundred and twenty seven dollars.

"Thank you, my Brothers," said Harry, adjusting his now empty derby. "You have provided, with my discount thrown in, just about a half year's provisions for Isaac and Ikey." He handed the cash to Joe. "Let's adjourn before our women come looking for us."

Robearde Turner waited outside the door for the rabbi. "You need escorting." It was a stated fact, not a question. He patted his shoulder holster. "My pistol, named him Roscoe. We will see you home."

"You know guns aren't allowed in Lodge." Joe smiled. "Thanks for wearing him."

"Knew there might be some money tonight. Besides, need to tell Isaac where the house is." The Constable grinned, crooked teeth showing in the darkness. "I was lucky that not all my rentals floated away during the hurricane, even if our own house did. T'was nice to have a spare to stay in while buildin' the new one. That's how come it's furnished."

Rounding the corner onto Avenue O, Joe chatted about his own house. "Ours lost some shingles and the back stoop blew off." Joe pointed. "The house stayed."

"Looks fine and strong."

"'Tis. Come in and meet the missus." Joe touched the *mezuzah* on the door frame with his right hand and kissed his fingertips. He smiled at his friend. "A blessing."

Waiting for them in the hall, Esther took her empty cake server. "Good?"

"Yes, ma'am, the best." Joe indicated their guest. "Dear, please meet my Brother, Constable Robearde Turner, a most generous man." He gestured to the settee. "We need to speak with Isaac."

Robearde nodded, touching his hat. "Ma'am, pleased to meet you. Is he home?"

"I'll get him. He's sitting with Ikey. The children are still very weak. Sarah's sleeping." Esther set the covered plate in the kitchen and tiptoed upstairs, avoiding the squeaky fifth step.

Soon all adults were in the parlor. Robearde told about the house, Joe handed over the start-up money, and Isaac bawled, his thin shoulders shaking. They all waited.

"I never thought anyone would ever do this for me," he blubbered. "I, I'm speechless." The sobs started again. "I owe you all so much."

Joe quirked his mouth at Robearde. "I think we'll have to continue this tomorrow. It's been a rough week."

The Constable stood. "Of course, please excuse me, Missus Esther. My own Beatrice will be wonderin' where I am."

Joe walked his Brother to the porch. "We need to get him on his feet and, now that the boy's on the mend, back to work countin' numbers right quick. You see how he is."

"I do, and we will. That man's hurtin'."

"Yes, my Brother, he is."

Chapter Nineteen
New House

Deathly pale, staring at a ghost, Isaac stood one step into the parlor with Robearde. Tears started. "I don't know what to do." He looked at the room. "I don't know what to do." Isaac stumbled to a strange chair where his should have been. The problem with the rental was that it was the very same layout as Isaac's destroyed house. It had two bedrooms, kitchen, side, dining, and sitting rooms. The only difference was that the porch shutters weren't painted green. And the furniture wasn't the same. And the carpet under the table was missing. And his Julia wasn't standing beside the kitchen stove.

"I can't do this, I just can't." More sobs.

Grabbing Isaac, Constable Robearde Turner shook him hard. "Shut up, man," he hissed. "Don't let the boy hear this. You're doing no good for anybody." He shoved Isaac into the chair. "Get ahold of yourself, for God's sake."

"Father, Father, look here. The rooms, they're just like our old ones, and we have a bathroom. Mother would have loved that. We never had a bathroom before." Ikey sauntered down the hall, smacking the third door he passed. "This one's mine," he announced. The boy walked out to the porch, vaulted the steps, and strolled back with one of his valises. "Look, Father, there's even a chest right where my old one was. I'm gonna move the bed." Sounds of drawers scraping and furniture sliding filled the air.

Isaac sniffled. "I, I'm sorry, it's just that--"

"What?" barked Robearde. "What the hell is wrong with you? You're acting like the hurricane was yesterday. All this boo-hooing is trying my patience." Robearde looked around the room. "Good God, man, do you want this house or don't you?"

"I do, I do, oh, I do." Isaac held out his hands in supplication. "It's just, well, I just don't know *what* to do."

Robearde waited.

"I don't know anything about keeping house." Isaac started crying all over again. "I don't even know how to make a good fire in the stove." His sobs got louder. "My Julia did absolutely everything. I can't...."

"My mother used to ask if I wanted a reason to cry." Constable Robearde Turner swung back his right arm, palm open. "Dammit, man, don't make me hit you."

"But—"

"But nothin'. Your wife is dead, but your arms ain't broke. All you're needin' is house help." He lowered his hand. "Ikey's heading so far wrong. Only you can bring him back."

"Yes, sir, I know."

"No, you don't. Your boy could've gone to jail the same as Junior. I saw them both that night." Robearde patted Roscoe. "Could've shot at 'em for trespassing, drunkenness, and mischief. Didn't. Myra and the family took care of Junior's punishment. Him goin' to sea with his step-daddy was the best thing that could have happened to the boy." He shook his head. "I let yours be invisible because of losing his mama. I didn't know you'd thrown him away."

"But..."

"The reality of this mess is that the boy thinks you did just that." Robearde offered Isaac his hand, pulling him out of the chair. "You have a second chance. For God's sake, don't let a little thing like stoking a fire stop you from showing your son what a man does, or you'll soon be visiting him in a jail cell. Mark my word."

"Knock, knock. Anyone at home?" Rabbi Joe stood outside the front screen, holding a small wooden box. "May I come in? I bring your *mezuzah.*"

Isaac wiped his face, sniffed, blew, and walked to the door. "Welcome, Rabbi, to our new house. We are happy to be blessed."

Joe nodded to his Brother as he entered. Robearde saluted.

Ikey caromed into the hall. "Everybody, come see my room. I have it all set up."

"Just a minute, son, Rabbi Joe is here to hang the *mezuzah.* Do you want to watch?"

"I'm not Jewish." Ikey turned to leave.

"I'm not either," said Robearde, putting a firm arm around the boy, clamping down on his shoulder. "I don't guess extra blessings'll hurt us."

They all stepped out on the porch. Joe pulled a small hammer and two nails from his pocket and handed them to Isaac. "This is your new house, your new beginning. You do the honors."

Isaac nodded. "Please, the prayer."

Rabbi Joe opened the box and held the charm against the door frame. "Blessed are You, Lord our God, King of the Universe, Who sanctifies us with commandments and has commanded us in affixing a *mezuzah.*"

Isaac nailed the piece, top leaning in. "I remembered."

Joe smiled. "It's a long way from Brooklyn."

Without a word, Isaac touched the *mezuzah* with his right hand, kissed his fingertips, and entered his house. He stood inside, holding the screen open. "Son, please come into our new home." Ikey looked at the amulet and then at his father. Isaac understood. "No, you do not have to."

"But I do," said Joe, with a smile. Ritual completed, Constable Turner followed his Brother to the hallway.

"Now can I show you my room?"

Chapter Twenty
New Hope

Isaac took some of the money to Dickinson's Grocery with the hope Ada would guide him through his very first food shopping.

"Land's sake, Isaac, you mean to tell me you've never done this before?"

"Never."

"What did you do during Julia's confinement? Oh, wait a minute." Ada laughed. "Now I remember. She'd give you a list, and I filled it. You'd stop by after work and carry everything home."

"Yes, I never ever looked at the paper." Ike shrugged, shaking his head. "She could be exacting, rest her soul."

"She was a blessing to the Guild." Ada tilted her head toward the checkerboard set up with chairs. "Wanna sit? I'll pour you some coffee. We need to talk about your basics." She eyed his frame. "You need to get some good food in you."

Ada soon served steaming mugs and a plate of crybabies, knowing it was one of his favorite sweets. She had a piece of butcher paper and a pencil stub from the meat counter, which she handed over to Isaac. "You write, I'll try to remember everything in my pantry."

"Yes ma'am." Isaac smiled. Julia had always told him what to do. "Go."

Ada started reciting. "You gettin' all this?"

The scribbling stopped. "Yes, just don't check my spelling. Did you say 'coffee'? Don't see it here."

Ada shook her head. "No, it's in the canister on the shelf. I'm still going through the pantry. Is there a grinder in your new house?"

"Didn't notice. Did see a nice pot in the box of things the church ladies put together." Isaac looked at his cookie. "Oh, Ada, I'm so hopeless. This house has running water, and I don't even know how to boil it."

Ting.

Ada stood and smoothed her apron. "Got a customer. I'll be back." She smiled. "Good morning, Margery. What can I get for you?"

"Good morning, Ada. I need a soup bone and some fat back. Makin' greens this afternoon. The family turns their nose up at turnip tops, so I always do collards." Margery stared at Isaac's *yarmulke*. "Is he related to Rabbi Joe?" she whispered. "Met his wife last week."

"The Cohens are dear friends of my nephew." Stepping toward the barrel and chairs, Ada called. "Isaac, come meet Margery. She knows Esther."

Standing, Isaac nodded. "My name is Isaac Jacoby. Pleased to meet you. Esther and Joe have cared for my son since the hurricane."

"I hear both children are recovering nicely. My, my," sighed Margery. "What a scare."

"Yes, ma'am, all is well, now."

"Isaac's a widower. He and his son are setting up housekeeping." Ada pointed at the butcher paper. "Show Margery, maybe she can help while I wrap her order."

The two were just finishing when Ada brought the meat over to the game board. Margery stood, shaking her head. "Ada, this man doesn't know a thing about housekeeping. I told him about a girl I met last week. Said she had a couple years' experience. Heard she rooms downtown. Think she's Jewish 'cause she wears one of those backwards kerchiefs."

Isaac smiled. "We call them *babushkas*." Tearing off a corner of the wrapping paper holding the shopping list, he scribbled his address. "If you see her again, please ask her to come by. Maybe I could hire her. That way we won't starve."

The next day a slim young woman knocked on the Jacobys' door. She was dressed in the plainest of clothes, and her hair was neatly covered. Isaac thought she looked more like dark Hungarian than Jewish, but he didn't care. He let her in.

"Sir, my name is Louise Dubin. Missus Margery sent me. Said you need house help." She waited. "May I sit down?"

Isaac nodded. "Thank you for coming, I am at my wit's end. My son and I were so spoiled by my late wife." He gestured to the kitchen. "I don't know how to fire the stove. Ikey and I are getting really tired of bread and sliced cold meat."

"I can help you. I did work for Matron Bernhaim in Austin. She ran a very big house there." Louise stood, her skirts brushing his trousers' leg as she strode into the kitchen. Within the hour she had made a good fire and set a large pot of water to heat, with Isaac watching from the kitchen table. "You have dirty dishes." The woman helped herself to the icebox. "You need more food. I'll start today."

Isaac felt the relief of familiarity. "Wonderful. My wife was just like you. She didn't ask, just told."

Louise smiled. "We'll do fine." She held out her fingers, ticking off her list of requirements. "I need twenty five dollars paid monthly on the first, meals included. You will give me a half day off on the Sabbath." She sniffed. "I don't smell diapers. That's good because I don't take care of babies."

"No little ones," chuckled Isaac, "My Ikey's soon fourteen. This is a house of bachelors."

She made a pot of spicy rice with the okra and peppers Ada added to his order. Louise sat with them to eat. Isaac had never tasted Jewish food like this, but he ate it, and the boy had two bowls full. After the meal, she washed, and Ikey dried. It was almost like home.

Louise let Isaac help her with her shawl. "I'll see you all in the morning."

"No, I won't be here," said Isaac, walking her to the door. "Now that we have you, I can go back to work. I am head man in one of the counting houses on the docks."

"Ooh." Right then and there Louise made a new list.

"Yes. I always breakfast at the new diner, but will make sure Ikey is up by five thirty. Please pack his bucket."

"I like toast bread for breakfast," hinted Ikey, "With butter and jam."

Louise snugged her shawl and adjusted her head scarf, tucking in a few auburn wisps. "I will be here at five." She headed down the front walk, turning out of sight.

Ikey slipped his hand in his father's. "I like her."

"Me, too."

"Wonder why her hair's kinda short?"

Chapter Twenty-One
Louise Makes Herself T' Home

Letting herself in with the key given the Wednesday after she was hired, Louise made herself at home.

"Goodness, Miss Louise, when did you get here?" Isaac wandered into the kitchen, tying his wrapper around him. It was nice to smell the coffee boiling.

"Early." She put a china mug on the table. "Do you take it strong and black? That's how I make it."

"Yes. How do you take yours?"

She pointed at her own mug. "Just like that. I put top cream in mine. You don't have any, so I used milk. Next time the milk man comes, I'll order some."

"Write down anything else you need. Delivery's tomorrow." Isaac gestured at the empty egg bowl. "We don't have chickens. Put eggs on the list."

"Didn't see any butter. Do you have a churn?" Louise was poking through the side cupboard.

"Write it down, maybe he sells it." Isaac sipped his brew. "What's in this? Tastes different."

"You mean to tell me you have never had chicory coffee?" Louise continued her sorting. "I'm going to empty all this and start over. You didn't lay paper."

Isaac sighed. "Julia always had the shelves covered. Ikey and I didn't know what to do. Just put things away when we got here." He took another drink. "Don't know if I like this."

"Sometimes it's good to make a change." She stood. "Did you wake the child? Look at the time. You should be going, and he should be ready."

"I did, but haven't seen him yet." He stood and retightened his wrapper. "I'll check."

Louise looked him up and down. "Goodness, you aren't dressed. Go take care of that, I'll get the boy."

Walking to his bedroom, Isaac smiled. It was nice to smell coffee, and have a woman tell him what to do.

As Isaac called "Good bye, everyone" from the front door, Ikey asked for more toast. "You Reform like the Cohens and my father? I was raised Methodist."

Louise smeared the bread with a thick layer of the F.R.O.G. jam she'd brought in with her. "Does that mean you say grace?"

"Only when someone's listening." He finished his glass of milk. "My mother listened."

Louise sat across the table, opposite from where Isaac left his mug. "Do you want me to?"

"Naw."

"Your dinner pail's ready. When you get home, tell me what you didn't like. That way I'll not pack it again."

"Miss Louise, I really like ham and cheese. Father said we can't buy anything piggy to eat." He looked up at her with the slightest frown. "Would it be wrong if *you* bought sliced ham, and hid it in the back of the icebox? Father doesn't need to know."

"You little stinker." Louise gathered his breakfast plate and handed him his bucket. "I know Jewish families don't eat pork. If I recall, you said that you are Methodist. Don't see why you can't have what *you* want." Laying her hand on his shoulder, she winked. "Our little secret?"

"Oh, yes, ma'am, our little secret."

"Off you go. Be good and learn. I'll be here when you come home."

The screen slammed, and he was gone.

Louise sat with her cup. She'd only worked in set-up kitchens with women who knew what to do. "Ding dang it, I can do this," she muttered. "This is my last chance. Gotta remember what I learned." An hour later she pushed her escaping hair behind her scarf, shoved the shopping list in her apron pocket and headed toward Dickenson's, the only store she had seen since stepping off the train.

Ting. A short, whitehaired lady looked up from the counter. "Hello. May I help you?" She walked around the apple barrel and put out her hand. "My name is Ada, Ada Dickenson. My husband and I own this mercantile." She smiled. "Have we met? You look familiar."

"Um, er, no, ma'am, I'm new in town from Austin, working as a house girl. I need to shop for my employer, Mister Isaac Jacoby. Does he have an account here?" Ada nodded. Louise showed her the list. "He's just starting out, and his supplies are incomplete."

"Yes, my dear, I know." Ada chuckled as she read. "I'm a guessin' you're the one Margery told us about. She helped him do his first shopping. I see you're rounding out his kitchen." She spied 'ham slices'. "For the boy? Used to feed him lunch. He loved my ham and cheese sandwiches."

"Yes ma'am, that's what he wants. Told me not to tell his daddy." Louise looked heavenward. "Guess his mama made them. It's the least we can do for the poor thing. Can you keep this quiet from Isaac?"

"Of course, after all, the boy's Methodist. How are you going to make his lunches if you can't touch pork? Margery said she thought you were Jewish, too."

Louise put her finger to her lips. "I'm not that strict."

"Oh, I didn't know there were different ways." Ada turned to the meat counter. "Maybe it's like what's between Catholics and, say, Baptists. They all claim they're the same, but, boy, oh boy, do they do things opposite." She placed a boneless smoked shank on the slicer and cranked out four pieces. "I set the blade to the thickness we have at our house. Four enough?'

"Five please; I'll make him a sandwich every day. What does he like on the bread?"

"Just butter." Ada wrapped the meat. "Same count for the cheese?"

Louise smiled. "I want him to be happy, bless his heart."

"You'll need to make breakfast rice." Ada pointed over to the staples shelf. "You want long grain? I'll add it to your order. Every day he'd eat it with sugar and cream as a dinner dessert. I'm guessin' about a filled half pint jar in his bucket." She looked at the spice section. "Does Isaac have cinnamon? I always sprinkled some over the cream."

"Please, and a tin of ground nutmeg." Louise smiled. "They say a way to a man's, er, boy's heart is through his stomach."

"You mean mace?" Ada was surveying the tins. "The only nutmeg we have is whole, and that's considered a fancy." She stretched to reach. "Isaac's wife bought mace like everyone else."

"Yes, mace, thank you." Louise looked at her growing stack of supplies. "Was his wife a simple cook?"

"Oh, Lord no. Julia, rest her soul, was a fantastic cook. She made the most wonderful angel food cake with orange sauce." Ada licked her lips. "I could eat a slice right this very minute."

"I'll have to learn."

Ada looked at Louise. "Where's your grocery tote? I thought all Jewish women used them."

"I didn't notice if there was one in the house. Could you box this up for me? I would appreciate it so much."

"Of course." Ada started packing one of the small wooden crates by the counter. "Now, I don't know what you're used to in Austin, but around here, it's expected that you bring it back next week. Makes it easier for those who forget."

"Oh, yes, ma'am, I understand." Louise gathered her purchases. "Thank you for all your help."

"Oh," added Ada. "I know your Sabbath is on Saturdays, our regular shopping day. Will I see you next Wednesday? That's when the others come in."

Louise gave a slight nod and left. Ada watched her go. "Wonder what she did in Austin? Humph, nutmeg. Must've been in a rich house. Next thing you know she'll be askin' for J.B. O'Donohue Mocha and Java beans," she muttered to herself. "Who does she favor? Forgot to ask her name. Oh well, she'll be back."

Chapter Twenty-Two
Chaw Choke

The first thing Louise did when she got back in the house was to check the pantry for a canvas sack. Her 'training' did not include any form of shopping. "Wonder if the boy knows where one might be?" she said aloud.

"Where what?" Ikey was sitting on the kitchen step stool.

Startled, Louise turned around. "When did you get home? I didn't hear the door slam."

"Couple of hours ago. Got sent home sick after dinner. Puked twice. Don't tell Father." He stood, swayed, and just made it to the kitchen sink. He wiped his mouth with the back of his hand. "Three."

Louise pulled out her hanky, covered her nose, and stepped backwards. Her 'training' did not include sickness. "Please rinse the sink. I'll clean it later."

"Aren't you going to feel my forehead? Mother always did when I got sick."

"Please rinse and go lay down." Louise spoke from the pantry door. "I'll feel your head in your room."

Ikey saw what was in the sink, gagged, and ran to the bathroom. "Four," he hollered. "Goin' to bed."

Louise approached the sink like it was a pit of vipers. Still holding her handkerchief to her face, she saw the mess. Surrounded by vile liquid was a glob of brown goo. She knew exactly what it was. Tucking her hanky back in her pocket and holding her breath, she scooped it up with the oldest spoon she could find, dropping it, spoon and all, in the rubbish bin. A rinse, a swipe, and the evidence was gone. She squared her shoulders and walked in Ikey's room.

Louise sat on the edge of his bed. "Child, let me feel for a fever, if that's what you want."

"Mother always did." Ikey's voice was soft.

"Even when you swallowed chewing tobacco?"

Ikey sat straight up, eyes popped wide. "Please, please don't tell Father. He might send me away again."

Her quiet voice matched his. "You should know better than to swallow your chaw. How'd it happen?"

"Got caught in history class. Forgot to spit after dinner recess. Knew I'd get the paddle, so I swallowed it." Ikey grinned. "The rest is history."

"You will not do this again, do you understand?" She stood. "Go wash out your mouth, and get to work on whatever lessons you missed. I have supper to fix." Louise stopped at his doorway. "And yes, I will not tell your father. This is between you and me."

"Will you write me a sick note for tomorrow? I need a day of recovery since…"

"No." Louise was half way down the hall.

"But I'm still…"

"No means no."

Ikey smiled. "You sound like Mama."

Chapter Twenty-Three
Domestic Tranquility

Each morning Louise arrived exactly on time. She always had fresh toast bread and jams on the table, waiting for Ikey's breakfast. Isaac learned to not be caught in his dressing gown, making sure he was presentable when she let herself in. The two would share coffee time, chatting about his day.

"I don't know much about a counting house. Do you actually go on the boats and tally their cargo?" Louise buttered herself a slice of toast. "That would be so very tiring."

"No," Isaac laughed, "I supervise the men who handle all the invoices for the buyers. I haven't stepped out to a boat in years."

"You must be exceptionally good with numbers." Louise took a bite.

"Well, our office won an award for our tight accounting." Isaac pointed across the way at the shining plaque mounted on the dining room wall. "I accepted that the day of the hurricane." He shrugged. "Since our old office blew away, I thought I'd better just keep it with me. You know, for safety's sake."

"That proves you are a smart man."

Isaac blushed. "I guess you're right."

Louise would ask what he wanted for his evening meal, and Isaac would often defer, saying she could buy and cook whatever the boy liked. This became a daily ritual.

One morning Isaac wandered to the kitchen, fiddling with his collar button. Before he could protest, Louise had it fastened. She patted his shirt front and picked a small thread from his sleeve. "Who does your laundry?" she asked.

"Oh, the old Irish woman around the block." Isaac inspected his other sleeve. No thread there. "You have a keen eye."

"So I've been told." Louise sat. "Just what do you eat at the diner every morning? Surely it gets tiresome."

"I've eaten breakfast there since Ikey was little. I can have everything I want on my biscuit and there's always a fresh newspaper for reading. It became a habit, I guess."

"Hmmm," murmured Louise, "what was it that you didn't like on your biscuit?"

"Orange marmalade; never learned to appreciate it, no matter how many times it was offered to me." Isaac stared off. "I know it's wrong to speak ill of the dead, but for some reason Julia, rest her soul, always insisted on passing me that instead of what I really wanted." He smiled. "She did put honey on the table after we, well, after we settled our differences."

"That's good to know."

That afternoon Louise bought honey.

Chapter Twenty-Four
Harry

Harry was woman free.

Ada had church Guild and was busy from ten until mid-afternoon. Their store clerk, Susan, was away attending to her mother and wouldn't be back in town until tomorrow.

"Hooray, time for cigars and shootin'." Harry flipped the OPEN sign on the front door to BACK IN 15 MINUTES, knowing he could hear the bell if any customers came in. He headed out to the dump with his .22 and a hot cup of whiskey joe. Rat shooting was one of his favorite things, and having a splash of backdoor booze in his coffee topped off the fun. He had been doing it for years, loving every minute of his 'men-only' pastime. Sitting in his favorite rat-shooting chair, the old one saved from the flood, he lit a brand new stogie, sucked in its delicious smoke, and aimed at the fat brown one chewing on a rotted apple. BANG. "Hah. Take that, Buster. Where's your skinny cousin?" BANG. He tasted his coffee. "Needs extra ammo," and added more than a splash of the liquor. "Yep, that's just right."

There was one rat, an albino with pink eyes, that seemed to mock him, therefore offering the biggest challenge. Harry watched. Suddenly there was a flash of white. Taking aim, he muttered, "Gotcha, you bastard."

BANG.

***

Ada found him there at three, frozen upright, teeth clenched tight on the butt, ashes scattered on his lap. Rigor had claimed him. Doctor said "apoplexy"; Reverend said "so sorry"; Masons said "Sister." She didn't hear their words.

Chapter Twenty-Five
Ada

"Mama, there's somebody at the door." Theo stood, looking out at a stranger.

"Telegram for Myra Ledbetter."

"It's the telegraph man."

"Hurry," Myra called from the kitchen, "and give him three pennies from the coin bowl. Mixing sausage. Can't come to the door."

Theo made the exchange and brought the missive to his mama. She rinsed her hands and sat down on the stool by the grinder.

MYRA LEDBETTER.

UNCLE HARRY DEAD.

COME NOW.

AUNT ADA.

Myra made into the pantry just before the screams started. She did not come out until there was no voice left.

Early the next morning the family, Marguerite included, was traveling south to Galveston. It was Marguerite who packed their cases, including Myra's funeral hat. A five dollar gold piece bought the two-way tickets. "No white folk better say nuthin'," she muttered, making sure Myra had twenty of the coins buttoned in her cape's secret pockets. "Missus Ada might need help with the buryin'. We don't know their money." She put lesser change jingling in her reticule for the porter. "Gotta pay our own."

Reverend Nicholson's wife, Linda Sue, greeted them at the station with hugs and tears. "Oh, praises, you're here. All Ada does is call your name, over and over. We must hurry." Linda Sue started trotting, dragging Myra by the hand. The children took her lead and ran. Marguerite, carrying the baby, followed behind.

Autos and horse carriages were scattered willy-nilly up and down the street, practically blocking the whole way. People stood everywhere, the mourning wreath already on the store front. Myra shook off Linda Sue. Hollering to the children to "stay put," she pushed through the crowds. Bursting in the front door, Myra stopped dead still.

Masonic Brothers stood side by side, on guard. In front of the meat counter laid a shrouded Harry. He was on several boards held up by sawhorses. "Oh, dear Lord," cried Myra. "Where's his casket?" She glared at the men. "My uncle is not a side of beef."

"Myra? Where's my Myra?" Ada's wavering voice drifted down the apartment stairwell.

"Missus Ada," boomed Brother Robearde, "your Myra is here. I'll bring her up in a minute." Robearde Turner escorted Myra away from the steps, off to a corner. "Sister Ada needs you. She seems out of her mind."

Myra looked hard at the Constable. "I was widowed on my twentieth birthday. I understand 'out of your mind'." She pulled her pins and set her hat on the checkerboard. "Is there anything else I need to know? Why isn't there a coffin?"

"We've kept him in the meat cooler since yesterday. Thank God he hadn't any hanging stock, so there was plenty of room. He's doing acceptable in this heat, but your auntie can't..." Robearde stared at the floor. "Well, let her tell you." Glancing upward, Robearde took Myra's arm. "Let's go."

Ada sat stiff straight in a black dress with her funeral brooch pinned at her throat, and her best handkerchief squeezed tight in her right hand. Nodding dismissal to Robearde, she opened her arms to Myra. Crumpling to the floor, Myra allowed herself to be petted as both women cried.

After a bit, Myra stood, straightened her hair, and planted herself directly in front of Ada. Coming straight to the point, Myra asked, "Where's his coffin? What's going on?"

Ada blew her nose. "Oh, my darling, he's hid all the money."

"What? Do you mean the store money?"

"Yes, and the house money, too." Ada chewed her bottom lip. "Darling, I can't pay the undertaker."

Myra fumbled with the clasp on her travel cape and reached inside. "How much does he want?"

"Thirty dollars, that's with the Lodge's discount. Dammit, Myra, I can't find the money anywhere." Stepping to the middle of the room, Ada pointed at the apartment's front door. "The Brothers downstairs think I'm staying up here out of my mind with grief. Only Robearde knows the truth. However, I told him there will be no charity collection."

Taking her auntie's hand, Myra whispered. "Here's burial money." Ada stared. "Shhh, don't say a word. We'll talk later." Myra walked to the apartment door and swung it open. "Constable Turner," she called, "could you please come here? We have a job for you."

Within the hour, Harry Dickenson was in an elegant casket wearing his Sunday suit and Masonic apron, ready to receive visitors. Ada and Myra sat to the side. The Brothers led in Marguerite and the children. Each one hugged their great aunt and stood in a row in front of their Uncle Harry. Marguerite offered Flossie Mae's cheek for a kiss and joined the family.

"Y'all ready? Remember not too loud." The children began.

"Jesus loves you, this we know,
For the Bible tells us so.
You will walk on Golden Street
And our daddy you will meet.
Yes, we will miss you.
Yes, we will miss you.
Yes, we will miss you.
Please say 'Hello' to our dad."

Ada and Myra hid their smiles behind fresh handkerchiefs as the cherub choir followed a sparkling-eyed Marguerite out the front door and down to the parsonage. Linda Sue knew the children well enough. She intended to feed and house them away from the all those people at the store. "I can put Franky and Benjy in the same bed, and Theo and Nora Lee on pallets. Not sure what I'll do with the Negress," she told her husband, "but I'll figure it out. Maybe put a cot in the back pantry?"

Two hours later, after Masonic rites and Reverend Nicholson's prayers, the mourners were ready to leave. Robearde approached Ada and Myra. "It's time to close the lid. Is there anything you want him buried with besides his Bible and his apron? The grave is ready."

"Yes. I'll get it." Ada returned with his favorite mug, the inside stained brown from the chicory coffee he drank every day. She also had the flask of the bad whiskey he'd pour into that cup when he was rat shooting.

Robearde nodded. "Anything else?"

Pointing above the front door, she smiled. "I'm way too short to reach the bell. Could you get it down so that my Harry can ring his way to heaven?"

Chapter Twenty-Six
Juneteenth

"Bye-bye, my darlings, be good for Marguerite." Myra stood at the store's now silent front door, waving Flossie Mae's hand at the departing children. "We will be home as soon as we can."

"Bye, Mama," they all called, holding hands like they'd been taught. The family, Marguerite leading, rounded the corner and was gone. Almost to the train station, there was a sound somewhere in front of them.

"Missus 'Guite, Missus 'Guite, can you hear it?" Franky was the first to notice.

"What, child? I don't hear nothin', nothin' except you all." The well-groomed line of children had devolved into a surge of skipping and chattering.

TOODLE LE BOOM TE BOOM TE BOOM.

"Missus 'Guite, it sounds like a circus." Nora Lee started running. "Can we go? Pleeeeese?"

"Stop." She grabbed the escaping child with her free hand. "You will not embarrass me in front of…" Marguerite froze. "Ooooh, will ya look at that."

The colored platform and the landing below were covered with ladies in gowns, all parasolled and gloved. They stood with suited gentlemen, each wearing a fashionable bowler and carrying a leather valise. All were watching a Negro brass band playing a march.

"Missus 'Guite, those ladies have really pretty dresses," observed Nora Lee. "Do you have any? I've never seen a fancy dress on a colored lady."

Marguerite stared. "No, Miss Nosey Rosie, I don't. Wish I did." She looked around, realizing the boys were not as close as they should be. "Gather up, everyone, hold hands. Let's get a little closer and see what's going on."

They wound their way through and up to the band. The tuba player puffed his cheeks and wiggled his eyebrows at them. All the children waved back. Marguerite suddenly realized she was standing next to Missylou, someone she knew from the Tremont Hotel. They had worked in the banquet hall together, serving meals and washing dishes. Missylou was dressed as fancy as any lady there.

"Excuse me, ma'am, is that you? It's me, Marguerite."

"Oh, Jesus in heaven, don't you dare ever call me 'ma'am' again," exclaimed the woman, giving Marguerite an arm's-length hug. "I'd squeeze you tighter, but I don't want to break the starch in my dress front." She stepped back and looked at the children. "You their mammy?"

"Lord, no. Remember my sailor, Jack?"

"Sure do." Missylou nodded. "Your mama would've been proud of how he courted you."

These are his best mate's young'uns. We all live together in LaPorte."

"Wondered where you ended up. How's that goin'?"

Marguerite looked hard at her old friend, and ignored the question. "You're not some kind of a left-handed wife, are you? You're dressed mighty nice."

"No," giggled Missylou, "I'm still at the hotel and still looking for a good husband. Just steppin' out today for the celebration."

Marguerite looked puzzled. "What's to...? Oh, don't tell me it's June nineteenth already. We came to the island for a funeral and have been *tres* busy."

"Almost, that's tomorrow. Some of us Bright Star Sisters and Prince Hall Brothers came down to welcome the Houston chapter. We all got floats in the parade."

TOOT

"Oh, train's a comin'." Marguerite stroked the fabric of Missylou's sleeve. "Do the Sisters all dress like this?"

"When we go out, we do." Missylou smiled. "We get them at Foley's. They give us a group discount." She spun around, showing off. "Wish you could be a member. Then we could be sisters."

TOOT

Marguerite gestured to the men. "What do Prince Hall men do? Never heard of them."

"They're colored Masons. They save us, save and raise us up," was all she said.

"Come on, Missus 'Guite," hollered Benjy. "You have the tickets. We gotta get on the train." He grabbed her hand and started pulling.

"Goodbye, *mon amie*," Marguerite called over her shoulder. "I am so glad I saw you."

Missylou blew her a kiss through kid gloves.

Marguerite settled everybody into the white car, thankful for the upholstered seats after a night on a cot in a closet. Not one passenger blinked at the mammy and her charges.

Chapter Twenty-Seven
Divel Divel Divel

Myra turned back into the store after waving her family 'Goodbye'. "Come on, little one, can't let you down on this oiled floor. Wish I had Marguerite here to hold you." She plopped the baby into a makeshift seat. "Ding dang it, child, what're we gonna do now?" she muttered as she tied her daughter to the chair rails with one of Harry's clean aprons. "Where did your Uncle Harry hide the money?"

"De da, de da hit," replied Flossie Mae.

"Goodness, Myra, you'd better watch your language. That baby's really pickin' up words." Ada shook her head as she came down the steps. "Um, *we'd* better watch our language. I was just cussin' up a storm, lookin' through the kitchen pantry." She shook her head. "Why did he have to go 'n' hide the money without tellin' me? How am I supposed to….?" Her chin trembled. "Oh, why did he have to go at all?"

"I don't know, Auntie, I don't know." Myra led her to the checkerboard chairs. Taking her hands across the table, she held on until she felt Ada relax. "Auntie," she whispered, "I think I might have an idea where the money is."

Ada perked up, her eyes widening.

"At least, I think I have a clue."

"Where? I've looked everywhere."

"Remember how he used to always call money 'cold cash.' Does, er, did he still?" Myra continued her soft voice.

"Yes. Why are we whispering?"

"The baby repeats everything. She's a real live Panama parrot." Myra looked over to the highchair. Flossie Mae was chewing her fist, staring at them. "Let me nurse her to sleep. Then we can talk. Watch this."

Myra picked up her child. "Nurse?"

"Noose, noose, mulk." Flossie Mae forgot her fist and wiggled for her mama.

"See. She's becoming a real jabber box."

Flossie Mae started giggling. "Ja ja ba, ja ja ba."

"Yes, precious, you are my jabber box." Mother and child disappeared up to the living quarters. Five minutes later, Myra was down.

"That was fast," observed Ada.

"Just about three sucks and she was gone. Laid her on the floor with the quilts and pillows from the company cot all around her. That way she can't fall out of bed." Myra frowned. "Uncle Harry would have had a fit over that. I can hear him now, grumpin' about 'proper crib for that baby'."

Ada nodded. "He was crazy about those children, would've done anything for them." Ada slammed her fist on the checkerboard, sending the game flying. "Dammit, man, where's the money? I can't buy milk for the baby, let alone pay the bills."

Myra scurried around, picking up the checkers. "Don't move, Auntie, you might slip and break something. Can't have you hurt, you gotta run the store."

"Oh, darling, I'm sorry I made such a mess. It's just that I'm so mad at him." Ada shook her head. "My grandmother used to say 'Divel, divel, divel, take your hands off' whatever was lost."

Myra looked up from the floor as she gathered the last pieces into her apron. "Did it work?"

"She'd stop saying it when she found what she was lookin' for." Ada grinned. "Oh, how silly, of course she wouldn't say it once she was done. Is it safe to stand?"

"Yes, ma'am, all the king's men are accounted for." Myra dumped her apron on the restored board. "Let's think about cold cash. Did you look in the kitchen ice box?"

"Right away. He was acting so forgetful these past weeks that sometimes I would find his socks behind the milk bottle. Guess he thought it was his dresser."

"Oh, Auntie, I'm so sorry. We didn't know."

"Darling, nobody did. I spent most of my day trailing behind him, fixin' whatever he would stir up or forget to do. Didn't want him gettin' embarrassed." One tear slid down Ada's cheek. "Oh, baby, I shouldn't have gone to Guild that day. I would have been here to save him."

"Now, now, didn't your doctor say the stroke took him in an instant? Didn't he say that's why you found him sitting with his cigar?" Myra looked at the walk-in cooler. "Do you suppose...?

"No," Ada made a face. "The men would have seen it when they put him there."

"What about the icebox under the meat counter? Did you look there?"

Ada bustled behind the glass display case and slid open the lower compartment. The cooling coils hummed. "Did you ever see the new equipment? Come over here, I'm somewhat afraid to feel around. Electricity's scary."

"Scoot over, I'll look." Myra peered into the dim contraption. "There's something in the back. Looks like a cigar box. I'll get it."

"Darlin, maybe...?"

"Not heavy enough for coins. Dollar bills? Here, you open it, my hands are shaking."

Ada set the box on the scale, slowly lifted the lid, and burst into tears. "Cigars, Charles Denby cigars. Oh Myra, why the hell was he hiding cigars?" She threw the box across the counter. "Divel, divel, divel, take your hands off *my* money," she shouted. "Now."

Chapter Twenty-Eight
Butter Me Up

"Come on, Auntie, let's eat. I made extra when I packed the train basket." Myra pulled out the plate of roast beef and horseradish sandwiches that had been sitting atop the big round of Colby in the store's display cooler. "You mind if I cut into this cheese?"

"Sounds good to me." Ada tore off a sheet a butcher paper and covered the checkerboard. "Maybe food will help clear my head."

"You want water or lemonade? There's some of each left from the wake." Myra brought the plate and two clean mop towels. "Don't want to chance wakin' the baby by going upstairs for napkins."

"Darling, lemonade sounds good. It's in a pitcher in the meat locker." Ada sat and reached for her sandwich. She snatched back her hand. "Oops, I almost forgot the blessing."

Myra fetched the pitcher and some coffee mugs. "I didn't see any glasses. I did find some left-over cake. Let's try a slice after we eat." Myra sat. "That cooler is jam-packed with all the food people brought. Think I'll give it a sort after we're finished." She sat and took her auntie's hands.

"Father, thank you for the blessings of the day and your gift of our meal. Please bless this woman whose hands I hold and the soul of our beloved Harry. Amen."

"Thank you, my dear. Let's eat." Ada took a big bite. "Gak," she choked, "Way too dry. Did you see the butter in there? He kept it in a wooden firkin. Don't try to lift it. Weighs over a hundred pounds."

"I'll get you some." Myra took the sandwich plate, grabbed a knife, and stood by the locker's door. "You want a chunk for upstairs, too?"

"Sure, how about four-inch square?" Ada tasted her lemonade. "Darn, this is Methodist tea punch. Please see if there is another pitcher in there somewhere. I could use a glass."

"Auntie, you tellin' me the lemonade's spiked? I didn't know you drank spirits."

"Shush, child, don't be shocked. You can't tell me you haven't had a hot tonic before?"

Myra smiled. "Yes, ma'am, I have. Guess we can call the lemonade cold tonic. I'll look for it after I cut the butter." She stepped into the cold depths. "Auntie," Myra called from the cooler, "there's two cases in here. Which one do you want me to open?"

"Didn't know he had two. See if you can lift them and bring out the lightest one. We'll see how much there is."

Myra brought the firkin and plopped it on the floor beside her aunt. "Wasn't heavy at all. Be back with the knife, plate, and the other pitcher."

Myra traded the cup of punch and poured a full mug of lemonade for her aunt. Ada pried off the top of the case and scraped a ribbon of butter for her bread. "That thing is almost full. How'd you lift it?"

"Doesn't weigh as much as Flossie Mae. Thought you said it was hundred pounds."

"Says so on the lid." Ada held up the top. "Don't tell me the dairy man shorted him."

"Don't be silly." Myra added a scrape to her own sandwich. "Yum, that's good," and took another bite. "I wish we could always shop here. The LaPorte stores are just not as friendly. I miss…" Myra stopped mid chew. "Oh dear God, I just remembered something."

"What, darling?" Ada reached for her lemonade.

"What did Uncle Harry say when he needed to be extra friendly?"

"Um, that he was going to butter 'em up?"

Myra took the butcher knife and stabbed the block of spread. *Thunk.* "Auntie, Auntie, there's something in the butter. Could it be?"

"Oh Jesus, oh Lord." Ada grabbed her niece's arm. "Get a dishing spoon from the back. We've gotta see what's in there."

Five minutes later Ada held up a solid roll of bills in triumph over the sacrificed block of butter. The baking powder can that protected the money lay forgotten on the floor. She laughed so hard, she got the hiccups. "Myra dear, your uncle was one smart man. No robber would have ever looked for the money in a hundred pounds of butter."

"Let me count," offered Myra. She unrolled the cash, flattening it on the checkerboard. "You have a lot of ones and fives. Did you know about all this?"

"He started keeping the account book high up on a shelf where I couldn't reach. Didn't think anything about it, figured he was just being tidy." Ada pinched her lips. "Now I wonder if he was afraid I'd see he wasn't making deposits." She counted. "This can't be all of it. We bank twice this much every month."

"Let me get some cake." Myra stared into the cooler. "You don't think he's hid the rest in the lard can, do you?"

"No, too small." Ada scratched her head. "So, we found the cold cash in the butter. We'd better find the rest, or we'll be in a real pickle." She chuckled. "He used to always say that. How in the world can you be in a pickle?"

"I don't know, Auntie, unless someone puts you there." Myra wrinkled her nose." Can't see anyone climbing into that stinky mess."

"O-o-oh, you mean like a robber?"

Ada was elbows deep in the barrel before Myra could react. "Bring one of those mop towels, I think I caught me a can of cash." She handed the dripping container to her niece and plunged back in. "Felt another one down there."

"I'll dry this and put it on the board."

"Here it is."

Myra scurried back with the other towel.

"It's heavier than that first one, might be coins." Ada looked up at Myra and grinned. "This is like shootin' fish in a barrel."

"Oh, Auntie." She took the treasure box from Ada, dried it, and set it with its briny companion.

Ada sat back at the checkerboard. "Pour some more of that lemonade. We need to make a toast, a toast with butter on it."

Chapter Twenty-Nine
Money Money Money

What a whirl of work, tears, and confusion those next two days brought. Keeping the baby off the oiled floor became the least of their concerns. Ada knew all about maintaining the front, keeping it stocked, stacked, and attractive. The back store business of product ordering and working the books was something Harry felt not to be 'woman's business'.

"Oh, blasted husband," lamented Ada, "just what did you think would happen to us? You were the older one, you know." She chewed her bottom lip, staring at the ledger. "I am the one who graduated eighth, not you. You should have…"

"Still can't figure it out?" Myra hugged her auntie's shoulders.

Ada closed the book. "Not only can I not figure it out, I can barely understand the numbers of the last month's entries, they're so scribbly. I think he hid more than his money and things. I think he knew how really sick he was."

KNOCK, KNOCK.

"I'll get it," said Myra. "You stay seated."

"Who could that be? Can't they see the wreath in the front window? That means we are in mourning."

"Now, now, Auntie, stop. It could just be the postman."

"Better not be another casserole."

"It's not," smiled Myra, "it's Rabbi Joe. May I let him in?"

"Of course, don't mind me." Ada joined her niece at the front door. "This bookkeeping's giving me a headache."

Joe entered, arms open wide. The ladies fell into his embrace, delighting in his hug. "My dears," he said after they both allowed their cheeks to be kissed, "I have brought you a present, something for good luck." He reached in his coat pocket and brought out a small box.

"Uh," stammered Ada, "you didn't bring us one of those Jewish door charms, did you? We're Methodist, you know."

Joe grinned. "Open the box. It's a chime, not a charm."

In the box was a brand new brass bell to take the place of the one sent off with Harry. "Oh-h-h," cooed the women in unison. Ada gently lifted it and gave it a tentative shake. It *tinged* almost the same, but a bit deeper and louder. She chuckled. "He would like this one. Always was complainin' that the bell we had sounded too soft for his old ears."

Rabbi Joe smiled. "So you like it?"

"Oh, yes." Myra glanced at the empty bracket on the doorframe. "Would you please hang it for us?"

"Only if you have some coffee on the stove."

"Silly man, you know we always have some waiting." Ada kissed the bell, and Joe soon had it in place with a hearty "*mazel tov.*" The three sat around the checkerboard with their mugs, munching on the latest plate of sweets brought in by well-wishers.

"Can't guarantee these are Kosher." Ada popped another cookie in her mouth.

"Reformed are not as strict as Orthodox. We watch what we eat, but as long as these aren't made of sausage, I'm a happy man." He swallowed another gulp and set down his cup. "So, tell me. What can I do to help? Pretty soon you're going to have to re-open the store. People are counting on you." Joe cocked his left eye at her. "And, I know for a fact that some of your customers did their Saturday shopping at W.W. Mac's over on Third Street."

Ada stared at Joe, weighing her words. Taking a deep breath, she plunged in. "I need a bookkeeper, someone who will hold our business private, someone to trust with the money." She swung her arm wide. "See these shelves? I can think up displays and sell things all day long. That man of mine never taught me the business side. How in God's name am I going to run this store?" Her voice rose. "I need help with everything." She shook her fist at the heavens. "Dammit, Harry, you know I can't do anything with meat."

"Auntie, watch your tongue."

"Ladies, ladies, it's all right," he shrugged. "We say *broch*, means almost the same thing." Joe looked at the displays. "Missus Ada, your hard work shows with all you have to sell. And yes, I agree, don't imagine you can handle a side of beef or even a pig, for that matter. I'm guessing you're going to have to send your shoppers to the butcher for their roasts and chops."

"I can't cut meat if I tried." Ada raised her eyebrow toward the cooler. "Do you think I could do anything like that after my beloved Harry spent time there, waiting to be put to rest?"

Nodding agreement, Joe started sliding the red checkers around the board. "Would you be comfortable selling cold meat for sandwiches out of the glass cooler case? Bet the butcher you choose to send people to would be happy to sell you sliced lunch meat as a business exchange."

"I guess I could ask around." Ada humphed. "Harry would have a fit if he knew we were doing that. He was so proud of his meat cutting and those home-cooked roast beef sandwiches he sold."

"Yes, ma'am, they were top notch. Loved the horseradish he used." Joe looked around. "I can see, however, that you and your clerks can't do this alone. You need shelf help. And, my dear, I know just who you can use to help with the books."

"Who?"

"Your nephews." Rabbi Joe stood. "I need some more hot. Where's the pot?"

"You are not going anywhere until you explain yourself."

"Yes ma'am." Joe sat. "You have the best bookkeeper right here in your own family *and* several strong boys startin' school vacation who could work and keep you company." He winked at Myra.

Myra patted Ada's arm. "I need the twins at home, but our Theo would do anything for his Aunt Ada, you know that."

He chuckled. "Yes, and for goodness sake, your nephew Isaac Jacoby is lead accountant for his company. I know he'll do it. Plus, he owes me one for keeping his boy."

"Oh-h-h, my stars and buttons, you're both right." Ada nodded to Joe. "The coffee's on the stove by the back room."

"Yes, ma'am, I'll be back."

***

Isaac stopped by the store that night. "Joe telephoned me at the office. Said you needed help with the business side of things."

"Bless you, child, we do." She gestured toward the front cooler. "Are you hungry? Do you want something to eat?"

"Thank you, no. Miss Louise fed us before I came over." Isaac patted his stomach. "She's one lucky find. What an interesting cook. She puts together foods in ways I didn't know existed. She even taught me to put honey on grits."

"I'm always glad to see her on shopping day." Ada smiled and took Isaac's hand. "Being from Austin and all, she's slowly learning our Galveston ways. Glad she's working out for you."

"I'm just happy to have my boy back."

Ada slowly released Isaac. "I hope he is doing better. I remember when he and Junior, well, anyway, I hope he's doing better."

"Ikey is such a good son. I am so proud of him. That little problem last year, ah, just a bump in the road. His end of school marks are tops," Isaac bragged. "Now I've got to find something to keep him busy this summer. Thinking about apprenticing him in the office."

"But, what about…"

"Auntie," Myra interrupted, "Cousin Isaac's here about bookkeeping. I'm sure the boy is *just* fine."

"Of course, of course, I'm sorry. It's just when I heard about him and the girl…"

"*Auntie.*"

Isaac held up his hand. "Whatever you need from me as far as numbers go, I'm your man. Let's see those ledgers."

An hour later, they struck a deal. "I will be proud to be your accountant. I'll come in the fifth of every month to do the books, and, Missus Ada, I only need one thing from you."

"And that is?"

Isaac's voice took a serious tone. "When I first got on my feet, Harry offered me store discount."

"I know."

"May I still have it as payment for the work?"

"Goodness, man. I'll double it if I never have to look at another number again."

Isaac stuck out his hand. "Well, then, I'm your man."

Chapter Thirty
Golden Opportunities

"Missus 'Guite, What's riff-raff?" Theo asked, brushing his brown wavy hair. Exchanged telegrams confirmed that he would be staying the summer in Galveston. Marguerite was giving him his traveling instructions. He was not to speak to strangers, keep an eye open for riff-raff, and be polite to the conductor.

"Gypsies, the worst riff-raff in the world." She smoothed his traveling jacket. "They're dirty cheats."

"Princess Lulah Marie's a gypsy." He turned away from the mirror. "You said so yourself."

"She is not a princess, and don't you ever mention that nasty piece of filth to me again."

"But she's your…"

"Give me that. You missed the back tangles." Marguerite began working his thick hair like she was threshing wheat.

Theo flinched away. "Ow, ow, not so hard, don't be mad at me that she's your…OW."

"Hush, don't make me brush you bald." She added a glop of pomade in attempt to control his mane. "Should'a gotten you to the barber," she muttered.

"Yes, ma'am."

Ten minutes later he was on the front porch, hair shining, ready to make his way to the station. Marguerite gave him a five dollar gold piece to buy the ticket and to have some spending change left.

"*Mon petit*, do not let anyone see that you have money in your pocket."

"Yes, ma'am."

"Do not let the coins jingle."

"Yes, ma'am."

"Did you say goodbye to the others?"

"Yes, ma'am."

Marguerite squeezed him close. "Tell your mama we miss her and the baby. Keep an eye on your shirt buttons; you know you always get them crooked."

Theo nodded. "Yes, ma'am. Please, can I go now?"

"*Oui.*"

Several hours, a tiresome train ride to Galveston, and lot of hugs later, Theo was settling into the back store room turned bedroom, the same place where his big brother, Junior, stayed before he got in trouble. The plan for him was to sleep there until his mama and sister went back home. He'd then move up onto the company cot in the apartment to help Ada feel safe.

Myra started emptying his valises. "Marguerite really packed you lots of clean drawers and socks." She shook out a pair of bib overalls. "Looks like she expects you to be diggin' in the dirt."

"Mama, I'll do whatever Auntie asks. Um, do *you* know what she wants me to do?"

"Baby, I think she needs a strong back and a quick mind."

Theo grinned. "Well, that's me."

Myra continued the unpacking. In the bottom of the bigger suitcase was a wrapped box, tied with string, a note attached.

FOR M
FROM M

It was heavy. Instantly she knew what it was.

"Darlin', would you fetch me a glass of water from Auntie's kitchen? I'm parched."

"Yes, ma'am."

As soon as the boy was gone, Myra made quick work of hiding the package, deep in the meat cooler where it belonged. When Theo returned, all his clothes were spread out over the bed. Gulping down the water, Myra shook her head. "Marguerite sent everything you would need, everything except tooth powder. You put all this away, and I'll see if Auntie can spare a tin. Come to the parlor when you're done."

"Yes ma'am."

Once upstairs, Myra whispered her secret to her auntie.

"You're what?" Ada exploded.

"Shhh. Don't let the baby hear."

"When did that happen?" Ada mouthed.

"Mama, Auntie, I'm all ready to work." Theo was grinning at the top of the steps, wearing one of Harry's butcher aprons, tied high under his armpits, the hem touching the floor in front.

"Good Lord, child, get over here. Let your old auntie fix you up." Eight rolls of the waistband and an exceptionally tight knot twisted in the back and bowed in the front provided a semblance of something boy-sized. She shook her head. "Land sakes, appears you got your mama's height," muttered Ada. "We've better find the ones your brother wore. Wonder where they are?"

"Don't know." Theo paraded around, giving a working boy's fashion show, not realizing his right shoe was untied. "Uh, Auntie, do you have anything in your icebox? Can I go see? I forgot to eat before I left."

"Darling, there is sliced meat, bread, and pickles. Make yourself something, but find a plate. We don't need crumbs. There's a rat dump out back, y' know."

"Yes, ma'am, I'll be careful."

"You can start being careful by tying your shoe," Ada chided. "Good Lord, you're almost ten. Can't you tell when your shoe is loose?"

"Please keep *all* your food in the kitchen," added his mama. Myra took her auntie's hand and led her to the steps. "Come down with me so we can talk" she whispered. "Don't need extra ears. I have something to show you and a wonderful story to tell."

Settled around the checkerboard, Myra handed her the box from the cooler. "Do you remember Captain Calhoun deeded the *Sallie Lou* and all her contents to CB and Jack?"

Ada nodded. "And?" She fingered the box.

"Oh, Auntie, just open it."

Ada pulled the ties, tore away the wrapping, and lifted the lid. "Oh, Jesus Christ, will you look at that." Clapping her hand over her mouth, the muffled apology, "Sorry, Lord," leaked through her fingers.

"Auntie, this is where Uncle Harry's burial money came from. Our root cellar floor is covered two crates high with treasure." Myra's voice choked, "We have so many five dollar gold pieces that we still haven't had the time to count them, just the forty-nine crates." The choke turned to gasps. "Auntie, CB and Jack have made us the richest people we know."

Ada scooped the coins out of the box, and chuckled. "You puttin' them in the cooler worked. You have cold cash, that for sure." She jingled them in her hand. "Why aren't you all living a higher life? Ding, dang it, I would."

"We can't spend it." Myra's gasps dissolved into pure sobbing. "We, uh, can't buy, uh, things with the coins. CB says a sailor cannot spend what he does not earn." She turned away from Ada. "Oh, dear God, we are the richest poor people in the whole of Texas. No one knows we have all this gold that can't be spent. We need paper money."

Thunk, thunk, thunk echoed in the stairwell. Ada had the box closed and hidden in the folds of her apron just as Theo jumped the last three stairs and skittered to a halt in the center of the store.

"Working man Theo is ready to go. Just tell me..." his bright face fell. "Uh, oh, Mama, why're you crying? What happened? Did I do something wrong?"

Ada stood, her hands inside her bib. "No, darling, it's just that your mama is, er, sad about Uncle Harry. Isn't that right?"

"Yes, I'm sad, so sad." Myra flashed her eyes around the room. "Come here, my big boy, and hug my tears away." She jerked her head to the cooler. "Auntie, is there anything cold to drink? I could use some lemonade."

"Me too, me too." Theo draped his arms around his seated mama and gently held her from behind.

Myra leaned back on her fourth-born's chest, her head bumping his chin. "Goodness, child, how tall *are* you?" She shrugged his embrace, sniffled, and stood. Extending her right arm she measured him just like she did all her children, by armpit height. He almost didn't fit.

Theo giggled. "With all the hard work I'm gonna do, I'll be grown as tall as your shoulder by the time school starts."

"Well, go upstairs and get your sister. I can hear her startin' to squall. Grab a dry diaper, just in case." Myra blew a kiss to the back of her stair- running son.

Ada was pouring the drinks. "So, my poor little rich woman, what are you going to do?"

Chapter Thirty-One
Store Front

"Auntie, I'm going to turn you into a criminal."

Ada swelled like a puffer fish. "Young lady, you are out of your mind. I will nev…"

"Shhh, now, not really a criminal," Myra grinned, "more like criminal's helper. I've done it before. It's kinda fun."

Ada, cheeks bright red, fish-eyed her niece. "You helped a criminal? Who?"

"CB, Jack, and…"

The fish exploded. "Our whole family? You mean to tell me that our whole family's a gang of, of…"

"Yes'um, we *were* jewelry smugglers." Myra wiggled her left hand, flashing the yellow diamond. "How do you think I got my engagement ring? This beauty was passage from some hopeful gold miner our men hid in the *Sallie Lou* on one of their trips to Panama."

The puffer fish deflated. "Go on."

"Like I told you, a sailor cannot spend what he does not earn, and, as the man-moving business grew, so did their payments. CB and Jack got cash and jewels from all the dreamers they transported." Myra shrugged. "They could spend the cash, but the jewels were another matter. That's where I came in." She smiled. "CB would hand me the gems when he paid for the sweets I sold him. I would then carry them to Julia…"

Ada sat straight up. "Julia? Our Julia?"

"Yes'm, did I forget to mention her?" Myra didn't try to hide the twinkle in her voice. "Julia had the most important job. She sold it all and took care that everyone got their fair cut."

"So-o-o," breathed Ada, "all that to-do at Guild about her needin' to hide her spending from Ike, er, Isaac, and selling her mother's wedding gifts, was just…"

"Yep, just a big fat lie to move the goods." Myra started laughing. "How in the world did you think I could afford the Chinese laundry? Not enough cookies to pay for that one."

Ada stared at her niece. "What does all this have to do with me? I can't sell five dollar pieces to the ladies at church."

"Nope, but you can trade me paper dollar bills and deposit some of the gold coins in the store bank account. Not so much as to draw attention, and Marguerite and I will have real spending money for the first time, ever." Myra clasped her hands. "Please, Auntie, please. We are so tired of hiding. It would be nice to have a new dress every once in a while."

"Well," Ada stood. "Can't see how a little bit of switch off could hurt anything. If you two could do it, I guess I can, too." Shaking her head, she started to the steps. "That boy's taking forever with his sister. Better go check." Tromping half way up, she turned. "Our Julia? Oh my stars and buttons."

***

Theo, properly attired, quickly learned how to clean and stack the shelves into perfect pyramids. Ada did have to remind him about his shirt tail if he had been climbing to the high shelves. Soon he was helping to fill orders and making deliveries for tips, just like his brother had. Theo liked sitting upstairs on the floor in front of the settee at the feet of his auntie while his mama rocked the baby, listening to the stories Ada read from her favorite magazine, *The*

Delineator. He would spin jacks on one of the old copies while she read. The words and the whirl soothed him.

"Mama, don't be upset with me, but I like being here. It's so nice 'n' quiet, real restful like."

Myra nodded. "Well, son, it's going to be even quieter tomorrow. Flossie Mae and I need to head home. I've been away from the others long enough. Are you going to be all right?"

Ada ruffled his hair. "Dear niece, this child has learned so much these few days. I think I'll give him a new title."

"But Auntie, I like it when you call me 'Theo the Tower Maker'." He grinned. "I can really stack 'em, can't I?"

Ada smiled back. "Yes sir, you can. But," she paused, "I like 'Theo the Tremendous Tower Maker' even better. And, some day, you might even earn the title 'Prince Theo, the Perfect Pyramid Producer'."

Jumping up, Theo swept an imaginary feathered hat and bowed low to his mother. "Prince Theo bids farewell to Queen Mama and Princess Flossie Mae." He giggled. "Go in peace, m' ladies. Your Prince will stay here with, uh…" he looked at Ada. "What does all this make you?"

"Sire, I am and always will be Queen Auntie." She looked at the clock on the side table. "Goodness, my royal one, it's your bedtime. Kiss your queens and skedaddle down those steps. Tomorrow waits for no one, and Saturday's the town's biggest shopping day."

Smooches around, and he was gone. Ada settled back into the cushions. "Niece, we need to talk about your coin exchange. How often do you need to do this?"

"Well, I thought one of us should come down to Galveston every month, if Marguerite's agreein'. There would be no notice of a loving mother or a child's nurse-maid checking on Theo's progress of becoming," she chuckled, "'Prince Perfect Pyramid Producer'. Oh my goodness, say that fast three times."

Both tried the tongue twister, neither succeeding. Ada nodded. "Once a month you'll bring me a box of fifteen coins. I will hide back the bills and add the gold to the last deposit. That way, the books will be good for Isaac when he comes in to settle up things on the fifth." She shrugged. "Let's start now. I'll go get the cash."

Standing slowly, as not to jiggle the baby, Myra kissed her Aunt Ada on her beautiful white curls. "Thank you for being a criminal," she whispered.

"Any time my darling, any time."

Chapter Thirty-Two
Rat Dump Deputy

"Auntie, teach me to cook like Uncle Harry. Please."
Theo, not one to sit, was wandering around the rear of the
store, not doing much of anything. "I miss the smells."

Ada looked up from her list making. "What,
darlin'?" She'd been to Guild the day before and realized
that her personal domain, the charity pantry, had been
seriously neglected. Reverend Nicholson promised her a
spot in the Sunday bulletin if she could state the specific
food donations needed.

"I said that I miss the smells of Uncle Harry's
cooking. You know, he always had rice and whatever on the
stove for the hungry people who came to the back door."
Theo smiled. "I remember the day Mama caught us playin'
hooky, eating rice and molasses at the old store. We all got
licks with the ruler."

"You deserved it." Ada went back to her writing and
added 'rice.' "Darlin', I won't be feeding the backdoor men
anymore. What if they're bad people?"

"Auntie, bad people can come through the front
door, too."

"Oh my, you are so right." Ada laid down her
pencil. "Your uncle always had the .22 close. Only used it
on rats." She looked at the boy. "Do you know how to
shoot?"

"No, ma'am, Daddy CB don't allow guns.
Somethin' about him shootin' Mister Jack in the backside
when they were boys. Said there's too many young'uns in
the house, and he can't let that happen again."

"Well, Uncle Harry didn't teach me, either. Can't even load it." She stood and walked two steps to the back and stopped. "Oh, ding dang, I think Constable Turner has it. Harry was shootin' rats when he died. If I remember, Robearde said he was worried about me being out of my mind."

Theo tilted his head, questioning, "Were you?"

"No."

"Are you now?"

"Lord, no, child."

"Good, let's get it back. I wanna learn to shoot." Theo ran to the front door, throwing it open with a *ting*. "I'll go get it."

"Hold your horses, boy, get in here. You're not off store duty yet, and you have no idea where the new sheriff's office is." Ada pointed to the dry-goods. "The calico needs sorting by color. And, do you really think the constable would hand over Harry's rifle to anyone but me? I don't think so."

"But, Auntie, I gotta protect you from bad people and animals. Mama said you needed a strong back and quick mind. You need a good rat shooter, too."

"I think you're right. We both could use some aimin' lessons." She picked up her pencil. "I'll finish my list and take it to the church. Reverend Nicholson can use the telephone and call the sheriff. If anyone answers, I will ask for Harry's gun and maybe Robearde will teach us both how to hit those critters."

"Yes, ma'am, sounds good." Theo gave her his wide-eyed 'please' look. "But, I still want to learn how to cook."

"Goodness, one thing at a time. Now scoot over to those bolts. Once they're sorted, pin a card of matching buttons to front of each one. Saves the customer's time."

Constable Robearde Turner returned the rifle the next day. "Missus Ada, I was wonderin' who was gonna keep down the rats." He looked up at Theo, who was balanced on packing crates, three feet off the ground, stocking the top baking goods shelf. "You been taught to shoot?"

"No, sir, but sure would like to learn." The boy hopped down from his perch. "We both would. My auntie needs me to protect her from varmints, but one of these days, I'll have to go back to LaPorte, you know, for school." He made a pouty face. "Summer's passin' quick."

"Boy, you been in town only a week or so. Your time with your Aunt Ada is just startin'. You have plenty of summer left."

Theo looked shyly at his aunt. "It's just that, well, I really like it here. It's so peaceful."

"I hear tell you've been makin' enough noise, yellin' 'Shoo' out back at those rats. Missus Ada says you been tryin' to scare them away." Robearde handed Ada a box of .22 shells. "I'm going to keep the gun with me until I know he can be trusted. You remember where Harry kept his ammo?"

She smiled. "Yes, sir, where he hid everything else. They'll be safe."

"Give me a handful. Guess we'd better get some shootin' lessons done. Bullets work better'n bellowing, ya know." He nodded at Ada. "Manners say 'ladies first,' but, if you don't mind, I'm going to take the boy out back to give it a try."

"That's fine with me. Susan has the day off, and a customer might come in." Ada looked down. "Robearde, truth be told, I don't think I'm ready yet for…well, there's that memory of finding him."

"Auntie, Auntie, I'll be your killin' man." Theo let the back screen slam behind him.

Constable Turner chuckled. "What's all this about peaceful? I think that boy's the next hurricane hittin' Galveston."

Ada shrugged. "He fills my heart. I'm blessed to have him here."

"Well, Sister Ada, you'd better talk to his mama about keepin' him."

***

Robearde stopped by three more times before he declared Theo 'Deputy Rat Dump Shooter,' and handed him the rifle. "You keep your auntie safe, you hear me."

"Oh, yes, sir. I'm her deputy, now."

Ada grinned. "I thought you were my prince." She took the gun. "I'll put it up."

Robearde shook his head. "Dear Ada, how are you going to do that? You'd have to grow at least two feet taller."

"Whaat?" She looked at the gun rack mounted above the apartment steps door frame. "Oh-h-h."

Constable Turner took off his hat, scratching his thinning hair. "Harry told me that when he had this place built, he wanted it handy. Don't think he ever thought *you'd* need to fetch it." He patted his ever-present side arm, 'Roscoe'. "Don't guess you'd want to wear a pistol, would you?"

"Land's sake, no." She tilted her head to Theo. "And, you, child, don't even think about it."

"Aw-w-w."

"We'll find a safe place to store it, won't we Mister Deputy Prince? Thank your teacher for his lessons."

Robearde plopped his cap on his 'Deputy.' "He already did, several times. You like being a shooter?"

Theo nodded so hard that Robearde's uniform hat went flying right back into the Constable's hands. "Sorry, sir."

"No harm done. Remember, keep it loaded. Can't shoot an empty gun." He looked hard at Ada. "You think about talkin' to his mama, you hear me."

"Yes, sir, will do it soon." Ada reached for his hand. "Thank you, again, my friend, for all you do. Give Beatrice my regards."

Snugging his cap, Robearde was gone.

Theo handed Ada the gun and headed to the cooler. "Can I have some lemonade?"

"May I," she corrected.

"Sure, I'll get you some."

Ada looked to the heavens, rolling her eyes.

He stopped. "Why does he want you to talk to Mama?"

Chapter Thirty-Three
Shootin' Varmints

Ada quietly took the boy, the gun, and two lemonades upstairs to the parlor, sitting him beside her on the settee. She leaned the rifle against the cushion.

"Auntie, you're scarin' me, actin' this way." Theo's brown eyes were big and questioning. "Does Constable Turner want to put me in jail? I thought I'd been good."

"Oh, precious boy, you've been fantastic. It's just that Robearde thinks it's not right for me to be by myself and that I should ask if you could stay here and go to school in the fall." Ada patted Theo's hand. "I want that, but..."

She caught the .22 just in the nick of time as Kangaroo Boy Theo jumped up, punctuating every hop with a "me too, me too." It wasn't until the painted porcelain vase on the side table started rocking did he realize that his energy had exploded all over the room. He plopped back beside his aunt, who was still balancing the gun.

"Pleeese, Auntie, pleeese ask Mama if I can stay. Pleeeeeese? You need a boy with a strong back and a quick mind, Mama said so." Theo took Ada's hand. "And, Auntie, I need a quieter house. Golly, sometimes things are so noisy, my jumpities can't take it. I hide under the porch until it gets dark so I won't get in trouble."

"Can't let that be happenin'." Ada smooched his cheek. "Gotta put this thing away before we have an accident. I'll send your mama a telegram tomorrow, and we'll see what they all have to say." Standing, she asked.

"You sure you want this? You won't be goin' to your old school. It blew away, but there might be some of your friends in the new one. However, you stayin' here with me means you'll be going to children's summer church every Wednesday and, of course, our Sunday services."

"I'd like that. There you can sing loud and nobody'll stop you." Theo puffed his chest.

"I love to tell the story of unseen things above.
Of Jesus and his glory, of Jesus and his love."

"Darling, please save it for Sunday. Do you want to be in the children's choir?"

"Can I sing loud?"

Ada smiled. "Yes, darling, that's the best place to do it. Now go wash up. I've got ham beans and cornbread on the stove."

"Don't forget the lemonade."

The rifle spent the night in the pantry.

Myra's next morning return telegram stated, "GOOD IDEA. WILL TALK LATER."

The small family living above the store settled into a routine of work, practice shooting at the dump, and cozy meals. That wonderful thing called electric lighting allowed Ada and Theo the evening pleasure of reading.

One night, soon after "Good night, sleep tight, don't let the bed bugs bite," Theo heard sounds downstairs. There was a *squeak* and a soft *thud*. Ada heard it, too. "Child, I think we got a possum in the back store room," she whispered. "Get the gun."

She pulled on her wrapper and tip-toed the steps behind Theo. At the bottom, they both heard scuffling. "Darlin', be ready. Aim good. Those critters can move fast."

"Yes, ma'am." Theo cocked the hammer. *Skitter, skatter. BANG.*

"Oh, Blessed Jesus!" the possum screamed.

Chapter Thirty-Four
On Account

"Don' shoot, don' shoot, ya done winged me." A very dark-skinned older man emerged from the shadows, hands up, his right forearm trickling blood. "I's jist hungry, not robbin' nobody. Lookin' for Mistah Harry. He always feeds me when I'm in town."

Ada stared. "Who are you? How in tarnation did you get in? Sit on the floor," she barked. "You're not going anywhere Theo, keep him lined up. I'll get a bandage."

"No need, jist a scratch. I's lookin' for Mistah Harry," the man repeated, folding like an accordion. "He got the sign painted out back." The man looked at his arm. "Could use a rag."

Theo braced his forearms against his chest. "You answer my auntie. My Uncle Harry's dead, and this thing's heavy."

Ada stepped behind the boy, and, keeping steady, relieved him of the rifle. *Click*, she pulled back the hammer. "Answer me."

"Is you Missus Harry? So sorry ta hear the news. Name's David Walker, but Mistah Harry always called me Walkin' Davey."

Ada released the hammer and lowered the gun. "I've heard that name. My Harry talked about a colored man who came for food. Said he was always walkin', never stayin'."

"Dat's me. Back in town, hopin' to work on the seawall. This time I'm a'stayin'. They say the buildin' company's got beds for the workers." Walkin' Davey looked up at Ada. "You'll mind if I stand? Got me some ol' legs."

"After you answer my other question. How'd you get in? The door was locked."

Walkin' Davey tilted his head toward the back. "Mistah Harry always had a key hangin' on a nail out by the dump. He told a few of us 'bout it. Said we could get a plate full from the pot left right inside." He licked his lips. "Don't 'spose you knew 'bout it, since'n you brung down his .22. Kin I stand, now?"

"Theo, give this man a hand." Ada nodded. "I know about old legs. And you, walkin' man, you give *me* my key. Humph, I always thought he left the pot there to feed the rats in the mornin'." Shaking her head, she smiled. "Can't have any more midnight visitors, might run out of bullets, shootin' the walls. Harry would o' been happy you stopped by. Theo, look for a clean rag, then run upstairs and bring down tonight's chicken and rice. It's in the blue pan in the icebox, Mister Walkin' will have to eat it cold."

"Thank ya', ma'am, obliged." Walkin' Davey looked around. "Never been this far in the store before. You sell ta colored?"

"Goodness, what a question, 'course I do. All that's expected is that the white ladies get served first. That's the way it is in all the shops." Ada crooked her eyebrows. "When you get work and settled in, come back. And for heaven's sake, use the front door. I'll think about puttin' you on account the first month. I know they don't give advances."

Theo arrived with rag, galvanized pot, and a big spoon. "Uh, Mister Walkin', I'm really sorry about shootin' you. It's just that I'm Aunt Ada's right hand man, now that Uncle Harry's gone. I'm her protection." He looked at Mister Walkin's arm. "Can I tie that up for you since I caused it?"

"Ain't bleedin' no mo'." Davey put a big spoonful of cold supper in his mouth.

"Pleeese," begged Theo. "I wanna make it right."

"Suit ya self, I'm eatin'."

Arm wrapped and stomach full, Walkin' Davey headed to the back door. Two steps out, he turned and nodded. "Thank ya, Missus, for the offer of 'on account'. White stores usually don't do that. Things kin git pretty tight."

"You're welcome. See you when you're working." Ada shut the screen.

"And, Missus…"

"Yes?"

"'Til you git a new man, ya better paint over the circle with the X on your back wall. Means us travelers is welcome. Put it there first time Mistah Harry fed me."

Ada just smiled.

Three days later another colored man came through the door, Theo's Jack. The boy was in his bear hug quick as a whip. "Mister Jack, Mister Jack, where's Daddy CB? Junior?"

"Comin' up behind, had to finish his captain duties. He'll be here soon. Junior stayed back with him."

Theo wiggled free. "Look at my shelves, my stacks, my pyramids. I'm a real hard worker." He ran from display to display. "See how all the cans have different rows of colors? I thought that up. I'm learning how to be a real good grocery man."

Ada heard the boy's to-do and came from the back room. "Oh, bless my heart, you're home. Where're my nephews?"

"Finishin' captain business," Theo answered. "Isn't that right, Mister Jack?"

Jack nodded. "And how are you, Missus Ada? Good to see you."

"And you." Ada gestured to the back room. "This is perfect timing. I happen to need a tall, strong man, taller than *my* strong man. Decided to empty the back storage room and turn it into an office."

"I thought strong man Theo was sleeping there." Jack headed to the ever-present hot pot on the stove. "You plan to keep this here?" He lifted a white porcelain mug off the peg. "You'd be the only mercantile around with an office coffee pot close by."

"Humph, fill me a mug, too. Let's go look at those top shelves before Theo decides to monkey climb and empty them himself." Ada led him into the room and quietly shut the door. "Jack, we need to talk."

Jack looked down at the top of her head. "Ma'am, why do you need to talk to me? Is there a problem?"

"Yes, I need to talk to you, and no, there isn't a problem." Ada set her chin. "It's just that, well, I met a colored hobo the other day and I can't get his situation out of my mind."

"You met a hobo? Goodness, Missus Ada, how did you do that?"

"All Harry's fault, long story, tell you later." She sat on an upturned crate, nodding to Jack to do the same. She took a deep swig of her cooling brew.

He waited.

"Jack, I never thought about travelin', workin' colored people." She shrugged. "People like you who stay in one place, have families and such, I know. But this man, called himself Walkin' Davey, is here to build the seawall. Harry used to feed him when he'd come to town. Seemed real nice." She stared into her cup. "I offered him 'on account' after he starts work. He acted like I'd given him the world, even though Theo shot him." Ada grinned. "Just grazed his arm."

"Well," Jack raised his mug in a salute, "CB shot me, so's I guess the boy comes by it honestly."

"Anyway, I've been doin' a lot of thinkin' about folks such as Walkin' Davey. Harry fed 'em all. I can't do that, not me as a widow woman, but, by golly, the colored workers have it hard."

"Yes, ma'am, that's true. But why do you want to tell me all this? I don't know how to help." Jack leaned forward, staring at Ada. "I'm always on the *Sallie Lou*, I have nothin' to give."

"Son, you have nothin'...except for a cellar full of gold."

Jack's eyes were wide. "You know?"

Ada smiled. "Myra told me everything. She thinks she knows what to do with her portion. Do you and Marguerite know what to do with yours?"

"Um, no ma'am."

"Well, I might. Think about it. Walkin' Davey sure could use a hand up."

"Huh?" Jack's face was pure perplexion. "A what?"

"The man had no startin' money. Didn't need a hand out, needed a hand up."

"And?" Jack's tone mirrored his look.

"And all he needed was some help, but there're no colored banks around. All we need..." Ada cleared her throat. "All that's needed is gold, five-dollar gold pieces."

"You're thinkin' of using CB's money to start a bank?" Jack shook his head. "Missus Ada, I thought you said Missus Myra had it all figured out for them."

"Not them, you, you and your wife."

"Oh, uh, ma'am," Jack stammered. 'I don't think so."

"Goodness sake, why not?"

"Uh, uh, because, we, um, that is, Marguerite and I never went to school."

"Oh?" It was Ada turn to be confused. "The two of you read, write, and cypher."

"Yes, ma'am, Mama learnin', but we're not smart enough to be bankers."

Rising, Ada wagged her finger as she walked to Jack's crate. "You listen to me, Mister Jack Smith. I heard how you did all the paper work that first roll off in Panama after CB got his neck sliced. Don't you dare tell me you're not smart."

His modest shrug did not deflect her.

Standing eye to eye, him sitting, Ada gave her best squinched eyebrow stare. "I want you to think about helping your fellow coloreds. All I can do is a few 'on accounts'. You could make a difference."

"Yes, ma'am, but I just don't think so." He looked above her head. "What you want me to do first? Empty those top shelves or shove the extra bed out of the way?"

Chapter Thirty-Five
Turn Around

Theo asked to tag along with the home-bound sailors, wanting to see his family in LaPorte. "Auntie, you feelin' safe without your deputy?"

"Yes, dear."

"I'll be back when the *Sallie Lou* is ready to sail."

"I know."

"I'll kiss everybody for you."

"Thank you, child." Ada gave CB a look that said "Git yourselves to the station, *now*."

"Come, son." He gently guided Theo to the front door. "See you real soon, Aunt Ada."

Ting. They were gone.

The travelers settled into their separate spaces. For once Jack didn't mind being in the colored car. He wanted to talk to his own, to see what was what. Sailing a white man's ship and living in a white man's neighborhood did not give him a clear view of his world, the Negro world. He nodded to a middle-aged gentleman sitting alone. "Ya mind?"

"Suit yourself." He extended his hand. "Name's Jefferson Lucas."

"Jack Smith." He sat on the thin worn cushion beside Jefferson. "You live in LaPorte?"

"Are you crazy, man? Colored don't live in LaPorte, just work there."

"I didn't know that."

"Well, that's what they say. My wife, Geneva's a house gal, workin' for a nice lady with kids. She's stayin' with her sister Karena, who's takin' care of a real old rich couple." Jefferson leaned back in his seat. "Got me two days off the wall. I'm a second line foreman," he said with pride. "Gonna buy a room in the new colored hotel. Heard it was for the visitin'." He scratched his moustache. "Can't wait to see my missus."

Jack smiled. "Me, too. I'm a merchant sailor." He did not mention he owned half the ship. "My wife lives and works in a nice place, too. We got a room there."

Jefferson grinned, elbowing his seat mate. "It's gonna be one hot night. That's all I gotta say."

"Yes sir, it sure is." Jack looked across Jefferson, out the window. "There's the seawall. "You know a worker that goes by the name of Walkin' Davey? Heard he just signed on."

"Naw, not if he ain't in my brigade. Too many new men comin' in to count." Jefferson looked at Jack. "You thinkin' of leavin' shippin'? I can tell you, the pay's real good on the wall."

"Good pay, huh? I'll keep that in mind." Jack leaned back, the rocking of the rails soon putting him to sleep.

In the white car, Junior'd given Theo the window seat. They were about five minutes into the trip when the boy started whooping and pointing as the train passed the seawall construction.

"There he is, there he is. There's Walkin' Davey."

CB's head whipped at the name. "You mean the one you shot?"

"Look, look, he's workin'. Guess I didn't hurt him too bad."

"Guess you didn't." CB cleared his throat. "Best not tell the others about all that, though. Mama wouldn't want any of y'all thinkin' you can get away with shootin' people."

Junior nudged his brother. "Gonna call ya Deadeye from now on," he stage-whispered.

CB's telegram said that this turnaround was short, so the LaPorte white platform was crowded with Ledbetters, hoping to get as much time as possible from the visit. Marguerite, posing as the family's mammy, stood holding Flossie Mae, and all were waiting for that tell-tale vibration that comes before any train appears.

"Mama, my feet tickle." Nora Lee, who insisted she wear her new satin Sunday shoes, felt it first. "Train's a comin', train's a comin'."

"Yes, baby, they'll be here soon." Myra flashed her eyes. "Now don't you say a word about riding in a horse coach. It'll be a wonderful surprise."

"We won't. The new bicycle and wagon Missus Annie and Mister Carlton had made for us is a whole lot bigger surprise than a horse coach." She mimed holding the handlebars. "Can't wait to show Theo how to ride."

Shadows crossed Marguerite's eyes at the mention of Missus Annie and her gift, an apology due Marguerite, but given to the children. She handed Flossie Mae to Benjy. "Tell your mama that I am going to the colored platform and that Jack and I will walk home."

"But, Missus 'Guite, don't you want to ride with us?"

"My husband's not a mammy. I will walk with him." With that, she was gone.

Benjy strolled over and stood by his twin, jiggling his wiggling sister. "Sorry Sweetie, can't let you down. Daddy CB's train might squish ya."

"Come here, baby girl, and let *me* hold you." Franky held out his arms and Flossie Mae nose-dived into his chin. The knock started her squalling, bringing her mama over from the front of the platform.

"Why are you holding her? That's Marguerite's job." Myra scooped the child into her arms, the cries stopping instantly. "Hmm, little girl, has your big sister been teachin' you all she knows?"

Flossie Mae pouted her lower lip.

"Yep, looks like it." Myra searched for her friend. "Where's Missus Marguerite?"

"Said she was goin' to the colored platform." Benjy shrugged. "Said they're walking home. Said Mister Jack isn't a mammy."

"Of course he's not a mammy, wonder what that was...oh." Her eyes grew wide.

Franky cricked his head. "Oh, what?"

"It's just that," Myra lowered her voice. "It's just that Mister Jack might not be allowed to ride with us in the horse coach."

"Oh."

Chapter Thirty-Six
Awakening

A sense of uneasiness filled the house. At dinner, Marguerite was exceptionally quiet, Jack filling the void with unnecessary chatter about ship business, not knowing what else to do.

Leaning over to her mother, Nora Lee whispered, "Missus 'Guite's grumpy."

"Hush, Nosey Rosy."

"Well, Mama, she is."

With that, Marguerite nodded her 'excuse me' and went to their room, leaving the dessert serving to whoever wanted to cut the biggest slice for themselves.

"Looks like I better go see why there's a storm brewin'." Jack nodded his manners and made for the stairs. At the newel post he turned. "Please save me a piece. Um, make it two. Maybe I can get her back down."

Several hours later the cake had gone unclaimed, and supper dishes waited, untouched on the table. Myra and CB were out in the gazebo with Flossie Mae. Benjy, Franky and Nora Lee were off to Sylvan Beach with their newly returned brothers, the "bestest place to play in the whole wide world." The Smiths were forgotten. Late that evening, Theo quietly did the dishes, hoping no one would come, breaking the peace. The trip to the beach with all the kids had given him the jumpities. "I'm Mama's Dishes Deputy," he thought.

"Son?" CB's voice startled the boy, and he dropped the spoons he was washing back into the soapy water, clanging on the bottom of the galvanized dish pan. "Son, you want me to wipe?"

Theo smiled shyly. "Yes, sir, but you don't have to. I'm the Dishes Deputy."

"That's a new one." CB picked up a clean tea towel. "Thought you said you were Rat Dump Deputy."

"I am, just made up the name. Hope Mama likes it."

CB picked up a wet supper plate and puzzled over it. "This new? Looks like your mama's been doing some shoppin'." He dried it and reached for another. "I don't remember little roses around the edge."

"Me, neither." Theo pulled the last rewashed spoon out of the rinse pan and handed it to be dried. "Here ya' go, I think the silverware's the same."

CB shook his head. "I heard about Nora Lee's new yellow kitty. We've never had a pet before."

"Yeh, she said her name is Miss Mimi Songsinger." Theo laughed. "She said it's 'cause the kitty doesn't meow, she says 'me me,' you know, like an opera lady."

The two finished the kitchen chores, covering the cake and putting it on the sideboard, "just in case."

"Good night, Daddy CB."

"Good night, son Theo. See you in the morning."

Theo sighed. "Aunt Ada says "Don't let the bed bugs bite."

"You missin' her already?"

"Yes, sir, but don't tell Mama. She might get jealous."

CB lowered his head, looking out the top of his eyes. "Can't do that with your mama, that's like lyin'. If she asks, I'll answer. I just won't bring it up."

"Thanks." Theo grinned. "Good night, sleep tight; don't let the bed bugs bite."

The next morning Marguerite and Jack were found in the kitchen, making breakfast, Cookie style. *Sallie Lou's* crew was always served the lightest, tastiest grits and that took a lot of elbow grease, whipping the mess hard until it boiled up thick. Marguerite took her turn at the pot, dropping in a giant cut of butter.

"I'm serious, *mon amour,* you need to think us up a spending plan."

Jack stood behind her, leaning in to nip the top of her left ear, remembering the night before. "Hmmmm, too busy."

Marguerite raised the wooden spoon, dripping with molten goodness. "Don't make me turn around with this," she threatened. "Reach me a tasting fork. Tell me if it's thick enough." She scraped off a glob, blew the heat away, and fed her husband. "*Bien?*"

Jack nodded, licking his lips. "Good." He stepped up to the stove. "I'll start the meat if you mix the biscuits."

Using a drinking glass, she rolled the dough and cut the circles. "Oh, *mon amour*, why can't we have our own house?"

"Huh?" Jack didn't hear her soft words above the sizzle of the frying ham. "What?"

"I'm tired of not having my own kitchen." She sniffled. "I want my own house." Marguerite swiped away the tears that had just begun, leaving a smear of flour on her cheek.

"We're set up good. I have the ship, and you live with Myra. Don't need to change." Jack looked at the rising biscuits. "How soon?"

"Maybe never," she whispered.

When it was time to head to sea, Marguerite said she would carry Myra's gold to Ada. Said she wanted to see Missylou and the others from the Tremont, knowing the manager, Mr. Brown, would let her stay in one of the unused rooms in the back of the first floor. She didn't say she was tired of being Myra's house gal and needed a

153 • The Cornerpost

break. She also didn't mention the extra weight of gold coins she carried in a separate pouch in her valise.

Mister and Missus Smith had never been on a train ride together. Luckily, not many coloreds were headed to the island, so they got to sit where they wanted. Holding hands, they chatted or dozed the entire way. Just before the station, the train passed the seawall. "*Mon amour*, look at that," exclaimed Marguerite, pointing out the window. "What are they doing? There are so many workers."

"That's the seawall. They say it'll stop hurricane waters." Jack shook his head. "I think the only one that can stop a flood is Moses."

Kissing his cheek, Marguerite leaned her head against his arm. "I'm glad they're trying. You never saw the waters up to the mezzanine of the hotel."

"No, but I did find you in that ruined dining room, or have you forgotten our first kiss?"

Marguerite's blush felt warm on his arm. "*Non*, I have not forgotten."

At the Galveston station, the sailors bid their family goodbye and headed off to the docks. Marguerite and Theo were soon 'dinging' the store's door.

"Auntie, Auntie, I'm home. I brought school clothes." Theo dropped his suitcase and ran from stack to display. "You need me. Look, look, the colors are all mixed up."

Ada grabbed the dervish. "Whoa, child, colors can wait, kissin' can't." She tapped her cheek. Smooch, and he was gone, back to inspecting the neglect of his hard labors.

Retrieving Theo's belongings, Marguerite smiled at Ada. "I think he's *très heureux* to be back."

"Pardon? I don't know what that means." Ada repeated the words. "*Très heureux*. I'm guessing it has something to do with being happy, what with that grin on his face."

"*Oui*, it means very happy." Marguerite stood, looking around the store. "Where do you want this? Does the boy still sleep in the back room?"

"Lord, no, he sleeps upstairs on the company bed, but don't you fret." Ada raised her voice. "Theo," she called. "Are your arms broke?"

"Huh?" He skidded to a halt in front of his auntie, flapping like a bird. "Look, they're not broke."

"Then carry your things upstairs. That is not Missus Marguerite's job."

"Yes, ma'am, can I get something to eat?" Theo snatched his case and took the steps, not waiting for an answer.

Ada turned her attention to Marguerite. "Where will you be staying? I'd offer you the back store room, got a camp cot set up, but, I'm sure your husband talked to you about what's going on."

The blank expression on Marguerite's face puzzled Ada. "Didn't he tell you about the plans?"

"*Non*." Wariness filled her eyes. "What plans?"

"The plans that maybe the room could be an answer to your half of the gold problem." Ada tilted her head. "He said you two were not schooled enough to do it, but I don't believe him."

Marguerite's color rose. "I do not have any idea what is going on, but I can assure you that we are both schooled, if not in the classroom." She spied the checkerboard and chairs. "May we sit down? Whatever my husband said to you needs to be corrected. Did you know that my Jack Smith taught your CB Ledbetter how to read and write? If that isn't schooled, I don't know what is. The skunk lied to you."

Ada joined Marguerite, bearing two mugs of hot joe from the stove. "Cream? Sugar?"

"No ma'am, thank you. May I have a saucer for the cooling?"

It was Ada's turn to look puzzled. She found one in the back.

Marguerite poured a bit of coffee into the saucer, swirled it around, and drank from the dish. "When you're thirsty, it's the quickest way to get it down without scalding."

"Hmmm, never seen that before." Ada smiled at her guest. "I'll try it Sunday."

Both mugs were half empty when Marguerite looked up, politely avoiding Ada's eyes. "Please tell me what I do not know. As much as I have begged, my husband refuses to talk about a spending plan. He thinks living on a ship is all he needs." She took a handkerchief from her pocket and nervously crumpled it in her left hand. "Missus Ada, just like Myra, I want more. My problem is not as easy to solve as hers." Marguerite looked at the valise resting by her feet. "And, yes, I brought her coins."

"Thank you, my dear." Ada patted Marguerite's free hand. "I figured you did."

"But," Marguerite extended her fingers under Ada's, "skin color makes all the difference in the world. Who ever heard of a rich Negro family?" She pulled from the touch and put both hands in her lap, twisting her hanky. "It can be real tiresome pretending to be somebody's house servant just to live under a good roof. Sometimes it isn't pretend."

"You mean to tell me that my Myra…"

"Oh, excuse me." Marguerite stood. "I've said too much." She took a step to the door. "I will go to the Tremont and be with my friends." She opened her valise and lifted one of the string-tied sacks. "Here's her gold."

"Child, sit. I never realized how things were, and I bet your husband didn't, either, or he wouldn't've ignored your need." Ada patted the checkerboard. "Please come and listen to what I told him."

After a quarter hour, they toured the new back room office. Ada pointed to the window, the one Junior got trapped in. "See that? You could be offering money help, for a bit of interest, through that window…"

"Like a real teller." Marguerite finished.

Ada nodded. "Like a real bank teller," she repeated.

Gathering her own belongings, and with a promise to "think about it", Marguerite was on her way to the Tremont, taking long, determined strides. "I don't have to think about it," she said decisively to herself. "I will do this, come stubborn husband, hell-fire, or sea water."

Chapter Thirty-Seven
Sisterhood Lost

The Tremont girls were thrilled to see her. Mr. Brown said that he would be happy for her to stay, but it was their beloved head butler, Mister Charles, the one Marguerite called grandfather, that made her tell her truth.

"Come, child, talk to me." The last time she saw the senior staffer was right after the hurricane. He sat high on the dais in the banquet room, observing and directing all of the work done for the refugees camped on the fourth floor. Mister Charles was the first one to meet Jack Smith, and to know his desire to wed Marguerite. Then he gave her away, just like family. Now he had an office on the first floor, with a fancy desk, settee, and matching leather chairs, a gift from the hotel for his tireless work during the disaster. "Come talk to me," he repeated.

Marguerite sat across from him, her face in utter misery. "Oh, *Monsieur* Charles, I have made a horrible decision, and I am not going to change my mind."

"My dear, what in the world are you talking about?" Mister Charles stood and very quietly shut the office door. He sat next to her on the settee, waiting while she cried a long, silent time. After the waves of heartbreak passed, she took a deep breath and told him everything: the gold, her treatment in the house upstate, and the fact that her beloved husband didn't understand any of it. "I am NOT going to be someone's 'colored girl' when I'm probably richer than that Rockefeller man."

"Now, I doubt that," soothed Mister Charles. "And, you must remember that you are not rich. You *and* Mister Jack are rich."

"I know." Marguerite lips started their tremble all over again. "I'm married to a man who only wants to be on a ship and visit me once in a while in the house he sold to CB. He thinks everything is just fine that way." The tears started again. "Oh, *Monsieur* Charles, I want to clean my own house, not Myra's."

"So, child, just exactly why are you here?"

She sniffled. "I'm going to start a colored people's bank in a white lady's store." Marguerite blinked and sat up very straight. "Oh, goodness, this is the first time I've said it out loud." She smiled. "I am going to take *our* money and make even more. And what that sailor man doesn't know while he's happily away, living on the *Sallie Lou*, won't hurt him." Her voice rose. "He can float from here to Timbuktu and back again, I don't care. Missus Ada, Myra's auntie, has a banking room for me in her mercantile, and it even has a teller window."

Mister Charles, index finger to his lips, nodded to the door. "Shhhhh, child, have you forgotten? Around here its telephone, telegraph, tell-a-gal. You don't know who's out in that hallway."

"*Oui*, I did forget." With an exaggerated look to the left and right, Marguerite made the lock lips gesture. "I can't let anyone know, not even Myra, that I'm leaving."

"How in heaven's name are you going to do that? The gold is in Myra's house, and you are going into business with her kin." Mister Charles leaned over, grasping Marguerite's chin in his hand. "Myra must think your friendship's as rock steady as that of those sailing men, or she wouldn't have started up with you to begin with." He waggled her face. "Think about it. Is what you want worth losing your only 'sister', considering that the men call themselves 'brother'?"

"She doesn't treat me like a *sister*." Marguerite's eyes glinted. "A *sister* doesn't not walk away from a table of dirty dishes without a care in the world, expecting her *sister* to do all the work. A *sister* doesn't assume the house work, including watching the baby, will be done without a how-do-you-do. She's treating me like a, like a…"

"Stand up, child, and calm yourself." He took both hands. "I hope you think long and hard about this change. Leaving a white house and a husband's arms can be very dangerous. Are you really ready to be treated like a Nigger? You know the color of gold cannot wash the brown off your skin." He squeezed her hands. "I doubt you will be able to rent a room, let alone a house, without your husband to sign. In the meantime," he squeezed tighter, "if you want, I will talk to Mister Brown about you staying with us once you make up your mind."

Marguerite pulled her hands free. "My mind is made. Please ask him as soon as possible. Tell him I'll pay." Stopping at the closed door, she turned. "I'm sleeping in the 'visit room' for a few days. Once we set up the bank, I definitely will need a place to live. *Monsieur* Charles, thank you for doing this."

"Well, then, dear, see ya directly." Sinking into his chair once she was out the door, Mister Charles closed his eyes and prayed. "Jesus, walk with her. Keep her safe from the devil and his wickedness. Amen." Just then his bell call rang three times. "Who's on third floor? Bet Mrs. Williams fell again. Lordy, my legs are gettin' too old for all this." He put on his suit coat, making sure his tails hung evenly, and tugged on his white gloves, adjusting the creases between each finger. After a quick look in the mirror by his door, he was gone. "Really do wish they'd let us colored use the elevator," he muttered as he climbed the back servant steps. "That'll be the day." He shook his head. "And to think our Miss Girl wants to start a bank. That 'bout beats all."

By the time Mister Charles was done with the hotel's 'falling star', his shift was over. As was his routine, he climbed one more round of steps, emerging into the banquet kitchen on the fourth floor. "Since I'm up here, might as well eat with the girls instead of in my room."

"It's jist me right now." Cocoa, one of the serving girls, was sitting at the staff table. "Mrs. Williams?"

Mister Charles nodded. "Won't let anyone else lift her ninety-five year old bones."

"Awww, she jist sweet on you." She made heart flutter gestures on her chest, laughing at his head-shaking denial.

"You know old rich ladies always have their house man. You be the head butler in dis here hotel. She 'spects the best." Cocoa lifted her left eyebrow. "She told me one time dat she always had good lookin' help in her house. Well, guess what, the Tremont's her house."

Noticing the empty room, Mister Charles changed the subject. "Why are you sitting? Looks to me like everybody else is on the floor."

Cocoa lifted the cane hidden under the table. "Sprung my ankle bad. Got took off the floor and put ta washin' dishes. Still gotta stand, but it's better 'en not gittin' paid."

"Sorry to hear that. Have you seen Marguerite? Our Miss Girl's somewhere around." He lifted the lid from the ever-present chafer on the side board. "Mmmm, smells good. I'll get me a bowl. You want this old butler to serve you?"

"Thanks, 'preciate it, and yes, I seen her talkin' to Missylou, somethin' 'bout the Bright Star Sisters." Cocoa gestured toward the swinging door. "Don't ya know, that gal grabbed an apron and is out 'ere right now."

The two fell into the rhythm of eating and talking. The chef always heated yesterday's dinner meal for the staff, so if the guests had roast beef with mushrooms on Tuesday, so did they, on Wednesday. This meal was chicken and dumplings.

An hour and a half later, Cocoa was dish washing and the rest of the girls were eating. Sitting next to the still present Mister Charles, Marguerite listened as they told the stories of their day.

"Did y'all see what happened at table fifteen? Dat man's no gentleman."

"Sure 'nuf did. I saw him try to swat yo bottom. Too bad you couldn't swat him back."

"Dat would've been the end of me."

Through all the chatter, only Mister Charles noticed quiet Marguerite flinch at some of the stories. "Miss Girl, you all right? You've not had a bite."

"Yes sir, just not hungry right now. Might come back up for something later." Marguerite walked up behind Cocoa, gave her a hug, and disappeared down the back steps. "Oh, Beloved Mary, it's been so long since I've heard colored talk," Marguerite thought.

When she hit the second floor landing, she started crying, and didn't stop until she fell asleep, fully clothed atop the still-made bed in the visit room.

Knock. "Miss Girl, you in there? It's me." *Knock.* "It's morning time."

Marguerite opened the door for Mister Charles. "Look at you, child, seems you slept in your clothes. You never did come up for food." He nodded to the rumpled, but still made bed. "You got something to tell your old 'grandfather'? What is in your heart?"

"*Grand-pere*, I thought I could go back, go back to the girls on the floor."

"And?"

"I thought it would be the same, that they could be my sisters like it used to be."

"And?"

Marguerite sank down on the edge of the bed. "I was right. It was just the same, none of the girls have changed."

Mister Charles nodded. "Yes, but you, my child, did, and that makes all the difference."

"*Oui*." Her eyes grew wide. "Oh, *Grand-pere*, there is no place for me. I cannot be who I was, I cannot be who I am. And," she blinked, "I can't even be a Bright Star Sister. Missylou said so herself."

"Good Lord, girl, of course you can't, you have no Prince Hall kin. Where'd you get the notion you could?" He took her hand, pulling her to a stand. "I'm stepping out. Do something to tidy yourself and meet me at the steps directly. You haven't eaten since yesterday. I'll get us something to drink and whatever else is sitting around."

Staring into the oval looking glass atop the oak dresser, Marguerite began working her hair. "Look at you. They call you the red-headed colored gal, and that is what you are, just that and nothing else." She disentangled her long back braid and dragged a comb through her soft, wavy hair. "Half breed with no daddy name, not colored, not white. You're a nothin', just a nothin'." Dividing her hair into three sections, she began the plaiting, twisting each strand tighter with the turn of the weave. "Look at me," she addressed the mirror, "can't be a Bright Star, or any other kind of star. Dang, not even an old lady falling star." Marguerite held one length to the side, making a sour face at what she saw. "I don't have the right kind of hair for a colored gal. And my skin's all wrong. And, and, and the only man who ever loved me lives on a stinking ship." She wrapped the braid into a knot and pinned on her snood. "All he wants is to play house, dammit, and all I want is to own one."

Marguerite threw open the door and stomped to the steps. There was one cup, a pot of coffee, and two ham biscuits on a silver service. Mister Charles was leaning against the stair railing, an almost empty cup perched on the top of the carved newel. He nodded to the tray. "Eat, child. Left you two. I'll be going to work soon, so bring everything up to the fourth when you're done. Can't expect 'just a nothing' to be waited on, now can we?"

"You heard?"

"Me 'n' half the world. 'Spect you'll be headin' back where you came from, you bein' all those names you called yourself." He pointed to the food. "Eat. You're lookin' a tad bit peaked, for a wrong haired, half breed, whatever else you said. I flat-out stopped listening after a while." He emptied his cup in one swallow with a grimace and set it down. He poured hers.

"Oh, *Grand-pere,* I'm sorry that you heard me." Taking a taste, she chewed silently, washing it down with a sip. "Hmmm," she took another bite, "This is good. Thank you."

Mister Charles watched her finish the first biscuit. "Miss Girl, I know you are feeling wronged by this world you've been put in. But remember, child, that our wonderful Savior never makes mistakes, so don't you ever think you're one." He waggled his finger at the dishes. "Don't forget."

"Yes, sir, I won't."

Two steps from the mid-landing Mister Charles stopped and looked over his shoulder. "Miss Girl, when you ever get over yourself, come find me. I'll introduce you to a real proper lady. She knows all about colored society here in on the island. Her name is Sister Givens, and she's *my* very dear friend."

Marguerite stared after him as he climbed out of sight. "I love you, *Grand-pere,*" she whispered. "See ya directly."

Chapter Thirty-Eight
NSC

Marguerite gathered her things and walked slowly to the mercantile, entering through the back. She sat on the cot in the room that once held her dreams. "Thank goodness Missus Ada didn't hear me. Can't face her just now," she thought. "Later's soon enough, I'll just rest 'til she finds me and sends me away."

Ting. Glancing up from arranging the cold meats and cheeses in her refrigerated glass case, Ada had to squinch her eyes to focus on her customer outlined through the glare of the opened door. "Yes? May I help you?"

"Missus Harry, it's Walkin' Davey. You remember me, don' cha? I'm the one your boy winged."

"Why, of course I do." She walked around the cabinet, wiping her hands on the side hem of her apron. Studying him up and down, she smiled. "I see you're as dirty as any working man I know. Looks like you got a job."

"Yes'um, sho did." Pride sparkled in his eyes. "Been on the seawall crew since the day after we met. Earned me a day off already."

"Good for you." She tilted her head toward the back. "Do you need fed? I can get you something."

"Oh, no, ma'am, thank ya, anyway." Walkin' Davey mirrored her tilt. "Do you remember what y'all said to me that day? Are you still offerin' 'on account'?"

"Of course I am. You do your shopping, and we'll see if it'll work out." Ada smiled. "When's your first pay?"

"Had it already, but some sommybeach, 'scuse my language, stole it out my knapsack that same night. Dey put all us new men in a big open room with cots. Call it a barracks, but it's jist a barn. So's I'm askin' you for help. Gotta rent me a room soon, dat's for sure." He shook his head. "Got no place to keep mah next pay safe 'cept wadded up in mah shirt. I knows the bills'll get too sweaty to use and I ain't got no place to lay 'em out to dry."

Walkin' Davey wandered the store, talking the whole time. "Can't pick nuthin' but canned and jarred. The crew cook feeds us hot dinner, takes it out our pay, and 'spects us to find supper somewheres else." He stopped in front of the sacks of grits. "Couldn't make me a batch of that if I tried. Got no money, got no kitchen." He continued looking. "Missus Harry…"

"Please call me 'Missus Ada'…"

"Oh, no, ma'am, wouldn't be right." Walkin' Davey was making his way toward the dry goods. "Will ya look at that, didn't know they made buttons to match fabric."

"Um, Mister Walkin', why don't you come back to the food side? We need to see what you can eat out of a can. I don't think pins and threads would be very tasty."

"Well, dat's true, but I used ta sew a decent stitch, and I need some mendin' things. Da boys on the da road were always lookin' for Walkin' Davey to fix their britches."

"Well, in that case, add some overall thread and a packet of needles to your order. Thimble? I'll count those as necessities." Ada returned to behind the refrigerated case.

"No thimble, I gots me some mighty tough fingers."

Pulling out a round of Colby, Ada nodded. "I bet you do. Don't you want a slice or two of cheese with some bread, on the house? I'll wrap it up for your supper."

"Well, ma'am, if ya don' mind. Next pay's in five days."

She handed him a thick slice, "for the tasting," cut one for herself, and proceeded to make him two sandwiches to take. Chewing on his sample, Walkin' Davey picked out enough canned food for the next while. Ada wrote all his choices in a ledger as he watched. "I's promise to pay, Missus...?"

"Missus Dickenson, you can call me that." Ada tapped the ledger page. "Just to let you know, when I do accounts for people, I don't charge credit for four weeks, but if you don't pay by the end of the month, it's an extra dollar each week you're late. You skip out on me, I call Constable Turner."

Walkin' Davey nodded. "Dat sounds fair. Gives a man a chance to get hisself set up. Jist hope I don' get robbed again."

"I need your mark here at the bottom of the page." Ada filled his knapsack and handed him the sandwiches. "I'll see you next week."

With a tip of his cap, *ting*, he was gone.

Ada turned, facing the rear of the store. "All right, Missus Marguerite, you can come out now. I know you're back there, don't know why, but I hope you heard everything he said." She busied herself with rags, vinegar water, and newspapers, cleaning the glass on the cold meat case.

A very gloomy Marguerite emerged. "I heard."

"You can help that man," Ada said, without missing a polishing swipe. "Banks get robbed a whole lot less than first-pay men."

"I know." She looked around the empty store. "May I have some coffee, please?"

"What happened to you at the Tremont? Of course you can. You shouldn't be askin', just gettin'." Ada squeezed her rag and hung it over the pail. Grabbing two mugs, she sat at the checkerboard, and Marguerite joined her with the pot.

Several sips later, Marguerite answered. "Missus Ada, I'm a nobody."

"Huh?"

"I'm too white to be colored, and too colored to be white. I'm a nothing." Marguerite stared over Ada's curly white hair. "Missus Ada, I got straight red hair."

Ada bit both lips together to hold her tongue and breathed deeply. "And?"

"And I don't fit."

"You get told that rubbish at the hotel?"

"No, I just saw." Marguerite continued her stare.

"I'll be right back. There's something you should see." Ada was up and down the steps in a slow blink, with the latest edition of *The Delineator.* She opened to the next to last page, folded back the rest, and pointed at a picture of a Negress. "See her. She's Annie Turnbo from St. Louis, Missouri, and she's rich enough to have an ad for her hair business in a white ladies' magazine. I'm tellin' you, that's sayin' something." Ada tapped the photo. "You're probably richer, smarter, and you sure do have a whole lot better hair than her."

"Ma'am, no white woman has ever said that to me. I'm just…"

SLAM. Ada smacked the picture so hard the checkers jumped. "Shush that talk right now. You heard Walkin' Davey. The colored workers need a safe place to get advances and keep their money. We have that place. Let me tell you about cold cash."

By time of the evening meal, they were in agreement. "Missus Ada, I don't know how to do this yet, but I will bring some gold to get us started. Thank you for offering me the cot in that office."

Ada smiled. "I already thought up a name for the window sign, a name that only certain people will know. You know like secret hobo signals."

"What is it, 'Missus Ada's Helping Hand'?" Marguerite started laughing. "How about 'Marguerite's Money Maker'?"

"Glory-be, what a name, but, if it's all right with you, we could call it the 'NBSBL', the Negro Benevolence Society Building and Loan."

"NBSBL." Marguerite savored the letters. "NBSBL. There's one problem with that."

"Yes?"

"We won't be loaning anything for building. We'll be all about helping people over rough spots and giving them a place to save." Marguerite looked at her lap and then straight at Ada. "I want to call it a saving cooperative. Heard about them, where people help out people. I want to call the bank, NSC, Negro Saving Cooperative."

"I like that."

"Thank you for this."

"My dear, *thank you.* I know, once the word is out, they will become my customers. And don't worry, as your banking partner, I'll take a cut for my own benevolence." Ada exaggerated her wink. "Need to save for that steamer trip around the world."

The next morning Marguerite lined her corset with the cash from both her and Myra's gold, pulling the laces extra tight. Standing at the door, ready to leave for the station, she once again thanked "Missus Ada" for all she had done.

"Child, do you have any female kin, a mama or an auntie?" Ada patted Marguerite's gloved hand.

"Um, my *maman* died right after the storm, God hold her soul." *Not gonna mention that gypsy trash sister.*

"I am so sorry to hear that." Ada's hand rested where she was patting. "I would like it very much if you called me 'Auntie Ada', if that's all right with you."

Marguerite's cheeks almost matched her hair. She picked up her valise and stepped to the door.

"Child, you forgot something." Ada took her in her arms in a tight embrace. "Good bye, *niece*."

Ting. "Oh my stars and buttons, that's the first time I've hugged a colored person," she said to the empty store. "Silly me, I thought she'd feel warmer, like a cookie that browned too long in the oven." Looking around, she realized her constant helper was at Wednesday Children's Summer Church. "Thank heavens the boy didn't hear all that. Don't want him to think his ol' auntie is such an ignoramus about colored folk…even if she is."

Chapter Thirty-Nine
What Was That All About?

"Missus 'Guite's back," Nora Lee trumpeted through the house. "Mama, Missus 'Guite's back."

"Thank God. Tell her to git up here right now."

"Can't." The girl was tapping on the stairway, two steps forward, one step back, turn around and do it again. "I'm busy."

"Don't you sass me, young lady," yelled Myra, "You tell Marguerite I need her, now."

"I'm not sassin', just answerin'." With a swing of her unbrushed curls, Nora Lee was out the front door. "Gotta practice my buck dancing on the porch." *Tappity tap stamp, tappity tap tap.* "Makes better noise out here," she hollered through the screen. *Stamp stamp.*

"Marguerite, where are you?" Myra called from her bedroom door. "Git up here, now." No answer, just the sound of fading footsteps on the stairs. Over the racket of the performing girl there was the squeak of the root cellar door. *Oh God, robbers.* Myra was down in a flash, pulling her dressing gown around her still night-clothed self.

Marguerite looked at the disheveled woman panting at the bottom of the steps, and turned back to moving boxes. There was a newly formed aisle down the middle of the dirt floor with even walls on each side.

"Dammit, you could've let me know you were here." Myra's tone had that familiar demand. "I counted on you to be home yesterday. Did you bring my money?"

"Hello to you, too, *friend*." Marguerite did not face her. "Yes, I did. It's on the sideboard, under the green glass bowl." She swiveled, hoisting a crate across the room to the other pile. "Why aren't you dressed?"

"Can't get anything done when you're gone."

"Hire a colored girl." Marguerite turned back to the moving. "Ask Missus Annie where to find one."

"But, but, you're my colored girl. I've got you."

SLAP! Marguerite didn't plan it, and Myra didn't expect it. "No. You. Don't." She set the crate on the growing stack and walked past a stunned Myra, up into the mid-afternoon light. She pocketed the cellar key as she passed the door.

There was neither hot food nor conversation around the evening supper table. Marguerite kissed each child and returned to her room. She did not come down in the morning. Myra sent Franky to fetch her.

"Knock, knock, Missus 'Guite," he called. "Mama said she's makin' breakfast." Silence. *Knock knock.* The unlatched door swung open. "Missus 'Guite? Mama said…" Franky was staring into an empty room, bed just so, made without *Maman's* quilt. Franky knew. "Mama, Mama," he yelled, running down the steps, "Missus 'Guite's gone."

"Huh, what? Can't hear you over all this yammering. Git over here." Myra spooned hot rice into the waiting bowls, and put the pitcher of cold milk next to the jug of molasses on the table.

"Missus 'Guite's run away." Franky started to sniffle. "Her Mama's quilt is gone." His tears started. "Oh, Mama, we made her run away, we made her run away."

"Stop that, child," Myra barked. "She can't run away, she belongs to us."

"No, Mama," Franky whispered, "she belongs to Mister Jack. She said that's what bein' a wife's all about. She's not married to us."

"I didn't mean that. It's just, well, she lives with us, and we need her."

Nora Lee shook her head. "Maybe so, but if she's run away, she didn't need *us*." Flossie Mae, tied in her highchair, was squeezing her breakfast through her fingers and licking her palms. "Mama, you want me to feed the baby since Missus 'Guite ain't here to do it?"

"Thank you, child." Myra sat to her own bowl. "Why would she go?" she wondered aloud between bites. "What in the world did we do wrong?"

Chapter Forty
The Congress of Mothers

Miss Mimi Songsinger, the family's pet kitty, pooped in Nora Lee's chifferobe. No one noticed. Teeny, tiny roaches were running rampant on the kitchen sink side board. No one noticed. The children were outside day and night, wearing the same dirty clothing. The neighbors noticed.

KNOCK. KNOCK. "Mrs. Ledbetter, are you in there?"

Franky came to the door with a mouthful of yesterday's bread. He squinted through the screen at a very tall lady with a dead bird on her hat. "Wa'chu want? Mama's upstairs. Said to leave her alone."

"Young man, I need to talk to your mother right now. Tell her it is very important because I do not want the law involved." The bird hat lady pulled out a matching feather fan and started fluttering it much harder than needed. "Tell her I am waiting, that I want to help, and I will *not* go away."

After a bit, Myra thumped down the steps, tying a sash around the only ironed house dress she could find. It was evident by her wild hair that she had been sleeping. The feathered neighbor lady was sitting on one of the porch chairs, still fanning.

"Yes?" Myra did not open the screen.

"Mrs. Ledbetter, my name is Mary Stoneking. I'm from our local chapter of the National Congress of Mothers."

"And?"

"And we want to help you before the sheriff's called to your house." Mrs. Stoneking closed her fan. "You don't know me, but my sister is Beatrice, Constable Robearde Turner's wife. She told me that you've had struggles with your children in the past."

"Uh huh, sure have." Myra stared down at her feet, realizing they were bare. "I, um, need to put on some shoes."

"May I come in? Please?"

"It's a mess. I lost my girl." Myra shrugged. "Don't know why."

"Please, may I come in?"

"I guess." Myra opened the screen and stepped aside.

"Thank you." Mary tried, but did not quite succeed in hiding her shock at the sight and smell of the house. "Where would you like me to sit?"

"One place's good as the next. Everything's dirty." Myra spied her house slippers kicked off in a corner and slid her feet in, not bothering to put on the stockings piled beside them. "I don't have any coffee made."

Missus Mary patted the settee. "Come, sit, and please don't feel embarrassed. The Congress of Mothers wants to help."

"How can anyone help?" Myra sat, her hands trembling in her lap. "My husband is always gone, my friend ran away, and nobody in New Town says 'Boo' to me. I can't get out of bed in the morning, and the children are running wild." Her tears were dripping off her chin. "I can't seem to do anything." She sniffled. "I don't even have a clean hanky."

Missus Mary produced hers and handed it over with a "Keep it." She waited a bit and then spoke. "My dear, I absolutely know how you feel about New Town, and that's what's so wonderful about the Congress of Mothers. All our chapter members are from somewhere else, and we know the loneliness of this place." Mary looked down at the beaded reticule on her lap. "After my second baby, I didn't leave the bedroom for two months. All I did was nurse and sleep, and even with that, they had to bring the baby to me for feedings, then take her away as soon as she was full. I couldn't stand her smell and didn't want to touch her."

"Oh, my," whispered Myra. "That's how I feel about all of mine, but it just started the day Marguerite ran away."

"Is Marguerite your Negress?"

"She's my best friend."

Mary looked confused. "But, but she's colored."

"She was my 'help'."

"My dear, how can this Marguerite be your best friend and your 'help'? That's not possible. No one would treat their best friend like that. "

"Mama did." Miss Nosey Rosy popped up from behind the settee. "Hi, Mrs. Stoneking, is Sharon with you? We're in the same class."

"Hello, Sweetie. Shar's at home."

Myra stared at her daughter. "What in God's name were you doing back there? Spying?"

"Nope, making a nest to hide from the boys. Got blankets and everything." Nora Lee wrinkled her nose. "You're right, they stink." She looked at Mary. "You got a dead bird on your head. Can I touch it?"

"In a minute." Mary looked at Myra. "May I ask her a question?"

"You can ask. She may not answer. Lately she's had a mind of her own."

Nora Lee skipped around the settee and the table beside it, landing in front of the women. "Wanna see me buck dance after you ask? I been practicin'."

Mary ignored the request. "I want to know who this Marguerite is."

"She's Mister Jack's wife, our god-mother, Mama's friend, and she has a filthy, that's what she says, gypsy for a sister. But I think her Lulah Marie's a princess." Nora Lee took a breath. "Mama made Marguerite do all the work in the house. Now can I touch your bird?"

"Yes, gently."

Nora Lee petted the hat and tapped across the room and out the door.

Mary shook her head. "Well, she seems to be a handful. How many children do you have?"

"Six. Two are away." Myra started crying again. "I'm such a bad mother. I just don't know what to do."

"You are *not* a bad mother. You are an alone mother." Mary stood. "I think I know what happened here."

"What? What did I do?"

"I don't know about having a colored best friend, but I do know that you don't treat any friend like a house girl." Mary looked around the parlor. "I don't know how you ended up in this place after the hurricane, but I do know it's way too big to keep by yourself. How in the world did your husband think you could do it with all those children?"

"He's always at sea. He's captain of the *Sallie Lou* and is only in port every three months. Marguerite's husband, Jack, and my CB come in for a week and then are gone."

"Oh, you poor thing, no wonder you're so lost." Mary stood. "All our Congress of Mothers members will want to help. May I ask a few to stop by and visit?"

"Well, I…"

"Missus Myra, just remember that once upon a time we all were by ourselves in this New Town. Now we are

together. You know, it's like they say, 'United we stand."
Mary smiled.

"And divided we fall," Myra murmured. "That's
what happened to me and Marguerite. Oh, Missus Mary, I
treated my best friend like a house maid. I've ruined
everything."

Mary stood by the door. "May I come back
tomorrow with a few Congress members? All we want to
do is help."

"Yes. Thank you," was the whispered reply.

After Mary left, Myra wandered into the kitchen
and took the milk bottle from the icebox. It was warm. The
smell was horrendous. It was evident there had been no ice
brought in for days. A large black field roach swan dived
from the edge of the box and ran across Myra's left slipper.
Down came her right one. "Gotcha." Leaving the carcass
for the cat, she walked out to the gazebo and sat. And
screamed. The neighbors shut their windows and pulled
their drapes.

Late that night, Franky, Benjy, and Nora Lee guided
their mother back into the house and up the steps. Nora Lee
opened her mother's dress front and handed her the newly
changed toddler. At least Flossie Mae got milk. The three
others finished the rest of yesterday's bread with water
from the tap. Myra didn't notice.

Chapter Forty-One
Women Folk

Nora Lee ran to her friend Sharon's house early the next morning and pulled the doorbell rope over and over. "Missus Stoneking, Missus Stoneking, please wake up. You said you would help." A medium dark-skinned woman opened the door. "You're not Sharon's mama. I need Sharon's mama. Tell her my mama's gone off her nut."

The uniformed maid had her employer to the door in a blink. "Hello, Nora Lee. Please come in. What did you say to Miss Geneva about your mama being out of her head?"

Nora Lee stood in the house's entryway. "I never saw you standin' up. Wow, you're really tall."

"That's true." Mary led the child into the first parlor and bent down, looking eye to eye with her.

"Well, anyway, yesterday you said you could help. Can you?"

Mary looked at her maid, mouthed the words "milk please," and led the child into the front parlor. "What happened?"

Well, after you left, Mama went into the kitchen, found out the milk was warm and all the icebox food was stinky, stomped a big roach, and went out to the gazebo. She didn't stop screaming for the longest time. Finally, when she didn't come in after dark, the boys and I pulled her back in the house and up to her room." Nora Lee plopped on one of the damask side chairs. "I changed Flossie Mae and brung her to Mama to nurse, but Mama couldn't remember how to undo her buttons, so I did it."

Nora Lee shook her head. "Gee whizzy Pete, that girl was hungry. Ya know, we can drink tap water, but a baby needs milk."

A shocked Mary took the tray from her maid and set it on the table in front of the settee. "Would you like some milk yourself? Miss Geneva brought some." It was gone in one long swallow and Mary nodded for more. "Nora Lee, how old are you?"

"Eight, same as Shar. Last year the teacher put us side by side on the birthday tree." Nora Lee looked around. "Is she up yet?"

"Oh my goodness." Mary looked at the girl. *I can't even imagine my sweet Sharon having to go hungry or unbuttoning my blouse.* "Not yet, dear. Come, child, let's see what Miss Geneva has for breakfast."

Nora Lee's hungry eyes looked toward the kitchen. "Oh, no, ma'am."

"Why ever not?"

Nora Lee turned her head down. "Not fair to the others," she mumbled.

"Oh, honey, we can fix that." Mary went in the kitchen and was soon back with another glass of milk. "Miss Geneva's packing a breakfast picnic basket. You and I are going to make a party on your kitchen table."

Nora Lee smiled. "Thank you." That glass was soon emptied, too. "Missus Stoneking, can your ladies group really help us? Mama's in an awful bad way."

"Yes, don't worry. I'll take care of things." Magically a full peck basket of food appeared on the sideboard in the dining room. "Thank you, Geneva. I don't know when I'll be back."

"I understand. You want me to telephone some of the others to meet you there?" Mary nodded. Geneva continued. "Don't you worry about nuthin'. Ya know, my sister, Karena, might could come by if her old folks can spare her. We'll just make sure our Sharon's little friend's family gits took care of."

Mary carried the basket in one hand and held Nora Lee's with the other. "Come on, let's go over to Lobit Street." Swinging hands, the two sang "This Little Piggy Went to Market" all the way home.

Two Congress women were already there, sitting in their autos.

Chapter Forty-Two
Start Up

*T*ing.

"Hello, Miss Susan." Marguerite nodded to the store clerk. "Would you please tell Missus Ada I'm back."

Theo jumped out from behind one of his pyramids, giving Marguerite a big hug. "You're back, you're back. I missed you."

She smiled at the boy and made her way straight to the converted storeroom. A cot was waiting and a sturdy desk was set up with a proper chair. Only then did she put down her very full valise, hiding it under the bed. Mixed in with her *Maman's* quilt and all of her best clothes was over a thousand dollars in gold coins, one fourth of one crate.

All that could wait. Nature was calling. "Miss Susan, is there an outdoor necessary?" Marguerite had been holding more than gold coins on the train.

"No, we have plumbing." Susan shrugged. "Why?"

"Does Missus Ada allow colored in her bathroom?" Marguerite was beginning to wish she were a man, what with the handiness of a tree. "I haven't used the facilities since LaPorte."

"I'll go ask her."

"Ask me what?" Ada was almost to the bottom of the steps. "Oh, my goodness, you're back already. That was quick."

Susan was wrinkling her nose. "Missus Marguerite wants to know if you allow colored to use the store toilet. I didn't think so, but I told her I would ask."

"Good God, woman, of course she can. She's…"

Marguerite ran into the room without further permission.

Several minutes later an enlightened Susan was back to her chores, and the other two were conferring in the newly appointed office, the door shut. Marguerite opened her satchel on the desktop and pulled out five sacks of coins. Teary-eyed, she lifted her mother's quilt and kissed one of the squares.

"Oh, my dear, this cover is beautiful," admired Ada. "Your family?"

"My *maman*'s. She got it from her mother." Marguerite nodded to the bed. "May I?"

"Of course, this is where you will sleep until things get settled." Ada cut her eyes to the door. "I want to apologize for Susan. You know how things are."

Marguerite nodded. "I do." She handed Ada a sack of coins. "I counted out forty two for each parcel. Didn't want to draw attention as I left."

"So Myra doesn't know?" Ada pulled and reset her comb. "What are you going to do about all that?"

"Oh, after what she said to me, she knows." Marguerite turned back to the bed and shook out her quilt. "She really hurt my feelings, but I'm not going to talk about it."

"Well, my goodness." Ada picked up one of the money bags, changing the subject. "Do you have a plan for all this? I thought you were going to make a safe place for the workers to keep their money. Looks like you need a place for yours, too."

Marguerite pulled a leather accountant's folder, and opened to the front page. The heading said "NSC," with neat lines drawn down, top to bottom, every inch or so. Numbers were written across in increasing order. She tapped the page. "I plan to make loans between pays. This is my bi-weekly interest chart."

"Good Lord, girl," Ada exclaimed, "where did you learn all that?"

Marguerite blushed. "At the Tremont. The *dames de la nuit* working on the second floor had *Maman* keep their ledgers. Most couldn't read or write, and they really trusted her."

"So your mama was, um, an accountant?"

"*Oui,* she was. When I got old enough to understand business, she taught me all about percentages, interest, and the like." Marguerite stood. "Oh, Missus Ada, my beloved Jack must never hear of this. I don't want him to think less of me."

"Don't worry about Jack. I know for a fact that he had dealings with whores long before he met you."

Marguerite's cheeks flamed. "You mean to tell me that, that skunk spent time with…" She slammed closed the ledger. "That rat told me he was fresh when he…"

"Now, now, child, I'm feeling quite sure he was. What I mean is, Myra told me when he and CB were moving men to the gold fields, it was the ladies of the docks who spread the word of the travelin' opportunities, for a small fee, of course." Ada reopened the book. "Your Tremont bookkeeping work is just like the boys advertising arrangement. Neither of you did anything wrong." She looked at Marguerite's interest charting. "When did you do all this?"

"Last night before I packed." She swept her hand over the bags of gold. "I will need to have these changed into money I can use. Is that something you can do for me?"

Ada nodded. "Of course. And once the bank is opened, you will have the workers' pay to use for the loans." She surveyed the desk. "Oh, my goodness, I forgot the pencils and a good pen set. I'll have Theo bring them to you from upstairs. There's only one thing I ask."

Marguerite sank into the desk chair. *"Excusez-moi,* the trip was more tiring than I thought." She looked up at Ada. "What do you need from me?"

"When you are ready, you must tell me what happen between you and Myra. I love her like a daughter, and if there's problem to be settled, I'll do it." Ada put her hand on the office door knob. "And, you let me know if Theo's jumpities get to be too much for you."

Marguerite started laying out her clothing on the bed, noticing there was no hanging rod, just a small chest of drawers. "We'll be fine. You must remember that I lived in that household for almost two years."

"Yes, you did. Yes you did." Ada clicked the door and swung it wide. "Theo," she called.

"Yes, Auntie?" Her deputy bounced over to the office.

"Please fetch a pen set and some pencils."

"Yes, ma'am." The boy raced up the steps.

"Oh, we have customers. Excuse me." Ada stepped into the main store room. "Hello, Missus Margery, hello Miss Louise."

"You want the pencils sharpened?" echoed from above.

"Hello," they both replied.

Marguerite stood frozen at the voice she heard.

Chapter Forty-Three
Almost

Isaac Jacoby was almost happy. Guilt for what used to be and a tiny bit of common sense niggled at his brain, but he brushed all that aside. His son, Ikey, sat with him two days a week in the counting house, learning the importance of bookkeeping. His maid, Louise, seemed to be able to run his household like magic, and she said there wasn't a bit of problem with her teaching his son on those summer days when the boy wasn't with him. Knowing Ikey spent time reading and practicing his arithmetic made him smile, something he had not done in a long time. Yes, Isaac Jacoby was almost happy.

"Miss Louise, I'm going out to play with the guys. Won't be back for dinner, got me a couple of sandwiches." Ikey put the sack of second best marbles in his pocket, tucking it up against his chaw and his coin purse. He pulled on his cap. "Um, I used all the sliced ham."

"Put it on the list, I'm going to the market soon, anyway." She raised an eyebrow. "You playing for money?"

"Uh huh."

"You know what I said."

"Yes, ma'am." Ikey patted his pocket. "You said, 'Let 'em lose 'til the bets get big. Then don't let 'em know what hit 'em'."

Louise inspected him. "Tie your left shoe."

"Yes, ma'am." He headed to the door.

"Now." She turned, feather duster in hand, to the parlor. "Be home before your father," she called. "Don't need him wondering about your day."

"Yes ma'am."

"Don't let the screen slam."

Ikey set off to the school yard, jiggling his marbles. "That Jay Jay doesn't have a chance against me," he muttered, rubbing the long disappeared bruise on his arm. "I'll show that little weasel who's boss." He licked his lips. "Gonna win big today. Could use the dimes."

Louise was almost done with the third shelf of the book case when the front bell rang. "Allo, dear, are you there?" It was Esther. "I brought you some more recipes."

Damn, it's Tuesday. Forgot today's Jewish day. "I'm coming." Louise quickly tied on her babushka, checking her face for tell-tale annoyance. The rabbi's wife was greeted with a smile. "Come in, Missus Cohen, come in. Show me what you brought."

Esther Cohen's had taken it upon herself to make sure her old Brooklyn friend, and his son, her foster, Ikey, had the good foods from their mothers and grandmothers. Many years ago Louise learned to pretend to learn. Now, at each of Esther's visits, she would nod, smile, and not listen. After Esther left, the written recipes would end up in a drawer, way in the back. *I'll cook his wife's recipes, not this trap. I know what he needs.*

"Huh?" Louise was startled into attention.

"Oh, don't tell me you don't remember *lokshen kugel*. It is on every Passover plate I know." Esther gave her upper lip a small lick. *"Oy,* so good."

"I'm from Austin. Maybe I know it by another name." *Better watch myself.* Louise looked at the written recipe, reading the ingredients list. "Oh, we called it noodle pudding."

"Well, dear, that is what *some* people call it." Running her finger down the list, Esther stopped at 'raisins', tapping the word with her index finger. "In Brooklyn we used what we could get." She chuckled. "My *bubbe* put in chopped figs one time. We never knew until she told us. Isaac was at that table. Hmmm, maybe you could make it with dried figs. Do you have any?"

Taking that as a cue, Louise stood. "Wonderful idea, I could make this tonight. Have to go to the market tomorrow, anyway. I'll just go a day early. Thank you for coming." She had Esther out the door before the woman had her shawl pinned.

What Louise didn't know was that Esther had another goal besides recipes. After every visit, she reported to her husband what she found. She noticed a lot, and, among other things, while the place was always clean, Louise never used Yiddish in their conversations, and the house never smelled of any of the shared recipes. Today Esther noticed that Louise had her two top buttons open, and her legs were bare in her shoes, showing almost too much.

What Louise did know was that her plan was working.

She went back to her dusting. *Might as well go, she could be watching.* Another few minutes, and Louise was out the door, the bundle of totes rolled up under her arm. She smiled, knowing that Isaac never checked the account bill, paying it with the discount he'd arranged with Ada for his bookkeeping. He let her do what she wanted. She would buy the necessities on the list *and* almost anything else that caught her fancy. He never noticed.

Chapter Forty-Four
Boy Oh Boy

Ting. Louise strolled into the mercantile, nodded her greeting to the clerk and Missus Margery, who was standing, looking at the stacks of canned goods. The two customers called their "Hello" to Ada as she walked in from the back. Louise was at the far side of the store, looking at cards of ornamental hair pins when she heard 'Do you want those pencils sharpened?' "Oh, Christ," she swore aloud, and was out the door. "Oh Jesus, oh Jesus, what is *he* doing here? He might have seen me."

Ikey was waiting on their front porch. "Where you been?"

"Shopping." She stepped around him, unlocking the front door. "Why are you home? Thought you were going to play 'til almost supper."

"You didn't buy anything," Ikey observed, walking in behind her. The mantle clock was chiming 'three'.

Louise busied herself in the pantry, stowing the still-bundled totes, working her face into a nonchalant blank. "Why are you home?" she repeated from the closet.

Ikey was sitting at the table, his marble bag flat in front of him. "Jay Jay cleaned me out," he said with a lip tremble. "He got 'em all and the dimes I brought, too." Ikey looked at his empty sack of hope. "Miss Louise, I think I'm in trouble."

"What did you do?" Louise opened the icebox, looking for something, anything to sooth the boy. "Did you hit someone?"

"No, worse."

She poured two large glasses of lemonade, setting them in the middle of the table. "What could be worse than that?"

"Well, you remember the story about me 'n' Sarah and the beer?"

"Yes." Louise felt a prickle on her neck. "And…"

"And Sarah and I did a lot of kissin' and stuff."

"I heard." Louise pushed his drink across the table. "Lemonade?"

He ignored the offer. "Well, I was braggin' to Jay Jay that Sarah and me almost did it. And the next thing ya' know, well…" he gulped. "The next thing ya know, I bet I could get Sarah to, uh, uh, you know."

"And?"

"And I lost." Ikey started sobbing, head in his hands. "I gotta get Sarah to kiss and pet with Jay Jay, or he's gonna tell my father about what I've been doin' all summer long." He looked up at Louise. "Oh jeez, oh jeez, he'll fire you for not teachin' the lessons, and he'll send me…." His sobs muffled his last words.

Very slowly, Louise lifted her glass of lemonade, took a sip, and threw the rest of it in Ikey's face, slamming the glass back on the table. The boy jerked upright. She snatched his glass and poured it over his head.

Long strides got her to the back screen. "See this mess I made? Clean it up. I'll see what I can do to clean up yours." She shoved open the door and held it wide. "I'll be out back. Do not find me until you have this room and yourself spotless." *Slam.*

Louise was halfway down the alley before she realized what she'd just done. "Oh God, Oh God, first *him*, and now this. What am I going to do? " She marched the rest of the alley, turned and was almost to the house when she stopped still, and remembered. "No snot-nosed brat is going to ruin this for me." She looked heavenward. "Thank you, Granny M, for what I know."

Sitting on the back stoop bench, Louise waited, completely at peace. Freshly bathed, dressed, and combed, Ikey finally came to the door. "I cleaned up the mess."

"Good. I'll take care of yours."

"Thank you, Miss Louise. I really did it this time."

"Yes, you did."

The three enjoyed a light supper. "I must do the Wednesday shopping tomorrow," was Louise's excuse. Isaac didn't mind. For the first time ever, he was noticing her buttons, and made it a point to help her with her shawl as she prepared to leave.

Chapter Forty-Five
Naked As A...

Soon as the breakfast dishes were washed and put away, Ikey was off, following Louise's instructions. "Stay away for three hours, and then bring all the guys back here for dinner. I'll be ready."

"Yes, ma'am."

"Do not lose your composure. This plan will work." She held open the door for him. "Remember, you are inviting the guys for food, and you are inviting Jay Jay for fun." She hugged his shoulder. "You can do this. Now get goin'."

Louise practically ran to the store, bought her shopping list and what was needed for the project. Exactly three hours later, Ikey called from the front porch.

"Miss Louise, Miss Louise, we're here."

No response.

"That woman," complained Ikey, "needs an ear trumpet." He held open the door. "Come on in, fellas. Sarah said she'd be here. Probably in the kitchen." He wiggled his eyebrows at Jay Jay. "She's a real good kisser."

Nobody was in the kitchen.

"Miss Louise," Ikey hollered. "We're waitin', where's our food?"

"Oh, lover boy," wafted from the pantry. The voice was high and soft. "Did you bring me a new sweetie pie? You said you would."

The boys stood frozen. Ikey shrugged. "She likes kissin' in the dark." He tapped on the door. "Honey baby, I brought you Jay Jay, just like I promised."

"Ooooh, is he cute?"

"Not as cute as me, but he'll do." Ikey turned. "Isn't that right, guys?" Ribald laughter was the response.

"Ooooh, are there more boys out there? I like boys."

"You listen to me, you only get Jay Jay. The rest are here to, uh, watch. Isn't that right, guys?" More laughs.

"Oh, lover boy, is he gonna be just like you are when we get together?"

"Uh, you want him to take off his…?"

"Uh huh," purred from the closet. "I like it that way. I've got everything ready."

Jay Jay looked around the room, his audience staring at him. "Jeez, I don't know about taking off my…"

"I did," was the sweet response from within.

Jay Jay was down to his drawers in two winks. "Back up, guys, big daddy gonna win this bet." To much applause, Jay Jay opened the door and stepped into the darkness. Ikey flipped the latch behind him, "For privacy," he said with a smile. He gestured toward the table. "Have a chair, guys. Probably won't take long, ya know."

Jay Jay screamed for what seemed like forever until Ikey opened the door.

"Oh God, oh jeezee, get me out of here." Jay Jay, covered with molasses and pillow feathers, lay rolled in a sheet on the pantry floor. He couldn't stand.

Louise stood over him, dusting off the few feathers that had not met their gooey destiny. Stepping around the crying Jay Jay, she nodded to the boys sitting at the table. "Gentlemen, let this be a warning to all of you. My Ikey will never again come home with bruises for doing his studies. My Ikey will never, never be mistreated by the likes of you alley rats, and you will never speak of Sarah Cohen. Do you understand me?"

"But he's the one…"

"I said, 'Do you understand me?'" Louise pointed at the sticky mess on the pantry floor. "Carry him out back. I want to see the face of the, ha, *man* who's met me in the closet."

Two of the biggest boys stepped forward, lifting the head and foot of the sobbing mummy. Louise held the door wide as they almost made it down the steps before the shroud slipped. "OW, OWWW," punctuated the last two steps.

"Stand him up." She nodded at Ikey. "I want our sheet back, if you please."

"Yes, ma'am." He grabbed the edge of the wrapping and pulled. Jay Jay stood in the back yard in his drawers, covered in nasty goo. "Hey, guys, you better get your Jay bird home. I don't want to see him lose his tail feathers over a bet."

Louise threw the bundle of clothing left on the kitchen floor across the yard, toward the alley. "Oh, sweetie pie," she purred. "You better get some clothes on, before your mother sees you. It would be a shame if she found out you was almost naked in a closet with a girl. Especially since, I'm presumin', you're supposed to be at Wednesday Children's Summer Church." Louise shook her head. "Tch, Tch, you don't want that to happen, now do you?"

"Oh, no ma'am, no."

"Then," she snarled, "Get the hell off our land." Louise gathered the sheet. "Come, Ikey, we have a lot of cleanin' to do before supper."

That evening, Isaac enjoyed the company of his household. For some reason, Ikey and Louise seemed full of joking and laughter. Isaac couldn't figure out why, but that didn't matter. It felt good and gave him courage as she prepared to leave.

"Miss Louise, I thank you for all you do for Ikey and me." Isaac blushed. "I was wondering if you would like to go on a picnic with us sometime, um, like friends."

"No, I'm sorry, but it wouldn't be right." She draped her shawl over her arm.

"Why not?" Isaac stood to walk her to the door. "I thought, well, I thought you liked us."

She tilted her head, looking up at him. "I like you both very much, and I really wish I could. It's just that I'm your house maid, and it would be totally improper for you to be seen stepping out with your *servant*."

Smiling, she let herself out.

Chapter Forty-Six
Expectations

Marguerite had her first depositor the day after she'd arrived. It was Theo. *Tap, tap.* The boy was standing outside, rapping on the storeroom window. "Missus 'Guite, are you open for business? I want to be a saver." A smiling teller took the boy's five dimes, earned from making deliveries, wrote him a receipt, thanked him for his business, and sent him on his way.

Tap, tap. Marguerite barely had time to enter the deposit on the newly titled ledger page, marked 'Theo Gallaway Ledbetter'.

"Missus 'Guite, Missus 'Guite, I want to be a borrower." The boy was bouncing in front of the teller window, a Sears & Roebuck catalogue in hand.

"Good Lord, boy, come in the front door. I'm not getting up again until a real customer comes."

"I am a real customer, Missus 'Guite, I really am, and I've got a real good idea."

"Just git in here, and bring your Aunt Ada with you."

"Yes, ma'am. Look, she's at your office door right now."

Ada touched her lips, tipping her head toward the window. "Just hear him out before you say 'No'. He's been on my tail all morning about this."

Marguerite put on the best 'business' face she could conjure, remembering how Mr. Brown would handle demanding guests at the Tremont. Ada waited as Theo beat the sound of the back door slam. He skittered into the office, waving the catalogue, and bounced into the desk in front of him, sending things flying.

"Woah, Missus 'Guite, I'm sorry. The jumpities grabbed me on the way in." Theo scrabbled up the miscellaneous scattered papers and plopped them on the open ledger.

Ada stepped in and did her special 'stand-behind' hug, the one that helped to remind the child to keep both feet planted. "Sometimes this works," she mouthed over his head.

"I know," Marguerite mouthed back. She stood. "Sir, I understand you want to make a loan. Just how much do you need?"

Theo, arms pinned by his auntie, flapped the book in his hands. "I need eight dollars and ninety five cents." He rocked his head straight up, looking at Ada. "You can let go, I'm all still."

"Promise?"

"Yes 'um." Theo slowly, feigning calmness, turned to Marguerite. "Ma'am, I need eight dollars and ninety five cents to help my auntie. Missus 'Guite, it will help you, too."

Marguerite kept her gaze on the boy, aware of his intensity. "Missus Ada, I just noticed this office has only one chair. Do you have any extras so that my customer can sit down?"

"Don't need to sit." Theo took a deep breath and began the speech he'd been practicing since breakfast. "I want to go into business. I want to buy a bicycle and a wagon just like the one up home. I want to make faster deliveries for my auntie's store, and I want to advertise for my Missus 'Guite's bank."

Theo showed Marguerite the page that was causing all the excitement. Sure enough, the featured Edgemere bike cost the requested loan.

Marguerite traced the picture with her finger. "Where are you getting the most important part of all this? Looks like something's missing."

"What?" Theo stared at the page. "Nothin's missing. There's the bike, the price, and where to send for it. Everything's there. Everything except…"

Ada's lips relaxed. "My darling, everything except the wagon. You forgot the wagon."

The young entrepreneur burst into tears and ran out of the office.

Ada shrugged. "You're right about needing a chair." She looked around to confirm Theo was out of ear shot. "When he comes back, tell him 'No, you're too young to go into debt'. There just so happens to be a new boy-sized bike and wagon at the Turners' house, waiting for him. Robearde wanted to give him something special, but I told him to hang on to it." She shrugged. "You know, they never had children, and they've taken a real liking to the boy. Talk about perfect timing. I'll make sure they're home this evening and send the boy on a delivery." She sighed. "Only wish I could be a fly on the wall, watching his dream come true."

***

Word spread fast thanks to Ada's quiet, but persistent chatting with all the help that came for their household shopping. The maids carried home the knowledge of a colored bank, "right there in the store, of all places, who'd a' thought." Theo carefully lettered "DICKENSON'S DELIVERY" on one side of the wagon and "NSC" on the other. He told his white customers the letters stood for "Not Slow Child." Those who knew Theo believed him. The maids taking the deliveries just smiled.

By the end of the month, he had deposited fifty more dimes into his account. Sometimes there was a line at the window, but most all the people waiting were really nice to him and often let him move ahead, even Walkin' Davey, who always told whoever was around, "Dat's da boy dat shot me. He's m' friend."

Banking business was good, and Marguerite glowed, her cheeks carrying the blush of excitement rarely seen. Ada said nothing.

It was Theo who brought up the unspoken. "Missus 'Guite, you gonna stay here forever?" The boy was working his magic, replenishing the stacks of cans recently disturbed by shoppers. "What's gonna happen if Mister Jack and Daddy CB don't stop here when they git in? Ya know, they just might go straight to LaPorte. That's gonna scare Mister Jack real bad if you aren't there." He left his pyramid and stood by the office door. "Don't you love him anymore?"

"Oh, *mon petit*, I love him more than the sun and the moon. It's just that, well, go read Ecclesiastes three, one through eight. My husband is at a corner." Marguerite kept her back squared to the door, not showing her tears. "I only hope he turns to me because I'm not turning back."

Theo shrugged and skipped off to find his Bible, knowing his auntie would explain the big words. Ada was behind the cold meat cooler, arranging the fresh butcher cuts delivered every day. Theo explained what he had asked and what he needed for her to read. "Sweetheart, I can't open the Good Book, my hands are all messy, but I know that passage by heart. The lesson is all about there being a time and place for everything as dictated by God. I'm guessin' that Marguerite feels that the banking business is her time." Ada did not tell the boy that Mister Jack disagreed.

"Is this the reason Mama hasn't sent a telegram, askin' how we all are? Has she made a turn, too?"

"Darling, that's something I just don't know." Ada shook her head. "Been wonderin' why things are so quiet up there." She looked at the calendar nailed to the post by the meat cooler, now a bank vault. "Hmm, will you look at that? It's almost time to get you signed up for school. Seems just like yesterday you got here. Are you absolutely sure you want to stay?"

"Yes, ma'am, it's just that I want to go to see mama before I start. Do you know when the *Sallie Lou* gets back?"

"No, but I'll ask Isaac. He knows every ship's schedule. Should be soon." She wiped her hands and riffled the calendar's pages. "I marked when Missus Marguerite started the bank, and that was about a week or so after they sailed. Oh my stars and buttons, that was almost two months ago. My how time flies."

Marguerite heard the exchange and cried even harder.

Chapter Forty-Seven
Ada Goes To Congress

Finally, Myra contacted the family on the island. The telegram was cryptic, saying something about mothers and congress, new help, and wanting to get a telephone. Ada couldn't make heads nor tails of it.

"What's the matter with that woman? This thing doesn't make sense."

"Huh, Auntie?" Theo was loading his deliveries, ready to hook the hitch.

"Oh, nothing, child, I thought I was thinkin', not talkin'," Ada stuffed the paper in her apron pocket.

"Is it from Mama?" *Thunk*. He dropped the wagon's metal tongue and hop-scotched over to her side. "I wanna see everybody before school starts, and that time's purtneer here. Does she want me to come?" His hopeful excitement was hard to ignore. "I think Mama misses me."

"I'll bet she does." Ada looked around the store. The stacks were stacked, the pyramids, tall. Her Perfecting Prince had everything in order. "What you think about the two of us making a trip upstate tomorrow for a quick two day visit? We can ask Missus Marguerite and Susan to watch the shop."

"But what about my deliveries? My customers like me to be on time."

"Darlin', they'll understand since it's only two days and, when they hear you're goin' to see your mama, they'll be real happy." Ada blew a kiss in his direction. "Now, get back to your loadin'. I'll get us some things together." *I don't know what this is all about, but my baby's got me scared.*

Marguerite nodded when asked to stay close by but did not send her regards, and Susan was happy to have extra paid hours. The travelers were on the morning train.

"What did Mama say when you telegrammed we were coming?" Theo's excitement bubbled just under the surface.

"We're surprising them." Ada felt him vibrating and squeezed his hand. "Won't that be fun?"

He squeezed back. "Wow…"

"Shush, not so loud."

"Wee," he finished, whispering. "They're gonna have a fit."

Ada looked out the window, pretending interest in the scenery. *Oh, my child, I think they already have.*

The travelers took the horse coach to the end of the street with the plan to walk in the back door with a big shout of "Surprise!" Halfway up Lobit they noticed several automobiles parked along the street. "Lookie, Auntie, there's autos everywhere."

"Dear God, they're right in front of your house. Oh, blessed Jesus, someone's dead." Ada grabbed Theo and ran the rest of the way, moving faster than her old legs should have, up the front steps, into the parlor…full of women holding tea cups and saucers, wearing identical hats with identical dead birds. All heads turned at the intrusion, a rainbow of tail plumage swaying in unison.

"Mama?" Theo thought he saw his mother. He shrugged. "Gettin' something to eat."

"Auntie."

Ada followed the sound, scanning the curious faces, finding her beloved as birded out as the others. "Oh, my baby girl," she panted, "who died?"

"Huh?"

"Say 'pardon me,'" came softly from somewhere in the room.

"Huh?"

Nora Lee bolted down the steps from the center landing, her favorite observation post. "Auntie, Auntie, Mama's gettin' lady lessons."

"Nobody died? How come all the traffic out front?" She looked around for a chair. "Pardon *me*, is there an empty seat available? Thought I'd missed a funeral."

Myra stood, setting her saucered cup on the table beside her. "Ladies, may I present my dear Great Aunt, Ada Dickenson, who appears to have traveled today from the island."

It was Ada's turn. "Huh?"

"I told you," informed Nora Lee, "Mama's gettin' lady lessons. That's lady talk. Ain't that right, Mrs. Stoneking?"

"Yes, dear." Mary Stoneking approached the thoroughly confused Ada. "Hello, my name is Mary Stoneking, president of the New Town chapter of the Congress of Mothers. We are friends of your niece."

"Oh, my goodness, when did all of this happen?" Ada couldn't stop staring at her hat. "I didn't know she had friends, especially ones with autos."

Theo tip-toed out of the kitchen and did a cupped-ear whisper to his aunt. Ada's eyes widened. "Really?"

"Uh-huh. Her name's Karena. She took one look at me and said, 'You must be one of them'." Theo shrugged, still whispering. "I said, 'Yep,' and she said 'You hungry?' and I said, 'Uh huh.' Auntie, I just thought you'd like to know there's food in the kitchen. Bye."

Ada watched her dervish disappear. Chuckling, she looked up at Mary. "That's Myra's Theo. He's my right hand man at the mercantile. We've come for a quick visit before school starts. He's missin' his mama." Giving the tall woman a strong look, Ada asked, "Are the ladies of your congress sincere? I don't want my Myra taken advantage of."

Mary gestured to the room full of women. "Ma'am, each of us is new to New Town, if you know what I mean. We only want to make friends with our neighbors." The room echoed a murmured 'yes, friends', sounding like a muted amen corner. She glanced at Myra. "She will tell you all about these last few weeks, won't you, my dear?" There was a nodded assent. Mary addressed to group. "Time to go. How many of you need your autos cranked?" There was a show of several hands. "Myra, can we borrow a boy to turn the engines?"

"Of course. Nora Lee, could you round up a brother or two?"

"Yes ma'am." The child made an exaggerated curtsy, calling "Bye, bye, lady lesson people." She headed upstairs, returning with Benjy and Franky in tow. "All I had to say was 'auto crank' and they 'bout knocked me over." Nora Lee spied the angel food on the dining room sideboard. "Can us kids have some cake after everybody leaves? Flossie Mae's wakin' up. I heard her." She looked at her auntie. "Wanna come up and get her with me? You ain't seen her since the funeral. She's big."

"Yes." She nodded to the Congress. "Excuse me. Pleased to meet all of you." Ada handed Nora Lee her valise and headed to the nursery.

As soon as the twins had all the autos running and the ladies on their way, Ada came back down, alone. "Lands sake, that baby's too big for me to handle on the steps. Nora Lee said they're going to stay upstairs, that you need to talk to me."

Myra unpinned her bird hat, setting it beside the cake plate in the dining room. She stepped into the kitchen to see her Theo, only to find a crumbed-up sandwich plate and no boy. She returned with two steaming porcelain mugs and sat next to her aunt. "I hate the china cups and saucers. Two swallows and it's empty." She held up her mug, and the women did a *clink* toast, each taking a sip, and placing them on the settee table to cool.

Staring straight ahead, Myra spoke. She told her auntie everything, including the long days of not remembering. Through sniffles and then sobs, Myra described Marguerite slapping her and why, and then her disappearance the next day. She told about Mary Stoneking showing up and rescuing her after those lost days, bringing the Congress women who took care of her and the household day and night, soothing her back to sanity. And she told Ada about having real colored help, named Karena, who came a few days a week and then went home at night.

Ada picked up her cup. "When is your husband coming home?"

"Very soon. Why"

"Because he will bring Jack here, and his wife isn't." She drank. "Jack has a right to know you have split his family before he goes to find her."

"I didn't."

"Yes, you did. Your behavior drove that man's wife away from the only kin he's ever known, not counting those on ship." Ada lowered her voice. "I know for a fact that Marguerite Smith will never live here again. You may have destroyed CB's home by ruining his 'brother's' home. Jack will 'cleave unto his wife' and leave this house, the house of his brother."

"Oh Auntie, what am I going to do? I never thought…"

"No, you didn't." Ada looked over at the cake in the dining room. "Right now you are going to cut me a slice. Do you have orange sauce?" The niece nodded. "We are going to enjoy it before the children turn into a swarm of angel food eating locusts," Ada continued. "Tonight, after I get my breath and the children are in bed, we will talk this out."

"Yes, ma'am. I am just so sorry."

"I know. Now cut the cake."

Chapter Forty-Eight
Decisions, Decisions

Isaac was distracted, a condition he'd never known. Broken hearted…yes. Lost… of course. Distracted…he didn't even recognize it until his senior clerk and longtime employee, Mr. Thomas, asked to speak privately.

"Sir," he began, "the men are talking. They're saying you must be ill. Are you?"

"Absolutely not, feeling fit as a fiddle." Isaac shut his office door, remaining standing. "Mr. Thomas, tell me what's going on."

"Well, they're saying that sometimes it seems like your head's in the clouds, that you're not yourself." Mr. Thomas shifted his weight as he stood. "Not me, of course, but some of the others have noticed a few, just a few, mind you, numerical errors. They're complaining that's it's not their job to tally after you, making sure things are correct."

Isaac opened his door, and with an abrupt "Thank you," dismissing the messenger. The rest of the morning was spent being extra vigilant with his columns. It was exhausting. At the dinner hour, he left the counting house and walked straight to Avenue O, hoping to talk to his rabbi. Joe opened the door.

"My friend, what brings you here, especially in the middle of the day? Come in, come in." Joe watched Isaac touch the *mezuzah* and nodded. "Do you want me or Esther? I think she's out back, but I'll fetch her."

"No, I need you and your wisdom. Do you have time?" Isaac looked around the parlor. "I think something is wrong with me." His voice was barely audible. "Please, can we talk?"

"Let's go into my study. Do you want a cup of tea? I do. Esther just brought me a pot and I have an extra mug around here somewhere."

"Please. It may calm me."

The worn places on the rabbi's rosewood desk were solid testimony to its use. Isaac recognized the craftsmanship and carving. "From Germany?"

Joe nodded, and gave Isaac a wooden coaster for his mug. "I made a water ring on it one time. Esther won't let me forget."

"I can understand why." Isaac looked at his pocket watch. "Joe, I need to talk about something, and you are the only one I think can help me."

"What is it?" Joe set down his mug. "Is it the boy?"

"No, it's Louise. I need to fire her." Isaac fiddled with his collar, trying to release the heat that was rising.

"Why do you need to let her go?"

"I asked her on a picnic and she refused. She said it wasn't right to be seen stepping out with a servant."

Joe was beginning to get the gist of Isaac's visit. "What are your intentions for this woman? Are you thinking of courting her?"

"All I know is that she has made that house a happy home." Isaac shrugged. "She and the boy are thick as thieves, and I can't stop thinking about the future."

"You haven't done that for a very long time."

"Yes, I know. Gosh, Joe, I don't want her to go away, and she won't let me court her as long as she's…"

Rabbi Joe nodded. "So, she can't work for you anymore, and you're afraid she'll move on to a new household."

"That's exactly right. Oh, my friend, what am I going to do?"

"The only thing you can do, ask her to marry you. She can only say "No."" Joe smiled. "And she might say 'Yes.' My question to you is what do you really want, a woman or a wife? There is a basic difference between the two."

Isaac studied his tea leaves floating in his mug. "Yes, I know. Julia was each of those at different times. But," he looked at his rabbi, "she was my wife when she was killed. We'd finally found happiness after many years of..." He did not finish his sentence.

"I want you to take these thoughts home. If you are looking for a mother for your boy, remember that children grow to adults and leave. If you are looking for someone to spend those later years with, is this the companion for you?" Joe leaned across the rosewood. "However, if she is tickling your fancy because you are lonely for a woman's charms and that is all, just remember that after the rose fades, the thorns remain."

"I don't want to be lonely, and Louise makes me happy." Isaac stood. "Thank you for your help. I will take your words with me."

"My friend," Joe walked him to the door. "I cannot advise you on whether you should propose to this woman. Please remember that very little is known about her family or her situation before she came to the island. Have you ever walked her home? Do you know where she lives?"

"Uh, no, she just shows up." Isaac scratched his head. "Never thought about her away from the house. Come to think about it, I've never seen her come in. She uses her key and is just there."

"It's not mandatory, but I will not marry you two without counseling."

That evening, after supper, right before it was Louise's time to leave, Isaac sent Ikey to his room to get ready for bed. He turned his dining chair to face Louise, and took her hands. "I want to go on picnics with you. I want you to stay with us. I want to get married. We will have to counsel with Rabbi Joe."

She jerked her hands from him and stood, whipping her shawl in place. "Sir, if that was a proposal of marriage directed toward me, you need to rethink your language." She strode to the front door. "I will be sick tomorrow, and maybe the day after that. Perhaps you can, by then, understand how insulting you are."

Isaac stared at her back in complete confusion.

Five o'clock three mornings later, Louise let herself in as she had since the first week of her employment. Isaac was sitting, fully dressed, at the kitchen table. She tied on her apron and went straight to her chores without a word, making the stove fire and preparing the coffee pot, keeping her back to him.

He watched. Finally, clearing his throat, he spoke very softly. "Thank you for coming back. We both missed you. I don't know what I did, but I am very sorry." He sighed. "Please?"

"Please, what?" Louise stayed turned and started cutting the morning bread for toast.

"Please forgive me, and please tell me what I did wrong." Isaac's voice took a note of pleading. "I want to make it right."

Louise, spun, bread knife in her hand, and glared. "You had better think about those words you used. You said that *you* wanted to go on picnics, *you* wanted me to stay with you, and that *you* wanted to get married. Then you tell me we have to talk to the rabbi. How dare you say things like that without once asking me what I want?" She returned to the toast. "If that was your idea of a marriage proposal, you're dead wrong."

Isaac murmured, "I'm sorry. What should I have said?"

"You're asking me how to propose? Go ask a man." Louise did not say another word until Ikey wandered in to breakfast, and then, all of her conversation was with the boy. Once again, Isaac walked to work, his mind on things other than columns. At work, he wrote words, not numbers, and ignored Mr. Thomas' pointed looks.

That evening, he again sent his son to his room. This time, he asked Louise to sit with him in the parlor. His suit jacket was on the coat tree, and he fetched a folded sheet of paper from his inside pocket. Flattening it on his lap, he began to read,

"Dear Louise,

I don't know how to do this, but please hear me out. You have made our house a home. You have shown so much care to Ikey and me. I want to give you what you want, but you never asked for anything. Please ask. I will listen. Then, after we talk with our rabbi, I will be able to propose properly.

Sincerely, with much affection,

Isaac"

Be careful. "When do you want the, um, time with the rabbi?" *Is he supposed to watch us do…?*

Isaac nodded. "I'll set it up with Joe."

"What's done here in Galveston? Is it expected?" Louise smoothed her skirt, picking off imaginary crumbs. "I must admit I didn't pay close attention to my lessons when I was younger." *That's an understatement.*

"Oh, it's nothing important. Rabbi Joe will want to affirm that we know everything about each other. You know, the usual things like the histories of our faith and our families." Isaac chuckled. "When Julia and I married in the Methodist church, the Reverend had no idea that we both went by different names and that we had never been baptized. In *our* faith, it is expected that the couples share their past before they can begin their future."

"Oh." Louise stood. "It's getting dark. Thank you for this talk." Once again she left without letting him help with her shawl.

She was almost to her boarding house when she calmed down enough to speak the foulest curse she knew, and spit.

Chapter Forty-Nine
Missus Odessa Givens

"We're home, Missus 'Guite, we're home." Theo ran to the apartment with their bags and was back down, bouncing at the bank's closed door before Ada was halfway across to the stairway.

Knock. Knock. "Missus 'Guite, you in there?" Silence.

"Go check the teller window, she might be away." Ada's heart was swelling. Myra'd given her all the papers needed to enroll him in school. It was official, Theo was staying. "Morning, Susan. Has it been busy?"

"Oh, yes, ma'am. Yesterday was almost too much. Missed you a lot." Susan cut her eyes right and left, making sure they were alone. "I ran the store by myself."

"You mean…?"

"Yes, ma'am. She didn't come out of that room. Never saw her, not even once. Didn't see anyone outside her window, either." Susan shrugged. "That's the way it is with *those* kind. You know, unreliable and lazy."

"You stop that kind of talk right now." Ada's anger was evident with her voice and in her eyes. "All I asked of Marguerite was to stay close by. Her bank is in my building, but she is *not* my employee, you are." She glared at Susan. "Thank you for minding the store. I think you need a day off, without pay. Good bye."

Theo was hollering through the back screen. "Her OPEN/CLOSED sign says closed. I'm goin' rat shootin'. Bye."

Taking the extra key, Ada slowly opened the office door. "Dear Heavenly Father," she prayed, "please don't let her be dead on the floor."

She wasn't. The room was in perfect order, with *Maman's* quilt on the cot, and a sheet of paper resting atop the pillow. 'Gone to see Grand-pere. Will be back.' "Praises," Ada muttered. "Hum, didn't know she had a grandfather." She folded the note, locked the door, and put on her apron. "With any luck, the rest of today will be a whole lot calmer than when it started." The store was still empty, so she headed to the dump. Her deputy was doing his job.

"How many?" she called, standing back a respectful distance.

"Three, I think. They all scattered at the first shot." The grinning Rat Dump Deputy shrugged. "Guess that's pretty good. Right, Auntie?"

"Yes, siree, you're my protector." She gestured with her head. "I, uh, gave Susan the day off, so I need your help inside. You hungry?"

"You betcha." He handed her the .22. "Did you find Missus 'Guite?" Ada nodded.

***

This time it was Missylou's turn to say "Ma'am." Marguerite, wearing one of her new banking lady dresses, matching black straw hat with white netting, and white gloves, climbed the back steps of the Tremont, and slipped into the open office of *Monsieur* Charles. There she sat until dinnertime. She knew he would bring in his noon meal and enjoy a quick cat nap for the rest of the hour allotted.

"Mister Charles, Mister Charles, chef asked..." Missylou froze. "Oh, excuse me, ma'am. Have you seen our head butler?"

The beautiful hat turned. "A friend of mine once told me never to call her 'ma'am'."

Missylou stared. "My good glory, look at you. What happened, you fall in a pot of gold?"

Marguerite just smiled. "I have a business. Tell y'all about it later. Right now I need to talk to *Monsieur* Charles. Has he gotten his dinner tray yet?"

"No, that's why I'm lookin' for him. Chef said his food's gittin' cold and told me to tell him to high-tail it up those steps." Missylou made a face. "Can you imagine any of us telling Mister Charles to 'high-tail it' anywhere? I sure can't."

Marguerite giggled. "Me neither. That'd be like telling your own grandpa to hurry up. *Maman* would have popped me a good one."

"My mommy would've booted me." Missylou headed to the door. "You bringin' your fancy self up to the kitchen? I know the other gals would wanna hear about your business. Oh, Lordy," she spun to face her friend, "are you runnin' a whore house?"

"No, my friend, I have a bank for coloreds." Marguerite started laughing, gesturing to her hat. "Honey, this is way too simple for a *madame*. I have only one little feather, and it's the wrong color."

"Did you say bank, like a money bank?" Marguerite nodded. "Can us girls go there?" Another nod. "Well, I'll be dipped in quinine water. Gotta hear more about this."

"I'll come up after I talk to *Monsieur* Charles. Please tell him I am staying the night in the visitor's room." This time it was Marguerite who blew a kiss through kid gloves.

That evening, after a quick chat with everyone in the kitchen, Mister Charles took Marguerite to meet Sister Givens. "Miss Girl, Sister Givens is everything you hope to be. She's the top widow lady of our church society, lives in a lovely home, has a maid…"

"A colored woman has a maid?" Marguerite's voice held disbelief.

"Yes, child, she pays her right well. And," he said with a twinkle, "Sister Givens is courted by the best looking head butler in the Tremont Hotel."

"*Grand-pere*, you are so silly. You're the only head butler in the Tremont."

"There ya go, Miss Girl, I rest my case." Mister Charles took Marguerite by the elbow, guiding her up a long front walk. "I want you to talk to her. She can help."

"Thank you, *Grand-pere*."

Mister Charles did a *push, push*, pause *push* on the little round button by the door, and grinned. "That's my electric doorbell signal. My Missus Givens meets me at the door, not her girl. That way she gets, well, just watch."

Marguerite heard a *click, click* on the floor inside, and then the door swung open, revealing a tall, strongly built Negress in very high heels. Mister Charles took her in his arms, bent her back, and kissed her deeply. In the middle of the embrace, he deliberately winked at Marguerite, who was blushing flame, her gloves covering her burning cheeks. Mister Charles uprighted his *paramour*, turned to Marguerite, and said, "May I introduce Missus Odessa Givens, the finest lady in town."

She calmly extended her hand. "How do you do? Are you the 'Miss Girl' he talks about? What's your name?" A shaken Marguerite answered her. Missus Givens smiled at her still red guest. "Well, my dear, come in. My Charles telephoned me before you all left. Fill me in on your situation. I know I can help." Missus Givens lead them to the second parlor, where a silver urn of still steaming mocha and fresh pecan pie waited. "Regina left these treats for us before she went home. I told her my Mister Charles was coming."

"She knows my favorite."

Odessa grinned. "She should, after all the years you have eaten pie in this house. Would you please cut us all a slice?" While Charles busied himself at the sideboard, Missus Given came straight to the point concerning Marguerite's needs. "I believe I have an empty house available. Let's talk about it." By the time the crumbs were forked, Marguerite was crying in gratitude, and the other two were holding hands, smiling like loving grandparents.

"Well, my dear, look at the time." Charles stood. "This old butler gets up at the crack of dawn, and our Miss Girl has had a long, long day." He offered his hand first to Missus Odessa and, after she was standing, to Marguerite. "Come child, let's get you settled in the visitor's room. You're missin' some color in those cheeks." He allowed both women to take an arm, pausing at the door. "You tell Miss Regina her pie hit the spot."

"Missus Givens, thank you for what you are planning." Marguerite blushed again. "Like I said, I'm not turning back."

"Oh my dear," soothed Odessa. "I don't see how you can. You've come too far." She leaned down to Marguerite and kissed her cheek.

"And, me?" Charles raised his eyebrows.

"And you." Odessa and her beloved repeated their door frame ritual. "Good bye, you handsome old rascal, see you Sunday."

"If not before." With a wave, Marguerite and her *grand-pere* were on their way back to the hotel. After walking about five minutes, Marguerite took his arm, and their pace slowed. "Tired, Miss Girl?"

"Yes, *Grand-pere*, but tomorrow things will be better. It's just that it's so dark out. I'd forgotten what a new moon evening is like. In LaPorte, I was either cleaning or tending children. This is my first time to be out and about in town since I came back." She squeezed his arm. "For some reason, I feel a haint close bye."

"Well, child, all I feel is my old legs hollerin' for my bed." He patted the hand holding tight to his arm. "You want me to tell you a secret while we walk?"

"Please. Is it about Missus Givens?"

"Uh huh, 'tis."

Marguerite heard a low chuckle. "Is it a funny secret?"

Mister Charles stopped walking. "Miss Girl, here's the secret: I love that woman."

"That's no secret. You two kiss like..." Marguerite's voice broke, "...like Jack and I do every time he comes home."

"Well the secret is that she won't marry me." He started walking again. "We have been courting for twelve years." He laughed. "I propose the first Sunday of every month. She always says to try again, three weeks from next Sunday."

"Same answer each time?"

"Yes. Do you want to know what she tells me?"

"Of, course."

"She says that I'm one fine devil, and she could never say yes to the devil on a Sunday." They both started laughing.

"Oh, *Grand-pere*, you're pulling my leg."

"That may be so, but remember that what I just told you is a secret. Can you imagine the mess I'd be in if the floor girls knew about this?"

"Cross my heart." In the dark, Marguerite made the sign. They were almost to the hotel. "*Grand-pere,* let's go in the front door. I've never done that before."

"That should turn some heads in the lobby. Let's do it." They did not notice the plain-dressed woman standing down the way from the marble stairs leading to those beautiful wooden doors, the doors that survived the flood. They did not hear her foul words or see her spit.

Two days later a package from Missus Givens was delivered to the NCS's teller window. It contained an address and a key.

Chapter Fifty
Chipped Cup

Sarah missed Ikey, and not just for the kissin'. "*Muter*, this house is too quiet." "*Muter*, I'm lonely." "*Muter*, why can't I go to high school?" Sarah missed Ikey because he'd been her best friend. They were each other's only companion, like real brothers and sisters, except for the kissin'. That turned it into something else. Then, after they got sick, Ikey left. "*Muter*, why can't I go out visiting anymore?"

Ignoring her questions, Esther continued to cut noodles, readying them for the new drying rack Joe'd made for her. "Your *abba* is such a good woodworker. He takes wonderful care of us." She handed the lifting sticks to Sarah. "My *tohkter*, please help. I am so glad you are here with me. You will make a good wife."

Sarah hung twenty strips of dough before she spoke. "I don't want to be a good wife, I want to go to high school."

"That's impossible. I will not let…"

"What, let me get educated, let me make friends, let me…"

"…let you get a baby like I did." Esther walked out of the kitchen, returning with the chipped china cup, the one from her *bubbe*. "Read it."

"I can't, it's in German." Sarah made a face. "You know," her tone dripping in anger, "if I went to high school I could learn something more than the Hebrew *Abba* teaches me."

"This cup was passed from elder *tohkter* to elder *tohkter* for many generations, but it was not given to me." Esther reached for the drying towel. "I stole it when I left."

"So, what does it say?"

"Oh, beautiful one, it says 'For a good Girl.' My *muter* refused to pass it down because I had a baby in me and no husband, just *suddech*. Then my beloved intended was killed by bandits." Esther started crying. "*Muter* said I wasn't a good girl and didn't deserve the cup, so I took it and ran away." She sat still until she could talk. "You are my elder daughter, my only daughter. After the sickness, I cannot let you go where there are bad things of this world."

"Where did you get the idea that I am not a good girl? Haven't I always obeyed?"

"You were found nearly dead with that boy, a pail of beer close by and…"

"And what?" Sarah snapped.

"And your top five buttons were open. You could have gone too far."

"You mean like you did? Well, I guess I'm just as good as you." Sarah slammed the screen door so hard the bottom rusty hinge broke. "I'll show her," she muttered, heading to her favorite bushy hiding place. "I can be *just* like her, wait and see."

"See what?" The voice was giggly and high pitched. A really little girl was sitting under the oleander, making what looked like a city in the dust. "Hi," she said, not looking up. "See my roads and grass houses? I like it here, it's shady."

Sarah plopped down beside her. "How old are you? What's your name? Do your parents know you're here?"

"You ask a lot of questions." The girl spat in the dust and stirred with a stick. "I'm makin' plaster for my houses. See how gooey the dirt gets."

"Watch out, this bush is poisonous. I almost died." Sarah scooped up a handful a dust and started her own plaster pile, stirring with her finger.

"You wanna use a stick? My name is Nellie, what's yours?"

"Oh no, Nellie, sticks around here can kill you. You better throw it away." She stood. "I'll get a couple of old spoons from the kitchen. Promise me you'll get rid of that stick?"

"Uh huh."

"Now."

"You sound like a grown-up. You didn't tell me your name."

"It's Sarah. I'll be right back. You hungry?"

Still not speaking to her mother, Sarah grabbed two old spoons and some apples. The spit mountains had grown while she was gone. "Here, you want one?"

"Uh huh. Look, I made more plaster." Nellie smiled. "I'm twelve. Thanks. I'm little 'cause I'm a midget. Not allowed to go to school. My pa tried to beat the short out of me. Didn't work. Ma shot him. Didn't kill him, but he can't make no more babies. Ma said that's all right with her. He never hit me again. Said he didn't know what she'd do next."

They sat, digging, spitting, and chewing. Nelly paused and looked at Sarah. "Why you wearin' your kerchief backwards? My ma says that only dirty Jesus-killin' Jews dress like that. You one of them?" Spit, stir. "Gonna put some plaster on these here grass walls." She reached for another apple.

After a while, Nellie said, "Ya know, I like you. Wish I could take you with us."

"I like you, too." The grass plastering job was almost finished. Sarah smiled. "You're a good builder. Where're you going?"

"Duhno, we're always goin'. Daddy says we gotta keep the dogs behind us. That's what he calls the law." Nellie shrugged. "It was nice way back when he was in jail. We stayed in a house with walls. Now," she shrugged, "we're hoboin' it. Fact is, my folks don't know I'm here. They're out seein' what they can get." She looked at the sky. "Uh oh, sun's down past the trees. That's my signal to go back to the tracks. Ma says if anyone sees me by myself or if I'm late, they'll sell me to the circus. I think I'd like that." She giggled. "In fact, they don't know it, but when I'm thirteen, that's exactly where I'm going. I'll be old enough to get a freak show job, or," she clapped in excitement, "get to be a clown."

Nellie hopped up. She was just the right height for a sit down hug from Sarah. "Ya know, you can come with me if you want. Hoboin' can get pretty lonely for a kid."

"Oh, I don't think so. My *muter* and *abba* would miss me."

"What'd you say?" Nelly cocked her head. "Never heard that before."

"I'm Jewish. It means mother and father."

"Well then, you can't come. No Jews allowed." She shrugged. "Gotta go. Thanks for the apples."

Sarah gathered the spoons, but did not touch the plasterwork. Very slowly she walked to the broken back door. She watched her mother through the screen. Esther was cleaning a chicken. "*Muter*, I'm sorry for my temper. May I come in?"

"Yes, my darling."

Going straight to the table, Sarah picked up the chipped cup. "May I put this back on the mantle?"

Esther nodded. "Of course."

That evening the family enjoyed chicken and noodles that stewed all day. Sarah put down her spoon, cleared her throat, and told her parents about the mysterious little hobo that played out in the oleander.

After the story was finished, her *abba* spoke. "What did you learn from this little one?"

"I'm not sure, but I do know this. I love you two very much." She looked at her plate. "Nelly's not allowed to go to school because she's a midget. That's just wrong. If she wasn't a hobo, I think I could teach her." Sarah looked up, straight into the eyes of her own teacher, the rabbi. "In the meantime, she knows what she's going to do, the only thing she can do, and she's excited. Oh, *Abba,* when I am ready, will you let me go to Normal School to get teacher training? I heard there's one in Denton."

"Well, I don't know…"

Esther interrupted her husband. "Joseph, don't say anything. Let us talk later." She turned to her daughter. "My beloved *tohkter,* would you like to drink your tea from the cup? I'll get it down for you."

"Yes, *muter*, thank you."

"Just be careful. It might scratch."

Chapter Fifty-One
Heartbreak At Homecoming

CB, Junior, and Jack skipped the stop-by to see Aunt Ada. Theo would get his visit on their return to the docks. All the husbands wanted were their wives. All Junior wanted was his mama and to be with the children.

"Gosh, Daddy CB, ain't it crazy that I'm missin' that stinkpot Nora Lee the most? Even more then Mama. You'd think it'd be the boys."

"Well, son, you don't need to ponder it, 'cause everyone has their own feelings, and you've got yours. I'm missin' your mama and Marguerite's good cookin'."

Jack grinned. "Yep, her good lookin' and her good cookin'. Can't wait."

"Do ya think they missed us?" Junior and CB were double stepping it, the latter trying to keep his bow legs up with Jack's long strides as they rushed from the wharf to the station. "Three months is a real long time." Jack looked over his shoulder. "Come on, mates, our women folk are waitin'."

No one at the LaPorte platforms, white or colored, waited for them. Junior grabbed his kit. "Either of you send a telegram?" Neither man responded, just looked at each other. "Dang. We can't go surprising Mama," worried the boy. "What if she's not got a cake made."

CB laughed. "And just when does she not have something in the pie safe? I don't think that'll be a problem."

"Y'all know darn well," offered Jack, "that if there isn't a cake or a pie, there's always…"

"Cookies." CB and Junior chimed in unison. "Come on, sailor men," Junior hollered, "follow this sailor boy home to the best eats in town."

"Aye, aye, sailor boy," saluted Jack. "Let's head on to Lobit Street for eats and sweets. Lead the way."

CB stopped the march at the end of the block. "Let's do a double surprise. I'll go in the front. Jack, you go in the back, and Junior'll tell us when to walk through the doors." He scruffed the boy's hair. "Let's hear that coyote call you been practicin' since Havana."

"*Ark, ark, arooo. Ark, ark, arooo, arooo, arooo.*" Junior nudged CB. "Ya think that's good enough?"

CB laughed. "Good Lord, boy, that sounded more like a dying dog, but for a signal to surprise them, it'll do just fine."

The three were almost to the house when Junior skedaddled up the walk and around to mid-point on the side. The men took their places, the coyote howled. Husbands threw open the doors and ran to their women.

Utter silence echoed in the empty parlor.

Deathly screams came from the kitchen. A strange woman in a maid's uniform was using a mop on Jack. *WACK.* "I don' know who you is, but you git outta dis kitchen afor I's use dat telephone an' call the sheriff." *WACK.*

Tree tall Jack easily grabbed his attacker, lifting the weapon and its wielder by her wrists. "You don't know who *I* am? Listen to me, lady, this is my house. Where's my wife?"

"Yo crazy, man, der ain't no colored livin' here." She looked Jack straight in the eye. "Good God, man, put me down before you break the mop."

He didn't. "Where. Is. My. Wife?" Each word was punctuated with a shake.

"Hi, Mister Jack, why you swingin' Miss Karena?" Nora Lee circled the two, studying the spectacle. "Miss Karena, this is Mister Jack. He's my godfather. Mister Jack, this is Miss Karena. She's our maid. I been watchin' Mama take lady lessons. You're 'sposed to say 'How do you do.' You can put her down now that you've met."

Jack gave the floor and the mop back to Miss Karena. "What in hell is going on?"

CB, not having a wife in the parlor to kiss, followed the sounds of the hullabaloo. Nora Lee ran for a Daddy hug and knocked him backwards. "Umph, child, when'd ya get so strong?"

"I buck dance. Makes muscles. Wanna see?" Nora Lee struck a pose. "I'm good at the bowin' part." She did a *tapity tap* and a spin.

"Where's your mother? The kids? Missus Marguerite? And Mister Jack is right, what in hell is going on?"

Tap tap shuffle. "Mama's at her meeting, the kids are at the beach, and Missus Marguerite ran away three months ago." *Tip tappity.* "I stayed home to keep Miss Karena company. She only comes three days a week."

Jack's eyes went wide. "She did what?"

"Yep, she took her quilt and everything. She 'n' Mama had a real bad fight. Don't cha know it, the next morning she was gone." Nora Lee shook her head. "Didn't leave a note or nothin'. Mama went off her nut."

"She did what?" CB's expression matched Jack.

"Yep, that's why she goes to lady meetings now." She smiled at Miss Karena. "Missus Stoneking sent Miss Karena after the Congress ladies got Mama straight. We're doin' pretty good now, aren't we, Miss Karena?"

"I seen better, I seen worse." Karena looked at Jack. "You gonna leave me alone?" He nodded. "Then I want to 'pologize for hittin' you. Ain't used to no men comin' in."

Jack sank into the kitchen chair and whispered, "My Marguerite, my beautiful golden honey, where are you?" No one answered him. Tears began. He looked at Nora Lee. "Little Missy, does your mama know where she is?"

She snuggled up beside him, petting his wet cheeks. "I think Aunt Ada does. She was here a few days ago and she 'n' Mama did a lot of whispering. Did y'all stop at the store before you came up?"

"No." CB spoke up. "Child, can you tell me where this meeting is? I need to talk to your mama right now."

"Suh, I do." Karena skirted Jack and walked to the dining room door. "Come out ta the front porch. I'll show ya the right house."

CB stood for several minutes with the maid, being filled in on the Mother's Congress and how they were helping "Missus Myra git herself back." Karena indicated the house, up a ways with all the automobiles in front. "Dat'll be where you find her." CB tipped his cap in appreciation and was gone.

Jack climbed the steps to his room. Marguerite had taken her quilt, her clothes, and left nothing except *The Sovereign,* the music book from his mother, the one he used to teach CB notes and words when they were boys. He sat on the empty bed, rocking the book to his chest like a baby, crying 'til his eyes were empty. That book was the only thing he had left. With a deep sigh, he lay it on the bedside table and fell asleep, snoring through the reunion ruckus on the first floor.

The next morning Jack hugged the children, assuring CB and Junior he would meet up with them at the *Sallie Lou.* He did not speak to Myra until he was at the door. "I don't know what happened, but I will find out from my wife. Good bye." All he took from the house was his book, leaving the gold behind.

Standing on the colored platform was a crowd of men, waiting and talking. Jack recognized his seat partner from the last trip, and, shifting the book, extended his hand. "Well, if it ain't Jefferson Lucas. How's the seawall buildin' comin' along?" *Gotta remember I'm a sailor, not an owner.*

"Jack Smith, good ta see ya. Buildin' comin' along fine and dandy. You headin' back to sea? How's the wife?" Jefferson wiggled his eyebrows. "Ya missin' her already?"

Jack swallowed. "Yes, sir, I'm missin' her." He looked to the other men waiting. "All them up for the visit time?"

"Don't know, we was jist jaw-jackin' about the weather." Jefferson smiled. "Need a seat partner? Looks like it's gonna be tight."

"I guess."

About fifteen minutes into the trip, Jefferson had covered the weather, the men at the sea wall, his good times with his wife, and all the gossip about the family she worked for. The continuous chatter was drilling a hole in Jack's head, and his chin dropped, feigning a nap.

"...and my Geneva's sister, Karena's, working two houses. One of 'em got troubles with wild young'uns."

"What's that you say?" Jack's head shot up at the name 'Karena'. "She's your what?"

"Mah sister-'n-law. She keeps two houses. One's got real old people. They don't eat much and can't hardly move around enough to make dirt. So my Geneva's boss lady talked her into gittin' Karena to go over to that house full of kids." Jefferson shook his head. "Genny sez Karena's had her hands full when she first got there. The Missus of the house was laid up in the bed with the vapors or sumpin', and the kids was scrappin' for themselves."

"Sounds bad. Y'all know the street this mess was on? My wife was workin' on Lobit."

"Same street. Mebbe your wife and my Karena's met."

"Maybe, maybe not." *Oh, blessed Lord, where is she?* Once again Jack let his chin relax. This time sweet sleep rescued him.

"Wake up, man, we's here." Jefferson stood as the train slowed. "Good talkin' t' ya. Don' fergit your book, it slid off your lap. Picked it up and put that envelope back where it was bookmarkin'. Hope it was the right page."

Jack blinked. "Uh, thanks man. Y'all be safe on the wall, ya hear."

"Same to ya. Mebbe I'll see ya headin' home to yo honey another time." Jefferson pushed through the aisle and was out soon as the doors cranked open.

Jack followed the departing men. First platform bench he could find, he sat. The envelope was tucked between pages 146 and 147. He knew page 147 by heart. It was the song he's sung with CB to signal traveling men that it was time to go to the Promised Land. The song was 'The Golden Gate.' The envelope was addressed to "My Beloved Husband." It was empty except for a scrap torn from a newspaper with a faded photograph of several colored women dressed like white society standing next to a colored brass band.

Chapter Fifty-Two
Don't Ask, Just Do

Theo was packing a crate, ready to load his bicycle cart with groceries, destined for one of his regular customers, Mrs. Swink. She bought the same thing every week, prepaying the boy for his next delivery. "Keep the change, child, but don't forget the Lord's due."

Theo wondered just how much the Lord was due. "Auntie, how much am I 'sposed to put in the church basket? Every time she tips me, Missus S. says to not forget the Lord."

Ada, sitting at the checkerboard, peered over the top of her new *Delineator*, smiled at her little business man. "What you put in the basket is private, but the Old Testament suggests one out of ten. How much does she pay you?"

"A dime every time." He pulled one out of his pocket. "So, if you make me change, I can put in a penny. Or..."

"...or you can put in the whole thing. Remember it's 'tween you and God. You'll figure this out."

He pocketed the dime, knowing where it would end up. "Auntie, can I ride my bike to school when it starts?"

"Child, you realize only big boys have bikes. Yours is made special to fit you. It's kinda like a pony instead of a horse." She shook her head. "Do you want some other kid to steal something as special as that?"

"Nope, I'll walk." He hoisted the grocery box on his shoulder. "Look how strong I got this summer. I'm what Mama said you wanted."

"Yes, dear, you're my strong back and quick mind." Ada wiggled her fingers in dismissal. "Say 'Hello' to Mrs. Swick. Tell her I miss seeing her."

"Yes, ma'am." *Ting*, he was gone.

Ting. The bell rang again.

"Good Lord, boy, that was quick. What'd you forget?" Ada looked up from her magazine. "Oh."

Three long steps and he stood beside her, hands tentatively extended. "Missus Ada, help me. Where's my Marguerite?"

"Oh, my dear Jack, sit down. Are you hungry? Do you want coffee?" Ada headed to the stove by the office door, where she discreetly tapped several times.

"No. I want my wife." Jack pulled out his kerchief to hide the start of his tears.

"Are you sure you don't want coffee, *mon amour*? I will pour it for you." Marguerite stood by her bank's door, glowing in joy and glowering in anger, all at the same time. "I will pour it on your head."

"Now, child, don't go wasting a perfectly good potful." Ada took her hand. "Come talk to your husband." She looked up at Jack who magically appeared at her side. "Do you want to kiss her?"

He nodded, 'yes'.

"Do you want to kiss him?"

She shook her head, 'no'.

"Will you at least show him what you've done? He needs to know." Ada stood between them, not moving. "It's only right."

Jack looked over Ada's head at his beloved. "Please," he begged, "say something." Marguerite turned and walked loud steps into her pride and joy. "We'll talk in here."

Ada returned to her magazine, keeping one ear wide open, just in case she was needed...by Jack. Soon

Marguerite called out, not for enforcements or protection, but for coffee with a promise to keep it in the mug. "And, if you don't mind, some sandwiches." Ada found Jack sitting in the banker's chair with his wife on his lap, kissing. "Good?" she asked. The two heads nodded as one. Ada set down the refreshments and flipped Marguerite's teller window sign to CLOSED. She quietly shut the office door behind her.

Less than five minutes later, the two emerged, flushed but not mussed. "Missus Ada, I am taking him to see my new house. We need a discussion where we can be comfortable." Marguerite leaned to hug Ada and quietly whispered a request. The couple walked out the front, *ting*, and down the street. Ada, informing Susan that she would be back soon, went through the back door and into the alley, following all the shortcuts to the church and its telephone. "Gotta get us one," she muttered. A quick call to the Tremont had Mister Charles waiting on the front porch when the two arrived. Jack was not pleased.

"Thank you, *Grand-pere*, for coming." She turned to Jack. "I asked him to be here. I love you, but right now, there are things to be said. *Grand-pere* helped us when we were courting in the Tremont. I want him with us when we talk."

"But I won't…" Jack knew what he wanted to do that night, and it didn't include Mister Charles.

"*Oui*, I know you won't listen, but you must."

"That's not what I was going to say." Jack's tone was sharpening.

"Ah, Jack," Mister Charles spoke for the first time since arriving. "You have a lot to learn. Please listen. I will help her explain all that she has told me."

Marguerite opened her reticule. "*Mon amour*, here is the key. Please go into this wonderful new house."

"How did you…?"

"Ah, my friend," Mister Charles interrupted, "now is not the time to be askin', just doin'." Jack unlocked the oak door, stepping into an unfamiliar, but nicely appointed, front parlor. The crystal sconces, the lace doilies, the velvet settee all were definitely trappings of a proper lady. There wasn't a bit of man things anywhere.

"Come, *mon amour*, into the study." Marguerite stepped toward the open door right off this beautiful room.

"Study? Dammit, woman, what are we, some kind of rich people? I'm just a..."

"Shush son, just do." Mister Charles herded Jack behind his wife.

"Oooh." The study was set up like a ship's cabin, only finer, with framed world maps hanging on mahogany walls. Jack stared at the one over the desk, snugged in one corner. "Oh my, you didn't."

"Yes, my love, they're all there. All ports are marked." Marguerite slid her arm through his. "See the strings? Your routes are different colors depending on the safety of the seas." She tipped her head, inviting *Grand-pere* to stand beside her. "I am living here and will not go back to LaPorte. This is for you if you stay. Missus Givens has offered to sell it to us."

"But, CB and the..." Jack's voice faded as he felt Mister Charles' reproving eyes.

"My husband, let me repeat, this is my home now. You have a decision." Marguerite turned. "Would you like to see the rest of the rooms?" Leading the men on a first floor tour, she paused at the bathroom and excused herself. "*Grand-pere*, please tell Jack how this wonderful house happened. There is lemonade in the kitchen."

Marguerite, returning from her 'necessary' time, found the men leaning back in their chairs, dozing. *BANG.* The half-emptied glasses bounced at her table slam. "Wake up, you're supposed to be talking."

Jack blinked and grinned. "We did, we're done." He pushed the full glass toward his wife. "Please sit. I think we should talk about…"

"Good Lord, man, are you that thick headed? Just do." Mister Charles stood. "I don't know why, what with the way you're actin', but my Miss Girl loves you. All I can say is let her lead until she can follow." He checked his jacket pocket for his white gloves. "Going back to butlering. Child, you two come by the hotel tomorrow. I know the gals would want to see him." Mr. Charles winked. "They took a real cotton to that husband of yours."

Marguerite walked her *Grand-pere* to the door. "Is he? Did you?"

"Now it's your turn to not ask. Just do." Mister Charles kissed her forehead. "He needs you to lead."

"I'll try. The question is, can he follow?"

The next morning Jack rolled over in a four poster bed, and kissed his wife. "You are the smartest, most wonderful woman I know, and I trust you completely. Headin' up to LaPorte and will be back this afternoon. I won't be disappointing you."

"Oh, *mon amour*, I know you won't." Marguerite stretched. "I'll see you at the bank."

Chapter Fifty-Three
Don't Worry About the Mule

"Eek, what are you doing here?" Karena was up to her wrists in ground meat, squishing chopped onions and bread pieces. "She still ain't come back."

"I know. Found her. Where's CB?" Jack rummaged through the pie safe, seeing only crumbs. "Caught the early train. Any breakfast biscuits left? Looks like Myra's not bakin' these days. "

"She does the best she can." Jack turned to the voice of his best mate. CB pointed out back and headed to the gazebo. Jack followed. The two sat silently across from each other, waiting.

CB finally spoke. "Myra got real sick. These ladies, the Congress of Women, are saving her."

"Why'd she act that way to Marguerite?"

"She doesn't know, but she's real sorry." CB shook his head. "The young'uns filled me in. Franky said that their mama needed slappin', and Marguerite did it. Things got real bad after that, but are on the turn-around now. Won't ever be the same, though."

"I know. That's why I'm back." Jack stood and paced the width of the shelter. "You are my brother, always will be. We know sailin's a whole lot easier than what our women go through." He stopped in front of his friend. "I'm taking my half of the gold."

"Huh, what? Why?" CB stared at him. "You leavin', too? What about our ship? Oh man, we grew up together. You're my brother. Are you leavin'…me?"

"Hell, no, we're partners through and through, but she's not ever coming back to this town. My love has a house on the island, and I'm going to her." Jack sat next to his brother. "Marguerite's got a real spending plan, and, thanks to Missus Ada, a decent set up for the gold with a safe hiding place." He looked hard at CB. "You're my only brother. She's my only wife." He stood. "Gotta load that wagon I hired. Can you help?"

"Don't want to, but I will." He took three steps to the house and turned. "Don't know about that Karena. Maybe we should send her out for a wild goose while we bring up your crates."

Jack laughed. "Ya need a new mop handle. Thought I heard it crack when I lifted her."

"That'll do." CB studied at the sun. "Takes six hours travelin' time. We better step on it."

"Aye, aye, you take care of Karena, I'll find Junior. We could use an extra mate in the liftin'."

CB gestured dismissively with his thumb. "He's asleep. This morning the kids begged him to go the beach. He just rolled over and covered his head. Last thing I hear was the twins were planning some sort of short sheet revenge. I'll go stir his bones."

Jack drove the mule out back and the three sailors loaded the wagon, covering the crates with canvas. With handshakes around, they all agreed to meet up at the mercantile when this visit was over.

The mule barely needed driving, giving Jack six hours of thinking. By the time he got to the front of the store, he knew exactly what he would say to his wife and all her ideas. Theo saw the weary traveler tying the animal to the hitch post out front. "Mister Jack, Mister Jack, you made it. Missus 'Guite's been lookin' for you. She told me to say, 'Mr. Smith, would you like to make a deposit in the NSC? Come to the side window, please.'" Theo hopped up on the buck. "How'd it sound? I been practicin'. Was it business-y enough? I got her bank name on my delivery cart."

"Whoa, boy, just a minute, I gotta stretch my legs." Jack eased himself down. "Y'all mind sittin' here, keeping an eye open? Is there a privy out back?"

"We got a bathroom," Theo said with pride, "and everybody can use it, no matter what Miss Susan said. It's by the old meat cooler."

Jack returned to the wagon, finding Theo and the produce barrow waiting. "Auntie told me to help unload. Wanna see if Missus 'Guite can hand us down the boxes? She doesn't have anyone at her window right now."

"Absolutely not, she needs to stay right where she is."

It was several hours into the evening before Jack returned the hired rig to the local livery, generously tipping the stable boy. Not knowing the way to their new house, he returned to the store and his waiting wife.

"You two come up here right now. I saved you some supper." Ada stood at the top of the stairway, holding a serving bowl of beef stew. "I know y'all must be hungry."

The Smiths looked at each other, smiled, and climbed the steps. After a delicious meal and a polite "Thank you and good bye," they slowly walked home. Enjoying the stars and the solitude, Marguerite squeezed her husband's hand. "*Mon amour*, you must be very tired."

"Not *that* tired."

"Good."

Chapter Fifty-Four
Almost Home

Mister Charles sent word that Missus Givens would have her lawyer draw up a sales contract for the house, selling it for $5001. Would Marguerite and Jack come to the hotel to talk? When it was ready, unfortunately Jack was already a' sea, but Marguerite could meet that afternoon.

"*Grand-pere*, why the one dollar?" Marguerite studied the contract.

Mister Charles held back a chuckle and looked to the ceiling. "She said it was to make a profit."

"How much did she pay for it?"

"Five thousand." He tapped the numbers. "Miss Girl, you understand that, as a married woman, you cannot sign this without your husband's signature?"

"*Non*, but I'm not surprised. Does Missus Given realize that Jack's probably to Belize by now?"

"Yes, dear, look closer at the contract. She dated it for three months from now. Until then, you can continue to rent, for another dollar, of course."

"Ohhh, how thoughtful." Marguerite touched the date. "I'll take this and put it with all the cold cash." She folded the paper, secured its envelope, and stood. "Thank you for this."

Walking arm in arm, they strolled through the lobby, pausing before they got to the entrance. "I love you, *Grand-pere*."

"I love you, Miss Girl." He stood, watching her go out those magnificent doors.

Chapter Fifty-Five
Tea Time

Louise didn't show up Tuesday morning. Isaac found a note in the door that read, "Gone to see my mother. Will be back next Monday. PS. Tell Ikey to make his own sandwiches."

That was another thing he didn't know about her. "Wonder if she has a father, sisters or brothers." Isaac looked around the house. "Want to eat at the diner tonight? I don't see anything on the stove."

"Sounds good, can I order pork chops?"

"Yes, Son, I don't know why not." Isaac cricked one side of his mouth. "I remember how tasty they were. Used to have ham biscuits almost every morning with my eggs and grits." He shook his head. "Those were the days."

Ikey wrinkled his brows. "Father, when did you go Jewish? While Mother was alive you were Methodist."

"Grab your cap, boy. I'll tell you about Brooklyn on the way." Isaac tapped his bowler down over his yarmulke. As they walked, he told stories of the tenements and living next to Esther. The two were almost at the diner door when Isaac stopped.

"And to answer your question, I went Jewish at my bris when I was first born."

"Did I have one? Was it a special party? I like parties."

"Son, Jewish follows the mother. Your's was Gentile."

"So no bris?"

"No bris." *Thank goodness I don't have to explain all that tonight.* Isaac guided his son into that wondrous emporium of smells...and ham. He ordered pot roast and watched Ikey devour his chops. They each had pie for dessert.

Ikey asked for another glass of milk. "Father, if Louise doesn't come back next Monday, can we eat here every day?"

"She'll be back, she said so." Isaac's eyes widened. "I just realized something."

"What?"

"She didn't leave her key."

"Good." Ikey used his napkin, getting almost all the milk moustache. "But just in case she doesn't, I want to eat here."

***

Louise was not at her mother's. She hadn't visited the woman since she was eighteen and had no plans to start. Nope, she was hiding in her boarding house room, getting ready for her grand experiment. After all, if, as was planned, she was going to marry a gentleman, she would have to practice being a lady. Her ten days served in 'training' in Austin didn't include anything like that.

For several weeks Louise would spend her half day off for the Sabbath sitting at her window, watching women dressed in their finest, going to Saturday tea at the hotel down the street. Louise had been to a tearoom, once. That didn't end well. *I gotta get the right clothes*, she thought. *Can't be too plain.*

One Saturday she went to Foleys. Louise did not wear her babushka, and, after spending a week's wage, walked out with a dress bag and a hatbox. It took another month before she could buy matching shoes. All this finery stayed in her chifferobe, waiting for the right time, but she knew she had to step out soon. It was Isaac's fumbling proposals that set the plan in motion.

Her dress and shoes were as green as the shimmering eye of the main plume on her hat. "Damn this hair." Louise was trying to pin her growing tresses into a semblance of an updo. "Damn that woman." She finally tucked what she could in a snood and tried on her new hat. The feathers were brilliant peacock blue. Turning her head this way and that, the mirror image made her smile. "Maybe, just maybe."

Tuesday at two Louise Durbin walked into the hotel's main lobby. No one stopped her. She asked the bell man standing by the registration desk where the tea room was. He answered her. The hostess seated her, and the waitress brought her Oolong with best cream and two vanilla sugar lumps. Nobody sent her home. That first day of experimentation was a success. "Tomorrow I will order pastries."

Wednesday the bellman nodded to her and smiled. Louise allowed the hostess to seat her, but she noticed it was at a back corner table, and the chair offered faced away from the door. She did not ask to be moved as the prickle of memory crept across her neck. She drank her tea, ate the sweet she'd ordered, and left, stopping at Star Drug. *Maybe I should wear face powder.*

Thursday's tea time was a repeat of Wednesday, her back to the rest of the ladies. Louise moved to face the front as soon as the hostess walked away. This time she ordered tea with best cream and two vanilla sugar lumps, cress sandwiches, and a plate of petit fours, *whatever all that is.* The waitress brought two slices of crust-less bread and butter with the pieces of bitter green weeds between. Just as she was taking a bite of the littlest cake she'd ever seen, a couple strolled past, stopping at the tea room door.

"Pha." Louise spat. "I knew it," her snarl muffled by the napkin, "that high and mighty whore."

"Ma'am?" The waitress, hearing the hiss, came to Louise's aid. "Are you choking?"

Calm yourself. "Thank you for asking, I must have swallowed wrong." Louise returned the cloth to her lap. "I see someone through the door who looks familiar." She indicated with her chin.

"Well, yes, that woman used to be one of our upstairs girls. She still likes to have special visits with Mister Charles." The waitress studied Louise. "May I introduce you?"

"No, thank you." *Hell, no.* "Does she live on the island?"

"Yes, ma'am, everyone here is so proud of her. She has her own business, now." The waitress noticed the empty cup. "Would you care for more?"

"No, thank you." Once more gesturing with her chin, Louise asked, "Just where is this business? It's rare for any colored woman to *own* a business."

"It's in the backroom of some store. The working men on the seawall go there all the time."

Humph, I'm not surprised. "Thank you, miss. Could I have my check, please?" By the time the money was settled, Louise saw no one she knew in the lobby. She laughed all the way home. In her room, she took off her hat, fluffed her hair and said to the mirror, "I win."

Chapter Fifty-Six
Hurricane Louise

Louise came back a day early. She pulled the bell. No one answered, so she used her key. Two hours later she had honey cinnamon yeast rolls waiting on the sideboard and a hot pot of joe on the stove. The beds were made with fresh linens and the steps swept, the open door allowing the wonderful smells to escape. She sat in the front porch rocker, waiting.

Father and Son ambled up the street, oblivious to everything except their diner-filled stomachs. The conversation was about yesterday's baseball game. The newspaper reported play by play of Dallas vs Corsicana, rivals in the Texas League. Isaac read aloud the entire article. Sunday morning meant the diner was empty, so Ikey stood between the tables acting out his father's narrative. Susanna, Isaac's favorite waitress since, well, forever, applauded the show, giving them each a free piece of pie.

"Gee, I wish Galveston had a team. We could go to every home game." Ikey was winding up to pitch an imaginary fast ball as they walked. "I play with the guys at school sometimes, but, stick ball isn't real baseball."

"Maybe someday..." Isaac glanced at their house. "Oh gosh, look. She's back." He quick-stepped it to the porch.

Louise collected Ikey in her arms. "Good to see you, son." Circling his shoulder, she guided him into the parlor, walking wide around Isaac. "I made honey rolls. Want one?"

"Just had pie, but yeah, smells good." Ikey smiled. "We missed you." He plopped in his spot.

Isaac hung his bowler and followed the two into the kitchen, sitting at his own place. "Hello, Louise. How are you?"

"Hello. I'm well." She poured him a fresh mug.

Suddenly Isaac felt bashful. "How was your visit?"

"I did everything I set out to do." She put the delightfully drippy rolls in front of them. "I know you like honey." She wiped the edge of the plate, scooping up the stray sauce, and licked her finger clean. "This is good."

Isaac studied her. "Do you remember what I asked you to do?"

"When?"

"When I read you the letter."

"Oh, uh-huh."

"Did you do it?"

"Yes." Louise flicked her eyes at Ikey. "We'll talk later." She cut herself a piece of the sweet. "So tell me, you two, what did you do while I was away?"

Ikey grinned. "Ate pork chops at the diner."

"Every day?" Louise bit into her roll.

"Every day," Isaac shrugged. "What did you do? Did you see your mother? I hope she's well."

"How nice of you to ask." Louise carried the dirty dishes to the sink. "I noticed the icebox is almost empty. Didn't either of you go shopping?"

"Uh, no, diner food every night."

She shook her head in disapproval. "I'll shop tomorrow, even if it's not my usual day." Keeping her back to the two, she washed what was in the dishpan. "Ikey, please let your father and me have a minute."

"Yes ma'am." The boy went to his room and plastered his ear to the wall. "Let's hope he gets it right this time," he muttered. "I want her to stay."

Louise dried her hands and sat down. "You asked me what I want. This is the list. I want a house with three bedrooms, two bathrooms, a telephone, an auto, unquestioned spending, and finally, a courthouse wedding." Isaac stared, open mouthed at her. "If you agree to all this, I won't leave, I'll marry you."

"But, but, I don't…"

"You asked me what I want. I told you." Louise's voice rose. "You have until next Saturday to propose with a ring. After that I quit being your maid, one way or another."

"But I…"

She stood, walked to the wall and rapped. "Boy, did you get all that?" She turned to Isaac. "I will see you bright and early in the morning."

"Uh, Louise, may I walk you home?" He stood, reaching for his hat.

She shook her head. "No. Like I said before, it wouldn't be right to be seen out walking with your maid." She smiled. "Perhaps next week." Linking her arm in his, she said, "Today you may walk me to the door."

For the first time, Isaac noticed she did not touch the mezuzah. *Must have a lot on her mind.*

Ikey peeked around his bedroom door frame. "Can we keep her?"

"Son, I don't see how. She wants a rich man's house."

"And you're not?" Ikey ran to the door just in time to see Louise disappear around the corner. "I thought you saved money every pay."

"I do, but that's for a rainy day."

"Father, this is a hurricane."

Chapter Fifty-Seven
Did She Say *Two* Bathrooms?

"Father, why does she want a big house? This one works just fine. It's the same size as ours when Mother was alive." Ikey gestured here and there. "It's even better because it has real plumbing. I like this place." He noticed the half eaten sweet roll on the table. "Can I have some more?"

His father nodded. "First we have pie dessert for breakfast, and then sweet rolls for a second treat. Me oh my, what a day." He cut them each another piece. "Dig in, boy. I think the coffee's still hot."

The two bachelors sat, discussing the possibility of living with a woman in the house. "She really is nice." Ikey smiled. "She's taught me stuff I wouldn't have learned, staying here by myself all summer. She's always on my side, you know, with food and cooking and, well, everything."

"I tell her to buy what she wants. I'm glad she's feeding you well." Isaac licked the drip from the last of his roll. "She buys what I like, too."

"Does getting married mean she'll be my mother?"

"Oh no, Son, she will never be your mother. She would be my wife and your step-mother." Isaac wagged his finger, "But not like a fairy tale step-mother. I can't imagine her turning mean and treating you like Cinderella."

"Oh, that only happens to girls. Mother Goose boys get to do whatever they want."

"Hmm, that's true, just don't start crying wolf." Isaac laughed. "My *bubbe* would tell the old stories from when she was a girl. I remember the one about a foolish boy who gets in trouble, gets punished, and has good behavior forever after. I think she made it up."

Ikey looked at his father. "Do you love Louise?"

"I don't know, I don't think so." Isaac held his mug, not sipping. "I don't think she loves me, either."

"So, why do you want her to marry you? Is it to take care of me?"

"Son, I think it's to take care of us. It's just that I really like having her here." He grinned. "She makes me happy."

"Makes me happy, too." Ikey shrugged. "Two bathrooms will make her happy."

"And a telephone, an automobile, spending money..."

"Don't forget a ring and a courthouse wedding." The boy carried their dishes to the sink. "What's the difference between a regular and a courthouse wedding?"

"The courthouse is all law and no God." Wandering into the parlor, Isaac sat, took off his *yarmulke,* and scratched his head. Absently turning the skullcap in his head, he noticed how dirty it was inside. "Son, would you get me a fresh *kippah* from my top drawer? They're on the right side by my handkerchiefs."

Ikey handed his father a clean cap and sat across from him. "Can you do all the things she wants?"

"I think so, everything except the house. I don't know of any with two bathrooms in this neighborhood. Too bad we rent this one, we could add on." He donned his cap.

"Goodness, Father, she wants three bedrooms, too. That would be a whole lot of adding on." Ikey stepped out on the porch, looked up and down the street at all the bungalows, and repeated his observation on house additions. "If we're keeping her, we're gonna have to move."

"I don't have enough money saved to buy her a nice ring *and* a new house, let alone an automobile, but we can get a telephone." He chuckled. "I could insist on a synagogue wedding but will trade it for staying here in this house."

This kind of talk interested Ikey. "No auto? How about all that spending money?"

"She can use it on a hired coach any time she wants to go anywhere."

"This sounds like *horse* trading to me," joked Ikey.

"I'd call it the negotiations of matrimony." Isaac stood, stretched, and headed to his study. "I'll check the numbers and then go to Goldstein's jewelry store tomorrow. Let's hope we can win her with a good ring, that and a ringing telephone."

Ikey looked toward his bedroom. "I'm so full of sweet rolls, I'm going to take a nap." He paused at his door. "Father, why would she want two bathrooms, anyway?"

"I have no idea."

Chapter Fifty-Eight
Negotiations

Isaac did not empty his rainy day fund, but the size of the dipper he used in the bucket was quite adequate. The engagement ring budget topped out at $500, with the hope of staying under. His *yarmulke* helped.

"Mrs. Goldstein, how are you?" Isaac smiled and removed his hat, revealing his covered head. "I believe this is the first time we've met. I'm Julia Jameson's husband."

"So sorry she's gone. Her family heirlooms were quite an addition to my heritage resale collection." She spied his cap. "Julia never mentioned that you are one of us. Orthodox?"

"Brooklyn Reform, born and somewhat bred. Long story." He tilted his head, looking at the shop owner. "You knew Julia well enough to realize she was Methodist and wanted to raise our son that way."

"Oh, yes, I knew your wife very well. Saw her here frequently. I miss her business."

"We miss her, too, but it's time to make a new family. I'm here to buy an engagement ring." Isaac blushed. "I'm proposing this week to a wonderful young woman."

"Then, *khaver*, let me show you my finest, with the 'friend' discount of fifteen percent, of course."

Isaac spent it all, but, thanks to taking off his hat, walked out with much more. The ring was "fit for a princess," worth an average worker's entire year's wage. "Hmm, maybe I should call her that when I show it to her."

The next step was a telephone. Southwestern Telegraph and Telephone was very happy to run a line to the house "if the landlord agrees."

Isaac kept a straight face when he said, "Call the sheriff."

The clerk looked confused. "Uh, sir, why? Do you see a robber?"

"No, he's the landlord."

Constable Turner was very happy to have Isaac pay for the installation and the monthly bill, since the family was still living in the rental gratis. "Son, make sure your first call is to me here at the office. That way I'll know everything's working."

"Yes, sir, will do."

The telephone line ran through the wall into his study. That beautiful piece of modern living sat on his desk. Thursday morning Isaac called Robearde as promised, and closing the office door behind him, left for the docks. "I will be late this evening, end of month accounts."

Louise and Ikey were playing checkers on the kitchen table. The two were exceptionally quiet, but for the standard call of "King me." Several games later, Ikey excused himself to the necessary, and waited.

RING. RING.

"Miss Louise, Miss Louise." The voice from the bathroom sounded urgent. "That's father's telephone. I'm, well um, I can't come out right this minute. Can you answer it?"

"Your father has a telephone? Goodness, when did that happen?"

RING. RING.

"Pleeeeese answer it. It's on his desk."

"How?"

"Lift up the thing on top and talk."

RING. RING.

Louise followed the sound to the study, and put that 'thing' to her ear.

"Hello?"

"Hello. Will you marry me?"

"Huh?" Louise started to cry.

"Isaac laughed. "I said…"

"I know what you said." She sniffled. "I will not continue this conversation. Goodbye."

Ikey was standing by the study door, crestfallen. "Why didn't you like your surprise? Father thought it would be wonderful."

"Well, I don't. That is no way to propose." She looked around the very tidy parlor. "I need a new feather duster. I'll be back later. Stay home." She returned several hours later, dressed in her tea lady clothing, including the feathered hat.

Ikey, having used the alone time to go back to bed without retribution, heard the front screen slam, and ran into the parlor. "Ooooh, look at you." He walked around, admiring her ensemble. "You look like a lady, not our maid. Gee willikers, I didn't know you had such red hair."

"I do, and I'm not your maid. My resignation is in that envelope over there on the receiving table. Your father has insulted me once too often." Louise sat in the center of the settee. "I will wait until he gets home and tell him myself."

"But…"

"There's nothing to be said. I'll wait." She flicked her finger at him. "I see, by the condition of your head, that you've been sleeping. I suggest you get back to it. By the way, I will not be cooking your dinner or supper, so if you're hungry, fix it yourself." Settling back into the comfort of the cushions, she waited…and waited…and waited.

It was deep dusk when Isaac burst through the front door into an unlit room. "What the...? Ikey, Louise, what's going on?" He groped for the light switch. "Louise, is that you?"

"Hello. I quit."

"No, no, no, you can't."

"Oh yes, I can and I did."

Isaac noticed no place to sit beside her, and sank to one knee, pulling out the jewel box he'd carried all day. Opening the lid, he repeated his earlier question, this time calling her his princess.

Louise took the box in her hand. *Steady, steady.* "This ring is beautiful, but you know my requirements. Where's the auto, the big house, the spending money, and the court house wedding?" She handed him back the box, leaving the lid open.

"I want Rabbi Joe to counsel us and marry us, but I will give all that up if you agree to stay in this house with its new telephone and unlimited spending. You can hire a horse carriage any time you want." Isaac reoffered the ring. "Louise, my princess, will you marry me?"

She took it out of the box and extended her left hand. "Yes, I will."

Ikey exploded out of his room. "It's about damn time!"

Isaac, grinning from ear to ear, spoke. "Son, watch your language, but I agree."

"Can we step out, now?"

"Yes, we can." Isaac offered his arm. "Come, my princess, would you care to dine with us? I would love for Susanna to meet you. After all, she's been feeding me long before you were."

The new almost-family thoroughly enjoyed the diner's offerings. Susanna highly complimented her ring.

"Been watching this man eat for years," she said. "Hope you have a big jar of honey on your table."

"That we do, that we do."

Chapter Fifty-Nine
Favorite Family Food Festival

On the first Sunday in September, Old Town LaPorte had a Family Fun Folderol by the bandstand in the central park. They'd been doing it for several years. All the registered home owners in the district got tickets from the mayor. Renters and colored help were excluded.

The New Town Congress of Women had begun addressing this in May. The discussion was still going on mid-August.

"Who does that man think he is?"

"We're part of this town, too."

"I'm so angry I could just spit."

"Now, dear."

The members were talking over each other, words flying every which way.

Mary Stoneking clapped her hands. "Ladies, ladies, we all know how it feels to be unwelcomed, but, Lord knows, we've been talking about it since before summer." She nodded at the gathering. "I suggest we table this once and for all, and get on to the next topic."

"No."

All heads turned as Myra stood. "Mary, you didn't ask for any new business, but I have some concerning this topic."

"Well then, the chair recognizes Myra Ledbetter, our newest member." Mary turned, looking across the room over her spectacles, giving unspoken reprimands to anyone wanting to interrupt. "Go ahead, my dear."

"I've listened to all the conversations, and I think I know a way every resident of New Town can have a party, too."

"How? Some of us are renters," came from the back of the room.

Myra smiled. "Y'all've seen that I have a house full of children. Do you know where they go almost every day? Sylvan Beach. It's a park open to everyone, no tickets needed. We can invite our husbands, children, help, and anyone else we can think of to an end of summer picnic. All we have to do is pack a basket and show up."

"Love it."

"Let's do it."

"I'll bring…"

This time the women did not stop talking until Myra clapped *her* hands. "Ladies, ladies, let Mary speak. What do you think?"

"I love it," she said. "Please give Myra a round of applause for her wonderful idea." The entire Congress stood, clapping and cheering. Mary waited until the room settled. "Let's spread the word to all of New Town. We'll meet at the picnic pavilion the first Sunday of September at two o'clock."

But that's the same day as *them.*"

"Yes, dear, I know." Mary smiled, raising one eyebrow. "We can have a picnic *any* day we want. They can meet in the park; *we'll* be at Sylvan, welcoming all who want to celebrate friendships." She looked at Myra. "Would it be possible for your entire family to be at the picnic tables early to greet people?"

"Certainly, but you know my husband's out to sea. What I can do is bring all the children for an early picnic play time, say, around ten, since we don't have a church yet." Myra rolled her eyes. "My Nora Lee could be a welcoming committee all on her own."

"She's a charmer."

"That girl could put on a dancing show."

"Good Lord, Myra sure has a handful."

CLAP. CLAP.

Mary stood statue still until she had everyone's ear. "Each family will pack their own main picnic food, and what do you think of each of us bringing a dish to share? I'm pretty good at making stuffed eggs. My mother-in-law's recipe is wonderful." Mary turned this way and that as she talked, noticing how lively the Congress had become. "Is there anyone else in our group who has a favorite family food?" She giggled. "Goodness, we could call the picnic the Favorite Family Food Folderol."

"No, don't use *that* word." said one lady sitting in a corner. "That's their word. Could we call it Favorite Family Food Festival instead?"

"I second that idea. Any objections to the name of our picnic?" Several members vigorously offered their thirds and fourths.

Mary asked Myra to stay after the others were gone. She stood, both hands on her new friend's shoulders. "You were very brave to speak up. I'm proud of you."

Blushing, Myra thanked her. "I used to sell sweets on the docks to support the children."

"I know. Beatrice told me everything." She took Myra's hands. "You had it really hard."

"When I first went out there, a twenty year old widow, all alone with those sailors, well, that was the bravest thing I've ever done." Myra shrugged. "Speaking up in a room full of talking women was a piece of cake." She blinked. "Oh, I could make the cookies I sold. They're Aunt Ada's recipes."

"Could you invite her and Theo to come up for the day? I'll telegraph Beatrice and Robearde to come, too. Maybe they could ride together." Mary gave Myra's hands a squeeze and let them go. "I hope we're helping you not to be so lonely."

"Yes, you are. There was a time when I just wanted to run away to anyplace but here." Smiling, Myra gathered her reticule and shawl. "Now I know where I'm going, where I'm staying. Lobit Street is my home, not CB's house, thanks to the Congress." She chuckled, remembering what she'd heard. "Those ladies seem to really know my Nora Lee."

"Yes ma'am, they do."

Chapter Sixty

You Can Take It To The Bank

*T*ing.

Isaac couldn't wait for the first of the month accountings. He knew he had to tell someone, and Ada was the closest thing to family. He found her in the corner by the calico, and, without warning, planted a big kiss on her cheek. "Aunt Ada, I'm getting married."

"Oh, my goodness, who is she, someone from your chur, er, synagogue? Have I met her?"

"As a matter of fact, you have." Isaac led her by the hand to the checkerboard, poured the coffee, and without asking, opened a box of Barnum's Animal Crackers straight off the shelf. "Care for a giraffe?"

"Why, so I can bite its head off if you don't hurry up and tell me?"

Isaac beamed. "I'm marrying Louise. We're going to the courthouse tomorrow."

"Your housekeeper?" Ada realized her tone too late. "Well, uh, I'm guessin' Ikey's thrilled. That girl buys everything he wants."

"I know, isn't she wonderful?" Isaac rummaged through the cookie box. "I'll take a lion." He popped the whole thing in his mouth. "I've known you since before you were my kin, what with church and all, and I know you love me as a nephew. I hope you can accept Louise as your niece."

Ada ignored his last statement. She'd heard too many gossipy women in the store discussing everything from the woman's hair to her skin to her manners.

"That Louise isn't from around here."

"She's not like any of the other Jewish ladies I know."

"I saw Ada cut ham for her."

"Just what did she do in Austin?"

Ada picked up on the last question. "Isaac, what do you know about her being from Austin? Does she have family? Are they coming for the wedding?"

"She said she wanted to visit her mother last week when she went away for a few days, but that's all I know. Never thought to ask." He scrabbled through the menagerie and chomped another lion.

"Does she even know that I call you 'nephew'?"

"Don't think so."

"Good Lord, man," Ada's exasperation rose to the boiling point, "What do you know about her? Is she really a Jewess? Her skin is darker than Esther's. She could be a mulatto, or even worse, a gypsy. Just remember, blood line runs with the mother."

Setting his cup on the checkerboard, he took her hands. "I don't care if she's a zebra. That woman has made our house a home, and we are getting married tomorrow. I want you to come stand with me."

"Oh." Ada shook her head. "My dear, I'm sorry, but I can't do that without asking her a few questions."

"Tomorrow's the day, and I really want you with me." He looked heavenward. "You know, Julia would want to know everything, too. I guess it's a woman thing."

"Not at all, child, it's an 'I love you too much to see you get hurt' thing." Ada looked at the big clock ticking away on wall by the cooler. "I will stand with you after you bring her to visit this afternoon, say about three, and she answers some questions. Humph, I'm surprised Rabbi Joe hasn't done that already."

Isaac and a reluctant Louise opened the store's door, *Ting*, at exactly three. Theo was out at the dump, throwing away some rotten cabbage. The boy kangaroo jumped through the back door and was halfway past the office when, "Princess, Princess Lulah Marie," rang through the store. Theo rushed her, knocking her back into one of his pyramids. *CRASH*!

"Oh, Christ, it really *is* you." Louise, staring wild-eyed in her one and only lady dress, lay spread-eagle on Ada's newly coal oiled floor, cans scattered everywhere. "What are you doing here?"

"Hi, Princess, This is where I live. Are you still a gypsy?" Theo's kangaroo hops were getting a bit too close to the pile on the floor. Ada grabbed his arm and pulled him clear, putting him in the calm down hug.

No one noticed the office door swing open. Marguerite, in her brand new lady-in-waiting dress, walked over to the assembled gawkers, looked at the floor and, in the calmest of voices, spoke to Ada. "What is she doing here? The last time I saw her, I'd just cut her hair, and she was being run out of town on a rail, sent to Austin, if I recall." She looked at Isaac. "Why are you here with this gypsy witch?"

"Wha—what? This is my fiancée, Louise." He stared at her. "Goodness Missus Marguerite, you must be mistaken."

"No she's not," piped up Theo. "She's the best gypsy fortune teller in the whole world. She's my friend."

Louise reached over and smacked Isaac's leg. "Get me up. Now." Standing, she turned to Marguerite. "Soooo, you little whore, is this where your *business* is? I can't believe Missus Ada would allow a cat-house in her store.

And look at you. Does your precious Jack Smith know whose baby you're carrying?"

Marguerite swung hard. Louise ducked.

"Hah, bitch, belly gettin' in your way? What cha gonna do with the brat, leave it at some poor house?"

SLAP. Marguerite made her mark. She stepped back before it could be returned, easing behind the cold meat cooler for protection. She pointed at her sister. "Isaac, for your information, this woman is Lulah Marie Dubonet, not Louise whatever last name she's using with you."

"And you are a half-breed bastard whore." Louise turned to her intended, smiling. "At least our father married *my* mother. "

"Good to know." Isaac looked for the checkerboard, and sat, shock setting in. "Good to know."

Ada let go of Theo, walked to the front door, flipped the sign, and stood, hands on hips. "I have had just about enough of this. Marguerite, stay where you are." She pointed at Louise. "You, do not move. Theo, get the gun, and Isaac, for God's sake, act like a man."

Theo returned. Ada walked to the center of the store, rifle in hand. She swiveled to Louise. "Now I know who you favor. Been wonderin' since the day I met you. There's one thing I want to know. Where did you get the idea my *niece* is a whore and that my store is a cat-house?" She looked at Theo. "Get me that box of bullets."

"Yes, ma'am."

Louise cut her eyes at Marguerite. "Missus Ada, did you know your *niece* is well known for her *business* with all the workers from the sea wall, and, she even makes special calls to old men at the Tremont. I saw her there, myself."

Ada handed the rifle back to Theo. "Load it."

"Yes, ma'am."

Low rumbling laughter came from behind the meat counter. "You idiot witch, my business is banking. I own the NSC, the only Negro Savings Cooperative available for the sea wall laborers. The old man is head butler at the Tremont and the closest thing to a grandfather, someone you will never have. And, for your information, Jack Smith's baby will be raised in a four bedroom, two bathroom house that my husband and I are buying. I live there right now, don't I, *Auntie*?"

"Yes, my dear, you do." Ada looked at Isaac. "A husband has to sign the papers with the wife, even if the house is paid for in cash, which they are doing." She held the gun steady at her side. "Are you really Lulah Marie, the gypsy I've heard so much about? Missus Annie talked about a flim-flam woman that robbed her sisters."

"Yes, Auntie, I remember when Missus Marguerite rolled her up like a mummy and cut off all her hair twists. Mama made us go home, but, boy, oh boy, did we hear all about it." Theo felt the fidgets starting. "Auntie, can I go shoot rats?"

Ada nodded, looking at her guests. "Here, take this before *I* have to shoot a rat."

Isaac, shaking his head in disbelief, walked to Louise. "I don't know who you are or where you come from, but you are my princess. Will you marry me tomorrow?"

"I will." The two walked out of the store, her oil soaked skirts leaving a trail of stain and filth behind them.

Ada shook her head. "Well, who'd of thought? Humph, Isaac marrying across lines and a gypsy t' boot!" She turned to the meat counter. "Come out, my dear, there's something I think we'd better talk about." Leaving the CLOSED sign showing, she led Marguerite up to the apartment.

Sitting beside her on the settee, Ada pointed at the telegram on the side table. "Do you remember when you first came to me? I told you that things would have to be mended between you and Myra. Read that telegram."
                    ADA DICKENSON.
BIG PICNIC HERE FIRST SUNDAY IN SEPTEMBER.
        PLEASE COME AND BRING THEO.
        PLEASE BRING MARGUERITE.
                    PLEASE.
                    MYRA.

Ada looked at Marguerite. "Will you come with us to LaPorte? You two are sisters, you know."

Marguerite stared at the paper. "I loved her."

"Can you forgive her?"

"Yes, I think I can." She looked at Ada, eyes brimming. "After all, who else can help me with having this baby?"

The End

About Jacqueline T. Moore

Jacqueline T. Moore works and plays in Murrell's Inlet, South Carolina. She says, "Living in the south makes me a sunflower…and a beach bum!" As a writer and educator, Jacqueline surrounds herself with words. She savors the sounds and sense of letters put together to create a lasting memory. Her debut novel, THE CANARY and its sequel THE CHECKERBOARD are inspired by a most beautiful yellow diamond that rests on her finger and the whispered family secrets about how it got there. THE CORNERPOST is our final visit with Myra, CB and all the children, but if you are hungry for more, take a look at THE CANARY COMPANION COOKBOOK.

Visit her at www.jacqueline-t-moore.com, on Facebook https://www.facebook.com/Jacqueline-T-Moore-476568419146045/, and on Instagram @Jacqueline. T. Moore for conversations and updates.

Social Media

Facebook: https://www.facebook.com/pages/Jacqueline-T-Moore/4765684196045

Website: www.jacqueline-t-moore.com

Instagram: https://www.instagram.com/jacqueline.t.moore

Email: Jacqueline@jacqueline-t-moore.com

Acknowledgements

With deepest appreciation I thank my daughter, Julie Anne Jacobs. She listens to every word I read, holding me true to story and style. Thank you, George James, for your point of view. Thank you, Uta Andrews, for your truth and Beth Winslow for being my 'Comma Mama', and, most of all, I thank Ellen (Cookie) Brenner and her husband, Gabe, for giving me their personalities and guidance in creating Rabbi Joe and his wife, Esther.

BOOK CLUB GUIDELINES

THE CORNERPOST title refers to decisions characters make to change the direction of their lives. For example: Marguerite turns three corners by leaving Myra, starting her business, and finding a house in Galveston. Think about her and the others who faced an intersection. Should they have taken a different path, and why?

Myra's breakdown comes from isolation and the challenges of a large family. How is this situation compared to modern mothers? How is it different?

Myra's children are prominent in the series. We spend time with Franky and Benjy in THE CANARY, Junior in THE CHECKERBOARD, and Nora Lee and Theo in THE CORNERPOST. Who is your favorite 'young'un', and why?

How soon did you figure out who Louise is? What are the hints you caught?

It's very rare at this time for a woman, especially a woman of color, to have money and properties. The book does not tell you the origin of Missus Odessa's wealth. What do you think her back story is?

The series ends with a couple about to get married and another couple expecting their first child. Take a look at all the characters we've met. Project their lives ahead five years, and discuss what lies in their future. For example: Did Sarah become a teacher?

Recipes from The Cornerpost

AUNT ADA'S CHOW CHOW
Adapted from My Pet Recipes, Tried and True (1900)

Ingredients
¼ bushel green tomatoes chopped fine
12 good large onions chopped fine
2 quarts vinegar
2 pounds brown sugar
1 tablespoon of allspice
1 tablespoon of cloves
2 tablespoons of ground mustard
2 tablespoons of black pepper
2 tablespoons of salt
1/2 cup grated horse-radish
Instructions
Mix all together and stew until perfectly tender, stirring often to prevent burning. Seal in glass jars while hot.

NOTE CB said the chow chow tasted like souse, only picklier. You decide. Jack said that souse tasted like slave slop, so he wouldn't eat it.

SOUSE
Adapted from The Virginia Housewife (1860)

Instructions
Let all the pieces you intend to souse, remain covered with cold water twelve hours; then wash them out, wipe off the blood, and put them again in fresh water; soak them in this manner, changing the water frequently, and keeping it in a cool place, till the blood is drawn away; scrape and clean

each piece perfectly nice, mix some meal with water, add salt to it, and boil your souse gently, until you can run a straw into the skin with ease. Do not put too much in the pot, for it will boil to pieces and spoil the appearance. The best way is to boil the feet in one pot, the ears and nose in another, and the heads in a third; these should be boiled till you can take all the bones out; let them get cold, season the insides with pepper, salt, and a little nutmeg; make it in a tight roll, sew it up close in a cloth, and press it lightly. Mix some more meal and cold water, just enough to look white; add salt, and one-fourth of vinegar; put your souse in different pots, and keep it well covered with this mixture, and closely stopped. It will be necessary to renew this liquor every two or three weeks. Let your souse get quite cold after boiling, before you put it in the liquor, and be sure to use pale coloured vinegar, or the souse will be dark. Some cooks singe the hair from the feet, etcetera, but this destroys the colour: good souse will always be white.

AUNT ADA'S FRUIT COMPOTE WITH GOOSEBERRIES

Compote of Blackberries, Currants, Raspberries, Strawberries, and other like Berries
Adapted from Hand-Book of Practical Cookery (1884)

Instructions
Prepare syrup of sugar, Put one pint of water in a tin saucepan, with six ounces of loaf-sugar, the rind of half a lemon, and set it on the fire; boil down until, by dipping a spoon in it, it adheres to it. Throw the berries in; boil from one to five minutes, according to the kind, take from the fire, and serve when cold.

Ada added gooseberries as a special treat. Uncle Harry thought it was funny and honked like a goose.

Gooseberries
Adapted from Hand-Book of Practical Cookery (1884)

Instructions
Select young gooseberries, make a syrup with one pound of loaf sugar to each of fruit; stew them till quite clear and the syrup becomes thick, but do not let them be mashed. They are excellent made into tarts. Do not cover the pan while they are stewing.

If you enjoyed this story, check out these other Solstice Publishing books by Jacqueline T. Moore:

The Canary

RECIPE FOR ADVENTURE: 1 spunky widow, 1 hateful church lady, 2 sailors & 1 checkerboard, 5 little darlin's + I smarty stinker, Add 1 apron pocket full of jewels, Mix well and bake in the 1890's Galveston heat. Myra Gallaway, a young widow with five children, supports her family by walking the wharves of Galveston selling homemade sweets. She never imagined she'd be joining forces with husband-hating church society queen, Julia Jameson. Myra's apron pockets are soon filling up with the unspendables man smuggling sailor friends Sure Foot and Black Jack need to move. The Klondike gold fields are calling hapless dreamers and the boys are all about obliging them, yet everybody knows that a sailor cannot spend what he does not earn. My goodness, those unspendables are one serious problem!

http://bookgoodies.com/a/B00N34SRVO

The Checkerboard

September 8, 1900
Five Thousand Lives Blotted Out

The headlines say it all. Death, destruction, and desolation is everywhere on Galveston Island. The papers don't mention the survivors.

THE CHECKERBOARD, sequel to THE CANARY, continues the story of Myra Gallaway, her new husband CB, and Black Jack and his new wife, Marguerite, the 'red-headed colored gal.' The men showed that, against all odds, a mixed ship sails well. The wives band together in the house in LaPorte to prove the same to their new neighborhood. All seems to go as expected until that crazy gypsy, Lulah Marie, shows up and practically sets the house on fire.

Myra's eldest, Junior, is in serious trouble and his rebellion landed him in jail on Galveston Island. His only hope for redemption lies in a very unusual punishment. The boy is forced to sail with the man he hates, his step father, CB Ledbetter. This voyage will either make or break Myra's family. After all, what do you do with a drunken sailor? Only time will tell.

http://bookgoodies.com/a/B017MFWS8M